# THY WILL BE DONE

★ ★ ★ ★ ★

by

## LOUISE S. APPELL

Bloomington, IN  Milton Keynes, UK

authorHOUSE®

*AuthorHouse™*
*1663 Liberty Drive, Suite 200*
*Bloomington, IN 47403*
*www.authorhouse.com*
*Phone: 1-800-839-8640*

*AuthorHouse™ UK Ltd.*
*500 Avebury Boulevard*
*Central Milton Keynes, MK9 2BE*
*www.authorhouse.co.uk*
*Phone: 08001974150*

*First published by AuthorHouse 11/27/2006*

*Printed in the United States of America
Bloomington, Indiana*

*This book is printed on acid-free paper.*
*ISBN: 978-1-4259-7030-7 (sc)*

Joseph Billieux (1850-1920)
m.1874
Rose Arquette
(1857-1938)

| Oscar (1876-1938) | Alphonse (1880----) | Maurice (1881- ) | Mathilda (1884- ) | Charles (1887- ) | Clara (1897- ) |
|---|---|---|---|---|---|
| m.(1896) Flora DuPont (1873- ) | -m.(1899) Grace Poulet (1873- ) | m.(1900) Simone Dion (1884- ) | m.(1904 ) Edward LaPointe (1881- ) | | m. (1917) Auguste Pelletier (1898 –1918) |
| Helene Louis Jacque George Jean | Artur Celeste Phillipe (1913- ) | Anna Colette Henri Robert (1925 - ) | Pierro (1908 - ) m.(1928) Angela Ciccione (1911 - ) | | |
| | | | Marie (1930 - ) Amy (1937 - ) | | |

v

To all families everywhere
and to
my daughter, Lissa
my son, David
my grandson, Nick

# ACKNOWLEDGMENTS

Finishing the second book of the trilogy about the fictitious Billieux family feels like having pushed the boulder over another hill. It could not have been done without the help of my friends. First of all, there is my special friend and writing colleague, Rachel Michaud, who is always encouraging, even when she's nagging. Thank you, Rachel, for your candor, your sharp mind, your loyal support and your generosity.

The Sunday Writers' Group offered insight, suggestions, and careful critiquing, along with fellowship. Naomi, Brenda, Connie, Constance, Lynne, I thank you all.

A wonderful circle of friends continues to encourage me and enrich my life, especially Marilyn, Sharon, Scott, Suzanne, Mark, Cheryl, Judy, Barbara and Ruth. Suzanne gets my sincere gratitude for her careful copy editing of the manuscript. My sister, Bea Erickson and my cousin, Arline Lula, have been wonderful cheerleaders and advocates. Thanks for your belief in me. The love goes both ways.

So many people responded to my questions about the WWII years, offering reminiscence as well as answers that it is not possible to name them all here, but I hope they know how much I appreciated every bit of lore they shared with me.

I am especially indebted to the readers of the first book, "Forgive me, Father," for their encouraging feedback. I promised to deliver the second book in a year and here it is.

# CHAPTER 1

## SUMMER 1941

Clara sat at the end of the gray plank deck in front of Mary Kowalsky's family cottage on Hampton Pond, squinting into the setting sun. She was watching for the rowboat to come through the concrete culvert under the road that split the pond into two sections. Pete and Ray had rowed over to LaFleur's Bait Shop to get more beer and sweet corn for their picnic. Now Clara was a little bit worried about whether they got held up by some of the guys that hung out at that place telling tales of their fishing and hunting expeditions.

She heard Angela coming down the path toward the dock, laughing with that rich, musical laughter that made everybody smile when they heard it. Then she heard the slap of bare feet on the boards behind her. She turned, her eyes widening, her brows lifting.

"*Mon Dieux*, Angela, where did you get that bathing suit? This is 1941, *cherie*. That looks like a relic from the thirties. Wool, yuk!"

Angela sat down beside her and tugged on the straps, "Itchy, too. I borrowed it from Mary because my own won't fit over my belly."

Clara hugged her nephew's wife, 13 years younger but still a good friend and much loved. "*C'est rien*. You are hardly showing yet. How are you feeling?"

Angela had suffered morning sickness much worse than with her other two pregnancies making her husband, Pete, and her in-laws all quite anxious about her health. Dr. Boucher patted her hand and assured her all was well, but privately Pete and Angela worried about it often. Two little girls already and they were hoping for a boy.

Behind them, Mary and Tom, a short, stocky blond with a tendency to blush bright pink and Mary's current boyfriend, slammed the screen door and ambled arm in arm toward the women waiting at the dock. Mary was flushed and glowing, a little disheveled, her pink flowered playsuit buttoned up wrong so the fit over her ample bosom was skewed.

Just then, Clara caught sight of the rowboat coming across the pond and she jumped up, waving her arms, shouting, "Hurry up. We're all hungry."

When the six of them were sitting around the picnic table under the tall stand of trees on the side of the cottage, the talk quickly turned to the looming prospect of war. All of them had seen the Pathe news clips at the movies, watched in horror the bombing of London, the rape of Europe by Hitler's war machine. They'd read the headlines on the front page of the Gazette and the Boston Globe of torpedo strikes in the Atlantic.

"Listen to me, all of you." Ray began, "We are sure going to go to war at some point. I don't care what the politicians are saying right now. Some people may think you can put your head in the sand, but sooner or later, it's going to happen. And when it does, I'll be first in line to enlist. Those bastards make my blood boil." He slammed his fist down on the wooden table so hard the beer bottles jumped up and rattled.

Echoes of agreement came from the other two men while the women looked on in horror, Angela crying out in her terror that Pete might actually enlist, too. Later, she would remember this moment with stark and painful clarity.

Clara was not surprised to hear Ray's passionate declaration, although she privately thought he was probably too old to be accepted into any of the services. *Mon Dieux*, he was 34. War was for young men. And, of course, Pete had a family, so he'd never go. They were just talking like little boys, fascinated with the adventure of fighting for a noble cause, to save the world from the monster, Hitler.

Driving back to town later that evening in Ray's comfortable Nash, which he kept spotlessly clean and polished, Clara began to talk in low tones of her first marriage and of the Great War. Pete and Angela were dozing in the back seat.

"I suppose you hardly remember that war, Ray, but let me tell you all the guys were so eager to go 'over there', to some godforsaken field in France. They had no idea at all about digging trenches and fighting in mud and filth and poison gas, scared, exhausted. There's nothing exciting or glamorous or noble about war, no matter what you think. And there's so much death and destruction, you can't imagine it. I can't even imagine it, though I've been told and I've tried to picture it. And when Gus was killed, I was damned angry. He'd been so happy to be serving his country, to be seen as a hero. And what did it get him? Dead. That's what it got him. Just dead."

Ray was staring straight ahead at the road. Clara could see his jaws clench. Then he reached over for her, where she was sitting close to the open window, separated from him by about 18 inches of leather seat. And he pulled her close to him, hugging her, the fierceness of his embrace speaking volumes.

The kitchen at 144 West Street was hot and sticky and dark as the tropical animal house at the zoo in Forest Park. *Memere* and Mommy were canning tomatoes, a messy job now that would be appreciated only come winter. Marie came down the back staircase, all skinny legs and sweating body, an eleven-year-old looking for breakfast, a loving pat on the rump and something to do on this wickedly hot August day.

She could go to the pool at Look Park, but not without an adult; she could go to the library, where the reading room had giant fans set in the high ceilings; she could pick hollyhock blossoms to make into elegant ladies in pink and white ball dresses; she could climb trees in the apple orchard and spy on the men working on the West Street Bridge repair. Nothing appealed. She was just cranky.

Betsy had gone to sleep-away camp, paid for by somebody Marie never heard of. Mommy wouldn't let Marie go and all her explanations for why not made no sense to Marie. Too expensive, too dangerous, not anybody Mommy knew in charge. Huh! Marie suspected it was more because Mommy wanted her help looking after her sister Amy who was a wide-eyed, sweet, angelic four-year-old who wanted nothing more in life than to tag after her big sister.

"*Bonjour*, Marie, *ma cherie, petite chouchou*. Sit down at the table and I'll fix you some cereal with milk and blueberries. Would you like that? Watch out for that pot. It's hot." *Memere* was wiping her hands on her apron and coming to Marie with a hug and a kiss.

Mommy turned from her position at the stove, stirring the contents of a huge blue enamel pot, and smiled at

Marie. "Did you sleep well, *cara*? Did you wash your face already? Is your sister awake yet?"

It was hard for Marie to retain her grumpiness in the face of such loving adults, so she smiled back at Mommy, hugged *Memere* and sat at the end of the table waiting for her cereal with blueberries. "No, Amy is still sleeping. I woke up because I could smell the tomatoes cooking and I knew you were down here already."

Canning chores were best done in the very early part of the morning, before the heat of the day added to the heat of the cooking and made the kitchen unbearable. *Pepere* had bought five bushels of tomatoes from Galusha's farm market stand in the meadows, getting them at the peak of ripeness, bright red, plump and luscious. The task of putting them up in jars could not be put off without risking a loss to their perfection.

First, the glass canning jars were sterilized with boiling water. They always used Ball's jars, the very best. Then, each tomato was washed and dried gently with an old linen towel before it was dipped into boiling water very, very briefly to make removal of the skin a simple, but slithery task. A swift flick of the wrist holding a very sharp paring knife removed the stem and core before the tomatoes were packed into the jars, squished down tight to get as many as possible in. A sprig of basil and a dash of salt went into each jar before the freshly boiled rubber flange was fitted into place around the mouth of the jar and the glass top added. The metal clamp that held the top on was the last task before the jars were lowered into the canning pot with the rack to hold them upright. The jars would cook in there for 30 minutes before they would be removed to cool, get labeled and be brought down to the wooden rack in the cellar that would be full of jars holding green beans, beets, squash, pickle relish and piccalilli. The piccalilli was Marie's favorite because it sat in large stone crocks on the back porch curing before it could be put up in the jars. It made the porch smell wonderful--spicy, vinegary and mouthwatering.

*Memere* and Mommy had bright red hands, almost as bright as the tomatoes, from handling the hot fruit, the hot water and the hot jars. But never mind, the job had to be done and they would do it. Not only did it save money so they didn't have to buy canned stuff in the winter, but it tasted so much better, it was worth a few burns on the hands and arms.

Amy came down the stairs, bumping along on her rump, a favorite mode of descending. She was rubbing her eyes and whining, "I'm hungry." Mommy turned from her task at the stove. "Just a minute, pumpkin, I'll be with you in a jiffy."

Marie sighed. She knew what was coming. Too late to escape. Mommy was going to ask her to watch over Amy until they finished with the canning. Maybe she would read her a story. Amy loved to hear Marie read stories to her. Even when they were books she didn't understand. The sound of the words never failed to enchant her.

Later, the two girls sat in the shade of the side porch, close together on the wooden swing, bright pillows at their backs, and Marie read the poems of Robert Louis Stevenson, while Amy listened, sighed and asked for some parts to be read again and again. They whiled away the morning like that until they heard the noon whistle from the laundry at the State Hospital. It was the signal that *Pepere* and Aunt Clara would be coming home soon for dinner.

By some unspoken, but common, agreement, nobody opened the newspaper before Edward and so, although Clara was eager to read the story below the black headline "Fierce Fighting Rages On Four Fronts", she waited. She went up to use the bathroom, lingering a little to re-do the heavy hair she kept fixed tight in a bun with large tortoise shell hairpins and which always came undone, damp tendrils plastered along her neck with the sweat of the morning's work at the hosiery. She heard the back screen door slam on its tight spring and knew her brother-in-law had arrived home for dinner.

Marie and Amy were already sitting at the table. Angela and Tillie bustled about the kitchen. Pork chops today, fried in the big, black iron skillet in bacon grease along with thick rounds of apple slices. A plate of tomato quarters, a stack of bread. Bring out the butter. Pour the milk and they all sat down.

They ate quickly and mostly in silence, except for Edward's compliments on the meal directed to Tillie and Angela and an occasional admonition from Angela to Amy, "Watch that you don't spill your milk." or "Don't play with your food, Amy." or "Eat all of those apples; they're good for you."

When Angela and Tillie rose to clear the plates, Edward picked up the newspaper and snapped it open. "Everybody at the library was talking about another ship torpedoed and I didn't get to see the New York

Times today. I wonder what those Nazis are going to do next."

Clara took a deep breath. "Would you read what it says about a fourth major Nazi offensive out loud, Edward? Please. I'm going to get the blueberry tarts."

Edward started to read. "A fourth major Nazi offensive, apparently aimed at Leningrad simultaneously with the southern smash toward Odessa, was reported today in Soviet war dispatches. ....."

Clara set the plate of tarts down in front of Tillie and returned to her seat at the table. "*Mon Dieux*, Edward, I hope we are not heading toward another war. How can this be? Didn't we learn anything the last time? What's the matter with those crazy people?" She was close to tears.

Tillie, sitting beside her, reached over and stroked her arm. Angela unconsciously rubbed her hand over her belly, not yet feeling more than a vague flutter within.

Walking back to the hosiery after dinner, Clara was deep in thought as she passed over the West Street Bridge, where the men there working on the repairs stopped in their sweaty labors to call out to her. "Hey, babe, what are you doing tonight? " and "How about a little smile?"

Another hot night, too hot for the red crepe dress with the elbow length sleeves. Clara rummaged around in the closet looking for anything that would be cool and comfortable. Dancing was always sure to make her sweat, but especially with the heat from the lights strung all over the outdoor ballroom at Mt. Tom Park, she was certainly going to need the coolest clothes she owned. With Tommy Dorsey there tonight, there'd be lots of swing, so it would be nice to find one with a full skirt.

She pulled out the pink flowered georgette with the fluttery short sleeves and the deep vee'd neckline. *Mon Dieux*, she'd worn this all summer, to nearly every dance, but it was perfect for tonight and nobody would say anything. Everybody else had as limited a wardrobe as she did. White sling backs and a white purse and she was ready to go.

Ray was already there when she came down the front staircase, sitting on the horsehair sofa in his cream linen trousers and pale blue sport coat. A little intake of breath betrayed Clara's reaction on seeing him. He really was a handsome man, wonderful to be with. She wondered how he ever put up with her continuing refusals to marry him. But he did, asking again every few months just to be sure she hadn't changed her mind.

There were two distinct dimensions to her relationship with Ray, the public one which her friends and family saw, the one where they dated every weekend and sometimes once in the middle of the week. And then there was a private one, where they went to one or another of the roadside cabins in the wide area between Massachusetts and Connecticut and enjoyed mutually satisfying, passionate, uninhibited sex.

Clara's family, meaning her sister Tillie and Tillie's husband Edward, along with their son, Pete, his wife, Angela and their two daughters, Marie and Amy, all lived in the house on 144 West Street. All of them loved Ray. None of them, except Tillie, could understand why Clara didn't agree to marry Ray.

Clara had been married very young to Gus Pelletier, her childhood sweetheart, and when he was killed in France on the last day of the Great War, what had been called "the war to end all wars," she had vowed never to marry again, deeply fearful of the emotional devastation of that loss. No argument that she would be equally devastated at the loss of Ray, whether they were married or not, was able to move her.

Besides, she had become entrenched in the comforts of living together in an extended family. Tillie ran the household, organized their lives around holidays, weekends, seasons and celebrations. She was the general, the rest of them her troops. Clara was glad to help with the chores, but she had no illusions that she was other than Tillie's helper, following her sister's lead, obeying her commands, even though they were always couched in requesting language.

# CHAPTER 2

## FALL 1941

Fall was Marie's absolutely favorite time of the year. She loved going back to school after summer vacation, especially now that she was going to Hawley Grammar, a big red brick building on South Street with a playground full of wonderful stuff like monkey bars and swings and a jungle gym. There were so many more people to meet and things to learn –geography and penmanship and history—subjects that hadn't been part of the program at Hospital Hill School. It was a longer walk to school, but no steep hill to climb and very interesting with houses and stores to pass.

Betsy walked beside her, both of them kicking at the dry leaves on the sidewalk. At Agawam Street, they were joined by Esther, whose wildly curling black hair, always escaping from her fat braids, fascinated Marie.

"We saw a boy kissing one of the college girls yesterday." Betsy smirked at the superiority of having had an adventure that excluded Esther. "And he was rubbing her back, too!"

"Where were they?" Esther's eyes were wide at such an experience.

"In the doorway of Gerry's Photo Studio," Marie answered. "It wasn't even dark out yet." Of course, none of the girls would be out after dark without an adult, but it was especially thrilling that such a forbidden activity might occur in broad daylight.

"Wow," breathed Esther.

When they passed the spot a few minutes later, all three looked intently into the doorway, but nothing was there to see today, especially at 7:45 in the morning. Mr. G, who smiled at the girls as they passed, watched over the burning leaves at the curbside. That was another thing Marie loved about the fall, the smell of burning leaves.

Passing the Forbes Library, Marie looked over the hedge to see if she could catch a glimpse of her *Pepere*, working outside today, but he was nowhere to be seen. Across from the entrance to the library and down Green Street a little way, the students who attended Smith College hurried from one place to another, oblivious to the life of the small town of Northampton and its inhabitants.

The three friends were moving steadily, not hurriedly, but still with a brisk pace, none of them eager to be tardy only three weeks into the new school year. They passed the tiny Methodist Church and turned down the alley shortcut to the school.

They climbed the worn staircase to the second floor, hung their jackets on pegs in the hallway and made their way to their desks in the drab green seventh grade classroom, on the right in the back corner. Since Marie, Betsy and Esther were all good students, they sat in the back of the room, while slower students, mostly boys, occupied the front seats.

Marie lifted the lid of her desk, took out a pencil and walked over to the pencil sharpener.

"Good morning, Marie." The teacher was Mrs. Miles, an unattractive, tight-lipped, stiff young woman, newly come to Hawley Grammar, who had already demonstrated that she could be stern and unforgiving of any disruption in class. Marie had not felt the sting of her ruler, but had witnessed it.

The seats were almost all full when the bell rang at 8:00 for the beginning of class, which always started with the Pledge of Allegiance and the Lord's Prayer. Marie, being Catholic, mumbled at the end to mask the fact that her version was a little different than Mrs. Miles'.

When the bell rang for recess, children hurried down the stairs and out the doors into a playground lit with the sunshine of a perfect autumn day. Boys quickly overran the equipment, and the sharp bark of a teacher monitoring recess reminded them to get in line, take turns, no pushing. A group of girls gathered on the blacktop with a long jumping rope, chanting familiar rhymes, skirts flying, while another group hastily drew a pattern in chalk to begin a game of hopscotch.

"Look at Irene Frenier over there. Want to go find out what she's saying?" Marie asked Betsy.

"Oh, I heard somebody say her uncle just joined the RAF and she's got a picture of him in his uniform. Want to go see?"

"Why did he do that? My *Pepere* says that we'll never go to war. President Roosevelt says so." Marie believed that nothing her grandfather said was to be questioned, because he knew everything.

"I think he had to because Canada is part of Britain, but I'm not sure. Maybe he just thought it would be exciting."

The two girls, arm in arm, strolled over to the cluster around Irene, peeking over shoulders to see if they could get a look at the picture she was holding. Marie put her hand out and asked. "Can I see it?"

"No, nobody can touch it except me. I don't want it to get messed up." Irene's voice was full of her self-importance at being the focus of attention.

Marie walked home with Esther; Betsy having been picked up by her mother to help mind her brother while she did her grocery shopping. The girls sang "Chattanooga Choo-Choo" and "Deep in the Heart of Texas," laughing when they forgot the words. And when

19

they tired of that, they ambled along until they reached Agawam Street and Esther turned right, leaving Marie to carry on alone.

As she passed the MacCallum Silk Hosiery, Marie looked into the windows just below the street level for her Aunt Clara, working at her inspection machinery. Stopping briefly, she blew kisses to her favorite aunt and caught the kisses coming back to her.

Clara and Ray lay spooned together, dozing on the bed in the Forest Mountain Cabins just south of Springfield. Clara woke slowly, languidly stretching. The shadows in the room reminded her that the afternoon was nearly over. She shook Ray's shoulder gently.

"Ray, wake up. We have to go."

Ray rolled over and reached for her, bringing her close, rubbing her soft flesh and lush breasts against his chest, fitting his thigh over her hip. "Not yet."

These afternoons, not as frequent as they would like and precious to them both, always ended too soon with some obligation or another keeping them from staying longer. Clara sighed, responsive as always to Ray's passion and expertise, and knew she would have to dress hurriedly and would still be late for Sunday supper with her family.

While they dressed, Ray again brought up the subject of marriage. For what seemed to him like it must be the hundredth time, he asked Clara to reconsider her opposition to getting married. He figured she would be most receptive to his pleas when she was flush with the evidence of his love and caring for her. But Clara was more resolute than ever since Ray had started talking about his strong conviction that the country would soon be at war again and his determination to enlist as soon as war was declared.

They had both seen the newsreels at the movies of the belligerence of the German regime under Hitler and the bravery of the Brits. Ray, who had had a year at Harvard before he needed to drop out when his father died, still kept up with some of his old classmates and knew that some of them had already gone to Washington to work on war planning, all very hush hush, of course.

He felt a strong obligation to "do his part." And Clara remained adamant that she would not risk being a war widow again.

"Ray, darling, you already know how I feel. Why can't you be happy with the way things are?"

Clara was weary of this discussion and silenced Ray with the usually effective strategy of a kiss. He was rueful but resigned. In the car on the way back to Northampton, they talked about plans for Thanksgiving. Ray was aware of Clara's need to help her sister and her nephew's wife, Angela, in the preparation of the Thanksgiving feast. He also knew his mother would not forgive his absence at his sister's home. For the past three years they had accepted the fact that they had to eat two Thanksgiving dinners and give the appearance at least that they were enjoying the abundance of food at both. It was a little tricky, but they managed it, sometimes with the simple ploy of pushing food around the plate and being animated in their contributions to the conversation so more attention was paid to the talk than the groaning platters before them. Fortunately, Clara's family tradition was an early afternoon meal and Ray's family ate in the evening.

Sometimes Ray reflected that they behaved as if they were, in fact, married. Of course they did not share a home together and he would certainly have preferred to have Clara in his arms and in his bed every night rather than the two or three times a week they were able to arrange. He knew, of course, that Clara was older then he and that it was extremely unlikely and maybe impossible that they would ever have children. He thought maybe she was coming to the point in her life where women go through the change, but he knew little about that except what he had heard in locker room talk and he certainly did not ever imagine talking to Clara about it.

Clara's insistence that she did not want to take the emotional risk of marrying again and facing possible widowhood again did not make sense to Ray. He was absolutely sure she loved him as he loved her and that married or not, if he died, she would be hard hit. But no matter how many times he told her this and even though she agreed with him, she insisted it would not be the same. Now with a war looming and Clara's terror at that, she was even more adamant in her refusal to accept his proposal.

"I hope you're planning to stay for Sunday supper tonight. I'm making pancakes and sausage."

"Oh, sure. How could I pass that up?" Ray reached across the seat of the car and took her hand, placing it on his thigh and squeezing it gently. He would have stayed if she was serving gruel just to be able to spend more time in her company, to look across a table and admire her beautiful eyes, her wide luscious mouth, her shining long hair coiled loosely in a bun at her neck.

Angela and Tillie were in the kitchen when they arrived, sitting at the table playing gin rummy while Amy played with her dolls by the stove and Marie sat in the rocker with her nose buried in a book. "I was thinking I'd be making the pancakes myself, *ma soeur.*" Tillie gently chided Clara.

"Sorry, we didn't notice the time," Clara replied and then flushed crimson when she saw the look Tillie gave her. "I mean, we were further away than we thought," she started to elaborate as her sister held up her hand in a gesture that clearly signaled she should stop explaining.

"*C'est rien.* You're here now. Let's get supper started. Angela, why don't you see if the men need a freshening of their drinks? They're so caught up in listening to the news they won't think to come and ask."

In the front parlor, Ray joined Edward and Pete around the big new Atwater Kent radio. Their faces wore grim expressions. The newscaster reported an air raid that took out a large section of homes in London, killing ten people who were not able to get into the shelters before the bombs came or maybe had not heard the warning sirens. One reporter, Gabriel Heatter, mentioned food shortages and talked about parents sending their children away from home for safety.

The Sunday newspapers lay on the floor all around them. Edward insisted that they get the Boston Globe as well as the Springfield Republican on Sundays, but waited until he got to work at the library on Monday to read the N.Y. Times. He read everything about the war in Europe and in Asia, as well. "I tell you both. We will be in this war by next summer. Maybe even sooner. You mark my words." Edward clamped his teeth down on the stem of his pipe and drew in sharply. "I know Roosevelt doesn't want to go to war, but something is going to happen that will force him to change his mind."

"Well, when we do, I'll be there in line at the recruiting station. I'm not waiting for the draft. I couldn't live with myself if I didn't do my bit to get rid of this bunch of monsters." Ray's tone was belligerent and determined.

"And how does Clara feel about that, Ray? You know she lost her Gus to the last one." Edward's voice was soft and mild, as was his usual habit. He believed that even painful issues could be discussed calmly if everyone kept their voices quiet.

"Oh, I know and I feel badly about that. But, you know, a man's got to do what his conscience tells him he must do."

Pete spoke up, "I'm thinking I'll have to do the same."

Edward scowled, "A man with two *jeune femmes* and a *bebe* on the way has no business talking like that. Forget about being a hero. Your place is here taking care of your family."

Just then Angela walked in. "Well. I sure agree with that. Now, who needs another drink? Clara just started supper, so you've got time if you want one."

Edward declined, Ray held up his nearly full glass and Pete said, "Sure, but I'll get it." And patted his wife's rounded belly as he rose from the chair.

Later, when Clara walked out to Ray's car with him to bid him goodbye, he asked her if she thought Pete was serious about enlisting, adding that he thought it unlikely Pete would be drafted.

"I really don't know. His passions run pretty hot. And he always seems to need to prove himself a tough guy. But we'll see how he feels when the new baby comes, especially if it turns out to be a boy. Maybe he'll want to stay home and be a bigger part of raising him than he's been with the girls."

"Yeah, maybe you're right. I know I would." The words were out before he considered how they might sound to Clara and he started to add other words to explain, but Clara quickly put her fingers over his lips and replaced them with her mouth in a kiss that made his gaffe a minor slip.

"I'll see you on Wednesday?" She asked as he climbed into his car. "Of course. You couldn't keep me away," he replied.

# CHAPTER 3

## NOVEMBER/DECEMBER 1941

Tillie bent over and checked the turkey, covered with cheesecloth coated with butter. It was just beginning to smell delicious. She stepped into the dining room and paused in pulling on her gloves to admire the beautifully set table. It was covered in linen with crocheted corners, set with the creamy china that had been in the family for as long as she could remember and graced with the silver peacocks in the middle. Memories brought the threat of tears, but she swallowed rapidly and headed out to the front door.

Standing in front of the hall mirror, she fixed her hat to her head with a long hat pin and called up the stairs, "Pete, don't forget to check the turkey. We'll be back in an hour or so."

Edward, Clara, Angela and her daughters were already in the car, waiting to go off to Mass on Thanksgiving morning. Tillie climbed in to the front seat, smiled at her husband and said, *"Allons, allons."*

Sacred Heart Church, called the French church by everyone in the family, was a lovely building on King Street set back from the curb with a wide lawn, now covered by a light dusting of snow. It was fairly small, at least when compared to St. Mary's up on Elm Street, where all the Irish and Italians went. Two priests and four nuns served the parish, which had a small parochial school in a building next door. Everyone from the French-Canadian community went to the French church. It served as a social meeting place as well as a religious one. It was a low Mass this morning and so, blessedly brief, and afterwards, they spent a few minutes chatting on the portico with old friends.

When they got home, Ray had arrived and was sitting in the parlor with Pete, drinks already in their hands. "Hey, Pa, sit down with us. Angela, get Pa a drink." Pete was full of bonhomie today. "I'll get it." Clara answered him. "You should go upstairs and lie down for a few minutes, Angela. I'll call you when we need you." Clara had a feeling that Angela was not doing too well today. She looked weary, her face betraying her attempts to assure them she was fine. Amy settled herself in her *Pepere's* lap and Marie wandered off to the little alcove to pick up her book. From the kitchen came the traditional smells of Thanksgiving, roasting turkey, sage, sausage, onions, and the sounds of pots and mixing spoons and the pantry door slamming.

"Did you see the paper yet today?" Ray asked. Pete reached under his chair and held up a paper. "This rag doesn't publish on holidays and we only get the Boston papers on Sunday. What have you seen already, so early today?"

"I got the New York Times at the coffee shop this morning after I drove my mother over to my sister's house. The front page has a story about a meeting of the US military chiefs and the President of the Philippines. It said the discussions were a 'closely-guarded secret.' That tells me they're getting ready for war."

The men settled into a discussion about world politics, Edward a staunch supporter of Roosevelt, the other two more skeptical.

"I tell you, if Roosevelt says we will not get into this war, he means it. Of course, something could happen to force his hand. But I trust that man." Edward repeated a declaration he had made many times before.

"I think he'll have to go to war if it gets any worse. He'll just have to. We can't be a player in world politics if we just sit here and pretend the world is not in chaos and the danger is not real." Ray had often said essentially the same thing.

When the whole family gathered around the table, each of them took a moment to settle into their seats, enjoy the sight of the big turkey with its crispy brown skin set in front of Edward for carving and inhale the lovely aromas of the feast. Marie and Amy were well aware of the expected behavior and folded their hands in their laps, waiting.

Edward bowed his head and the rest of them followed suit. Sensitive to Ray as well as Angela in their midst, he spoke in English. "Heavenly Father, we thank you for this feast before us and for the loving family around us, including our great friend Ray Carpenter. We remember today *Gran'pere* and *Gran'mere*, Clara's beloved fallen husband Auguste, our brother Oscar and all those other friends and family who have gone from us, but who are surely in your kingdom of Heaven with you now. We remember our brother Charles and pray he is well. We thank you for the good health we enjoy, the bounty of our table every day and the beauty that surrounds us. Also, we pray for peace. Amen."

Heads came up and hands reached out to pass plates as Edward rose from his seat and began carving turkey slices. But under the murmured voices requesting butter or salt, most around the table were remembering other Thanksgivings. It had been only four years ago when Oscar and Charlie had a terrible fight, right here at the table, during the feast.

*Gran'mere* was still living then, though her health was failing and she was losing her sense of herself, forgetting faces, her mind wandering into the past. Oscar, the eldest son of the family, was determined that her entire estate would come under his control when she passed on. Charlie, the youngest son, the one who had assumed responsibility for the tenant houses on their land that provided substantial family income, was enraged at his brother's arrogance. Oscar tended to be a bully even in his youth, had always been aloof from the rest of them and resisted his French-Canadian heritage. When Oscar criticized Tillie's care of *Gran'mere*, Charlie dragged him into the kitchen and tackled him. It had been a Thanksgiving never to be forgotten.

Then, early the next year, after *Gran'mere* died and Oscar removed the gold cross she had always worn around her neck before her casket was closed, Charlie confronted him at the cemetery. When Oscar spoke sharply to him, and struck him with his hands, Charlie picked up a shovel lying by the gravesite and hit his brother. Oscar's heart was stopped by the blow.

Ray had offered to help. He contacted the man who had been his roommate during his one year at Harvard, a man who had become a well-known and extremely skilled criminal attorney, who agreed to represent Charlie. When Charlie was convicted of manslaughter, an accidental killing, Oscar's family was enraged. Alphonse, the next to eldest son and his family sided with Oscar's widow in the belief that Charlie deserved to die for murdering his brother. Another brother, Maurice, a sensitive man, moved his family to Connecticut to help him overcome his grief. The close knit family was broken apart, never to be the same. And, although most of the family forgave Charlie, believing he hadn't meant to kill his brother, Charlie was unable to forgive himself. None of them had been able to visit him in prison because he forbade it. He was due to come out of prison next year. They all wondered whether he would ever come home; whether he and Aphonse and Maurice would ever sit down to eat Thanksgiving dinner with them again.

On what would turn out to be an especially memorable Sunday, Ray and Clara had lunch at their favorite Italian restaurant in Thompsonville, just across the state line in Connecticut. The food was always good; the place smelled of the luscious oregano that Chef Luigi used liberally; and the various jazz combos that played background music every Sunday created an atmosphere that was at once homey, comfortable and romantic. High backed booths along the back wall gave some illusion of privacy. Ray had been a customer for so long that Sergio, who owned the place along with his brother Luigi, made sure a booth was available for the handsome couple.

When they left there a little after two o'clock, they went to a cabin on the Old Coach Road, west of Springfield, back in Massachusetts. Driving there in silence, thighs touching as Clara sat in the middle of the front seat, each of them anticipated a couple of hours abandoning inhibitions in a wild frenzy of glorious, satisfying, breathtaking sex. Ray made love with all his heart and soul, tender and fierce at the same time, demanding response and reveling in it. For her part, Clara welcomed every kiss, every caress, and every stroke and gave back in equal measure.

Later, passions abated for the time being, Ray asked Clara again to marry him. It had become a familiar after-sex ritual, this business of asking and being refused. This day, Ray did not immediately begin to press his usual argument about the advantages of marrying him and instead was humming a tune as he helped Clara with the back zipper of her blue wool dress.

"What's that you're humming?" Clara asked as she turned around, kissing the little hollow at the base of his throat before she buttoned up his shirt.

"I don't know. It just popped into my head. I must have been thinking about you when I heard it. And right now I was thinking about how much nicer it would be if we were in our own house together and didn't need to get dressed again and drive back to Northampton for Sunday night supper with the family."

Clara swatted him on the arm. "Oh, stop, why don't you? Why can't you just enjoy what we have and quit trying to make me argue with you? Besides, you're too young for me. I'll be an old lady and you'll still be a gay young blade, bored with me and looking for a replacement in just a few more years."

Clearly exasperated, Ray grabbed Clara's shoulders and shook her lightly. "What does it take for you to realize how much I love you? I want to be with you forever. I want to take care of you forever. I want to watch your hair turn white. I want to kiss all your wrinkles when you have wrinkles." He would have continued but, seeing the tears gathering in Clara's eyes, instead he pulled her to him fiercely and put his lips to her ear. "Ah, don't cry, babe. I can't bear it when you cry. I won't say any more. Let's go have some supper with your family."

When they opened the front door at 144 West Street, they were surprised to see Edward, Pete and Angela with Amy on her lap, all sitting in the front parlor around the big Atwater Kent radio, with the volume turned up much louder than normal. "What's happening?" Clara's voice was anxious and strained. The voice of

John Cameron Swayze continued reporting on the radio.

"War. We're going to war now for sure. Those crazy Japanese have attacked Pearl Harbor in Honolulu. President Roosevelt is for sure going to the Congress tomorrow to ask for a declaration of war." Pete's face was white, his hands gripping the arms of the chair, the muscles in his forearms tight, reflecting the tension they all felt.

A look passed between Ray and Clara and in that moment she knew for certain that Ray would be going to war. A shiver went through her body, the sudden strong memory of her young husband going off to fight in 1917, so eager to do his part, so excited and full of patriotic fervor, and so dead by the end of that war. Grief, loss and bitterness overwhelmed her. Without even removing her hat and coat, she ran up the front staircase to the bathroom, slamming the door behind her so she could cry angry tears, banging her clenched hand on the rim of the sink. She wrenched the faucet handle to run the water full force in a futile attempt to cover up the sounds of her despair.

Down in the front parlor, Ray shed his coat and pulled up a chair next to Pete. "When did this happen? How many people dead? I thought the Japanese delegation was still in Washington presenting some kind of peace proposal."

"I don't think they know yet how many people have been killed, but one whole battleship is sunk, full of Navy guys. It began early in the morning in Honolulu, a little after two o'clock our time. Waves of fighter planes came over the island, so many the sky was dark and they just kept dropping their bombs. It took a while for our own guys to get to their planes and start fighting them off, but most of our planes were shot up anyway. Our antiaircraft gunners on the ground got quite a few, but, you know, nobody was prepared for a sneak attack from those bastards. " Pete's voice was thick with venom.

"*Attendez, attendez,*" Edward interrupted, gesturing toward the radio.

A Major somebody or other was analyzing the situation, saying the Japanese must have launched their attack from aircraft carriers because they had no bases close enough to the islands. He called it a risky strategy because that would put their aircraft carriers within striking distance of retaliatory forces of the United States.

"Who gives a shit about that, anyway?" Pete burst out. "If they bomb all our ships in the harbor and all our planes on the ground, who's going to be there to retaliate?"

The front door opened. Marie and her *Memere* came in with a whoosh of cold air. They were returning from a Bing Crosby movie. "Did you hear about the Japanese attacking Pearl Harbor? The manager at the Calvin came out on the stage just when the movie finished and yelled out that we were going to war because the Japanese are killing our people in Pearl Harbor." Marie's face was flushed, her eyes bright. "Will they come here next?"

Angela lifted Amy off her lap and stood up, a little awkwardly, now that her pregnancy had begun to affect her balance and put out her hand to Marie. "No, no, *cara mia*, you don't need to worry about that. We're a long ways away. Come with me; you and Amy can help me get some supper started and you can tell us all about the movie you just saw. Would you like waffles tonight?"

Tillie took off her coat and crossed the room in front of the three men sitting there, pausing to put her hand on Edward's shoulder as she passed him on the way back to the kitchen. *"Mon Dieu, Mon Dieu,* what's to become of us?" She murmured.

Ray didn't say much, but he wondered how the Navy could have allowed itself to be surprised. After all, the Japanese had been on the march through Asia for quite a while. The reality of war throughout the Pacific was frequently in the news. Maybe those Navy guys in their smart white uniforms thought they were invincible. It certainly wasn't the first time in history that the enemy was woefully underestimated. But now there was no question. The country would go to war, and not just with the Japanese, but with the Nazis in Germany. This attack would be the trigger to an all out fight to beat back the bad guys. He knew it would be harsh, bloody and painful and he had no doubt that the United States would be victorious. And he also knew he would be a part of it.

Clara, eyes still red despite the cold water she had bathed them in and the Max Factor she had patted all over her face, came into the kitchen from the back staircase. "Want me to set the table, Tillie?"

"*Non, merci*.  The girls are doing it.  We'll just have waffles and sausages.  Maybe you could boil some water for cocoa."

Later, when Ray was getting ready to leave, Clara stood in front of him, her face challenging.  "Now you're going to want to go enlist, aren't you?  Will it be the Army or the Navy?"

"Definitely not the Navy.  I don't like the idea of being a target in a boat out on the big ocean and besides, I'm afraid I'd get seasick and embarrass myself."  He smiled and lifted her chin up with this finger.  "Come on, babe, no tears.  I'll be careful.  And I won't go until I get my affairs in order.  I have to think of my Mother and talk to my sister and her husband and make sure they'll be all right."

"Don't go.  I'm scared.  I've got a bad feeling about this."  Clara's throat was tight, her efforts at control taking a toll.  "Will I see you later this week?"

"Sure.  Of course.  Aren't you going to be my date for New Year's Eve?  We'll be together for the holidays.  I'm not doing anything before they're over.  Now, where's

41

that beautiful smile I always get to remember all the way back to Hartford? You know, you're the most beautiful girl in the world to me."

With an enormous effort, Clara sighed and put on a smile, hugged Ray to her with unusual ferocity and sent him on his way.

In the front bedroom, Angela and Pete were carefully avoiding any discussion about the probability of war being declared in the morning. When she removed her dress and slip, Pete came up behind her and surrounded her with his arms, stroking her breasts and the swell of her pregnant belly. He spread little kisses beneath her ear and down her neck and, turning her around, began the familiar and comfortable ritual of arousing her with his expert and passionate kisses, whispering love words in English and French.

In a very short time, they were in the bed, naked and panting, their thoughts far from war and separation, happy in each other, eagerly enjoying the dazzling euphoria of two bodies joined in passion.

When they lay on the bed afterwards, shoulders and hips touching, Angela's head resting in the crook of Pete's neck, she asked the question she knew he didn't want to hear, "Pete, you won't have to go to war, will you?"

"If you mean, will I be drafted, no, I don't think so, but you never know. Probably not at first, but if it goes on for a while, and it might, I could be."

"But pretty soon, you'll have three children. Won't that disqualify you?"

"I don't know about that. Maybe. Why worry about that now, though? Go to sleep, darling. Don't go borrowing problems that may not happen. Are you cold? Do you want me to go get your nightgown?"

Ignoring his question, Angela pressed him yet again, "But I know you, Pete. You want to go. It appeals to your need for adventure, excitement, danger, like buying that dammed motorcycle." Her voice was getting higher. Pete rolled onto his side and slid his arms around her, kissing her face, pulling her to him, stroking his hands down her back. "If you're not going to sleep, I've got a better idea than arguing about something that hasn't even happened yet."

In the back bedroom, Edward watched Tillie take out the hairpins and unroll the tight pug at her neck, a hairstyle she had worn for many years now. He remembered when her hair was her pride and glory, thick, rich chestnut brown, rolled in an elegant French twist, pouffed at her temples, with little curls grazing her cheeks. But ever since her father died and she had committed herself to care for her dying mother and the rest of the family as well, she pulled it all back with a severity that made her cheek bones look stark and took away the soft prettiness of her features.

Taking the brush from her hands, he said, "Let me, *cherie*, I like to do it." and he gently drew the lovely silver backed brush through her hair, in long strokes from her forehead to the ends of the long strands. "I know you are worried, *ma coeur*, but there is nothing we can do except support whatever he decides to do. He is a grown man now, with a wife and children. We cannot order his life as if he were yet a boy."

Tears slowly rolled down Tillie's face. "He's still my boy, my only child. I want to protect him. These young kids don't remember the last war." She shuddered.

"We sent away boys and they came back broken men. Missing limbs. Gassed. Shell-shocked. Never to be the same."

Edward pulled her to her feet and put his arms around her. *"Ne pleut pas.* We will do what we have to do. And maybe he won't go. Maybe Angela will have a little boy and he won't want to leave even if he is drawn to the excitement of it. I really don't think they'll draft him." He took his handkerchief and wiped away her tears. "Come, *cherie*, you need a good night's sleep."

Tillie quickly fashioned her hair into a single braid and dropped to her knees at the side of the bed. *"Je vous salue, Marie, pleine de grace, le Seigneur est avec vous.........*

When Ray pulled into the driveway of his mother's house in West Hartford, he noticed the light burning in the living room and thought it strange, since his mother was usually in bed by the time he got home on Sunday nights. He knew she had been to his sister's house for Sunday dinner, going there directly after attending church services with Anna's family and spending the afternoon playing cards or watching the children. And after a light supper, Anna's husband, Randy, drove her home.

He opened the door to see her huddled in her bathrobe on the couch, an afghan over her feet. Her face was blotched and streaked with tears. "Ma, what's the matter? Are you sick? Should I call the doctor?" He sat down next to her and put his arm around her shoulders.

She pushed him away. "You should have gotten married long ago. There were plenty of girls you could have married. And you could have had a houseful of kids, too. And they would never have come to get you to go fight. Now, look."

Ray took a deep breath and sighed. "Ma, we've talked about this over and over. I love Clara and that's all there is to it. No other woman will ever do for me. Let it go, please, please."

"She's a nice person, Son, but she's too old for you. She'll never give you babies. You should have a son, at least."

Ray decided to ignore the comment and asked, "Did you listen to the radio over at Anna's house? I know Randy won't be called up because he works for Pratt and Whitney and they've been making airplane engines for a while now. I'll bet he wasn't surprised. I'll bet those guys have been talking about getting ready for war for a long time now."

"He thinks you should try to get a job there too and maybe you won't have to go. You're 34; maybe they'll cut off the draft at 30."

"Ma, I don't have any desire to work in a factory. God, I would hate it. Anyway, I won't wait to be drafted. I'm going to enlist right after the first of the year. Then maybe I'll get some job in the Army that will be better than crawling on my belly with a gun. Stop worrying, I'm not gonna go and get killed. "

His mother burst into fresh tears, wailing loudly, "I knew it. I told your sister that's what you'd do. You always were looking to go your own way."

Ray stood and held out his hand to his mother. "Come on, Ma. Time to go to bed. You'll worry yourself ragged and it won't change a thing. I'm going to do what I have to do and that's all there is to it."

At 144 West Street in the dead of the night, Amy woke up and slipped out of the big girl bed she had so recently graduated into and went to her sister, fast asleep in the matching twin bed.  She shook her sister's arm.  "Marie, Marie, wake up," she whispered.  And then, a little louder, pulling the covers off and poking Marie's shoulder with a pudgy little finger, "Marie, I have to ask you something."

Dazed, sleep fogged, Marie raised her head and looked at her little sister, "What do you want, Amy?"

"Marie, what's war?"

# CHAPTER 4

## CHRISTMAS 1941

The Christmas season had lost much of its quality of joy and festivity. Almost every family had someone who had already enlisted or was making plans to do that right after the holiday. Everywhere there was evidence of patriotism, fear, and a well-hidden, but still powerful excitement. People who had been in despair over the economy and lack of jobs now realized that the country would need all sorts of goods to fight this fight. And not just munitions and equipment for the troops, but sturdy shoes and uniforms and packaged food and a nearly endless list of goods and services, and that meant jobs.

Some of the men hanging around the Franco-American Club on Strong Avenue groused about being too old to go to war.  Many of them voiced their outrage at the Japanese and the Nazis in Germany, giving their theories on how to beat back the "Hun" and the "Japs" to anyone who would listen.  Some predicted shortages and started to hoard cigarettes and whiskey, fearful that these staples in their lives might turn out to be hard to get later.  And some of them predicted a swift end once our boys got over there.

Still, Christmas would be observed at 144 West Street. Cards were mailed, gifts were purchased and wrapped and the decorations came down from the attic to be hung on the tree Pete hauled into the front parlor.

On Christmas Eve, Santa came to wake up the girls; one of Pete's friends from the Franco-American Club pressed into service after Charlie went to prison.  It just wasn't the same for Marie and not just because she no longer believed in Santa. Christmas made her think about her Uncle Charlie and the wonderful friend he had been to her before the accident. He had always been there to take her sledding at the first big snowfall and he always let her help pick out the tree when he went to the woods to cut it down.  Mommy reminded her that Amy deserved to have this little tradition preserved and so Marie went along with good grace.

Amy loved her baby doll, which came with a tiny bottle that could be filled with water and then they all laughed at the drama of the wet diaper. Marie got four new books and was in heaven. Pete bought Angela gold earrings with tiny diamonds in them. He hid the box in the bottom of a new coffeepot he bought her. When she opened the package and thanked him for it, he said, "Well, now you'll have to use it right away." So she took all the packing stuff out and there was the box with the earrings. "Oh, Pete, you shouldn't have...," she said with tears rolling down her face.

Everybody, even Pete, went to church on Christmas day and then, Maurice and Simone and Ray all came to dinner. The ham was delicious, the green beans were covered with little bits of bacon and they had the special bread from the Polish Bakery. Marie even got a small glass of watered down wine.

As soon as the meal was over, the men all went into the front parlor to loosen their belts and smoke and talk about the war.

"I heard about a guy I used to work with on a construction gang who got killed in a training accident at Fort Dix. His gun blew up on him. Pretty sad, huh?" Pete looked up at the ceiling, blowing smoke rings.

"Of course, that sort of thing is going to happen and probably more than we'll ever know. Still, it's all in the numbers. They'll get enough guys and they'll train them and some will be savvy or lucky and they'll make it through the war like it's a big game. And some will get wounded and some will get killed. But we'll win anyway." Ray's voice was quiet and thoughtful.

Edward lit his pipe carefully and when he was sure it was going well, he took a deep breath and let it out in a long sigh. "May *le bon Dieu* bless them all."

The ballroom at the Roger Smith Hotel in Springfield was crowded, filled with couples in evening dress and a fair sprinkling of military dress uniforms. Nearby Westover Field Officers' Club always held a huge party, but there were some that preferred the relative privacy and anonymity of a big hotel. Red, white and blue streamers hung from the ceiling and a huge banner of gold cardboard letters spelled out Happy New Year over the bandstand.

Ray and Clara, out on the dance floor, swayed gently to the music of Sammy Kaye's orchestra. Clara wore an ice blue satin gown, cut on the bias to flatter her lovely body and spike heels on a strappy little shoe that would ensure her feet would absolutely be killing her tomorrow. Her long dark hair was styled in the chignon she wore low at the nape of her neck, anchored with bobby pins covered in rhinestones. Her face was slightly flushed from the heat of so many bodies in close proximity. Little tendrils of hair escaped from her sleek hairstyle and curled around her face. She wore a crystal necklace and crystal drops on her ears, ornaments that she had worn with her wedding dress, a gift from her mother and father.

Ray endured the discomfort of heavy starch in his tuxedo shirt, well aware that this was expected and even a source of rueful comment by many of his male friends. Still, he knew this was a special night and he wanted it to be as perfect as possible.

"You know, I hate to say this, because God knows I don't wish Angela sick, but I'm glad they weren't able to join us tonight. I'm really, really glad we're alone." As he said this, Ray drew Clara a little closer to him.

"I know. I'm happy to be by ourselves." She hesitated. "I told Tillie I probably won't get in tonight, so she shouldn't wait up for me."

Ray raised an eyebrow and smiled broadly. "Good, then it wasn't a mistake for me to arrange a room in this hotel tonight? I wasn't sure, but I was hoping you'd be willing to stay."

"Willing? You must be kidding. But you do know how awkward it can be with my sister."

"You know what I think? I think she knows what we are doing and she won't say anything until you do. And you know something else? I think she'd be all in favor of our getting married."

"Maybe, but let's not spoil tonight by talking about that. How about some champagne? I could stand to rest my feet for a few minutes."

They left the dance floor and made their way to the tiny table where a bucket of ice sat filled with a bottle of champagne. A waiter hurried over to pour and asked if they wanted anything else. Around the room people were laughing, talking, smoking, drinking, but with a subtle heightened sense of urgency, as if it were important to demonstrate to each other that they were upbeat, optimistic, as if nothing was hanging over them, as if the world was the same as it had been last year. Every one of these people knew very well that the men among them were very likely to be off to war within weeks or months and that some of them would never return.

In the darkened hotel room in the early hours of January 1, 1942, after they had made love, after they had declared their pleasure in each other, Clara whispered to Ray, "You're really going to enlist, aren't you?" and he responded simply, "Yes." Quiet tears slipped out and ran down into her ears and her hair. It took a minute or so for Ray to realize Clara was crying. He rolled up on his elbow and bent his head to kiss the tears away. "I have to do this, babe. I just have to. Please don't cry. I promise to come back to you. Nothing is going to happen to me."

With a horrifying sense of déjà vu, Clara realized those were the very words Gus said to her when he went off to war in 1917, never to return.

Ray was surprised to see a line at the recruiting station in Hartford, especially since it was seven thirty in the morning and the doors didn't open until eight. He sighed, lit a cigarette and leaned against the brick wall behind him. He'd spent a restless night agonizing over this decision. On the one hand, he knew he felt compelled to do this by every value he held dear. He was a physically fit man, unmarried, and there were monsters out there threatening the world he lived in. He knew from all he'd read and seen in the newsreels at the movies that the Nazis and the Japs had committed unbelievable atrocities. He knew they needed to be stopped and he was sure it would take a lot of men to do it.

On the other hand, his mother and his darling Clara were dead set against his enlisting. They both urged him to wait and see if he got drafted. And they also felt it to be likely he would be rejected, partly because of his age and partly because he was his mother's sole support. His mother would probably move in with his sister's family and of course, she would get an allotment from the Army. But Clara was a different thing. She kept refusing to marry him and she was convinced he would be killed as her first husband had been killed in the Great War. He heard her pain in every conversation they had about this and when he put his arms around her, he could feel her tension.

The line was moving now. He noticed the guy in front of him looked to be about 15 years old, his face covered with adolescent spots. And in back of him was a guy who looked like a bum and smelled like a sewer, dressed in clothes that were little better than rags. There were some who looked to be college kids, dressed in their gray flannels and white bucks and some who looked much older than he. There were faces that bore the stamp of Italy, Poland, Ireland. It was a reminder that this was a country made up of all these different nationalities, often living their whole lives in little enclaves of people who shared the culture of their country of origin.

Ray was sure that they'd all be thrown together in barracks, living side by side with a lot of different ideas about how life should be lived. In a sudden flash of insight, he realized that this line at this recruiting station represented the acceptance of an allegiance to this country and the need to be a part of preserving the values that made the old USA an attractive destination for immigrants.

Ray was inside the door now. He could see the two sergeants at the desks in the front room, asking questions and writing answers onto a form. Some of the potential enlistees got up from the chair and left abruptly, brushing past those still waiting, careless of the physical contact as they had not been before. Ray heard one yelling at the recruiter, his face red, his fists clenched. But most of the men were sent into the back room. Ray already knew that a rudimentary physical would determine whether they were accepted or not. The youngster who had been in front of him got up from the seat at the recruiter's desk and came toward him, headed for the door, the sheen of tears in his eyes. Ray heard the call, "Next."

It didn't take long for the mayor's office to start setting up committees for this and that. Everybody, especially anyone who was an official, wanted to demonstrate a commitment to helping win the war.

When Edward read in the Gazette that a Civilian Defense Corps was forming and volunteers to be air raid wardens were desperately needed, he decided this was something he could do. On Tuesday night after supper, he drove downstreet, parked in a spot in front of Foster Farrar's Hardware Store and walked to City Hall.

The room where the meeting was to be held was filled with men, most seated already, many dressed in casual shirts or sweaters, but some in suit and tie, probably thinking, as Edward did, that this was a sober occasion requiring some formality. The smoke in the room was heavy. Edward decided to abandon his pipe.

When a tall, red-faced man he didn't know stood on a chair and called the group to attention, the immediate hush was broken only by someone coughing. "My name is Joe Kelly. I'm the mayor's son-in-law and I volunteered to help set up the Civilian Defense Corps. Don't believe those rumors that the mayor twisted my arm. Well, maybe a little, but I'm glad to be able to help." There was a ripple of nervous laughter and someone called out, "Did your wife have to twist anything, Joe?"

Joe ignored him and went on, "Thank you for coming tonight. We have to get our community prepared for a possible enemy attack and we will need you to help us do that. First, please take one of the forms being distributed right now and fill it out with the requested information. Does anyone need a pencil? I have some pencils here."

Chairs scraped, pockets were searched. A young boy walked down the aisles of chairs with the forms. "As soon as you are finished, pass the forms to your right and my son will collect them."

"This is what air raid wardens will have to do. Make sure people in your section have blackout curtains in place. Walk around the neighborhood and check often. If you see someone in your neighborhood who doesn't belong there, ask questions. Report suspicious activities. When the air raid siren goes off, chase everybody off the streets into shelter. Sometimes it will be a drill to make sure people understand the way to do it. You will need a big flashlight for checking out dark places to see if anyone is hiding. We will issue armbands and hats for you to wear so they will know you are an official air raid warden and not just being nosy. I expect there will be some people who will give you a hard time. Remember always to be polite but firm."

Edward thought to himself this might be difficult with some people who lived in the alley and he raised his hand. "What if somebody is drunk and doesn't want to obey the rules?"

"Then you will have to report them. The police will follow up with these people. We have to be sure that we don't invite the enemy here to bomb our town."

"*Mon Dieu*," Edward thought, "this is going to be a hard job."

When Ray met Clara as she exited the hosiery at the end of the day on Wednesday, she slid into the seat of his car and looked at him sharply. She knew. Just from the look on his face, a mix of excitement and anticipation and concern, she could tell that he had done it. "You enlisted, didn't you?"

"Yes."

Twisting her body on the seat, she reached out awkwardly to strike him with her fists, hitting whatever she could reach and shrieking, "Oh, how could you? How could you do that to me? You know how I feel. I told you and told you."

Ray grasped her wrists in one strong hand and pulled her toward him with the other. "Shhh, shhh. I do know, but I had to do it. You have to try to understand." Clara started to cry, great wailing wordless cries of anguish and pain. "Please, please tell me this is not true. I cannot bear it."

Ray wanted to be patient, to understand her acute distress, but he could not hold back his annoyance. Holding her face in his hands and looking directly into her eyes, he explained, "Clara, for months now I've been telling you I would enlist if it came to war. I feel very, very sure that I have to do this. You've just been ignoring everything I've said, thinking it would go away. Why can't you see it from my point of view? I'm fit, I'm unmarried, and I hate what is happening in the world. I'd be a slacker if I didn't enlist. Wouldn't you hate me to be a coward?"

"No, I wouldn't. I just want you to be safe. You just don't know how horrible it is to wake up every morning wondering if you'll hear today that something bad has happened. The waiting is so painful, it's like a knife twisting your insides all the time and you have to go on and work and cook and shop and clean and make conversation with people like your world isn't falling apart every minute. You'll never understand." And she started sobbing again.

Ray's voice took on a hard edge, "Well, I hope you don't think I did this because it would be fun, do you? I expect it will be a lot of hard work and boredom and fear and pain for me, too. That doesn't change the fact that it has to be done. We can't just let these bastards take over the world, can we? This war has to be fought and fought to win. Am I supposed to let someone else do it for me? How could I hold up my head if I did that?

I wouldn't have a shred of self-respect left." He pushed Clara back to her side of the car and engaged the clutch. "I'll take you home. I don't think there's any point in beating this dead horse all night. We can talk later when you calm down."

Clara was crying quiet tears as they drove down the street to her home and when Ray pulled up in front of the house, she opened her door before he could get out of the car to come around and help her.

"Don't do this to us, Clara. I'm going to need you to be here waiting for me."

Clara nodded her head, but didn't trust herself to say a word.

☆ ☆ ☆ ☆ ☆

Tillie took one look at Clara and went to her with open arms. Hugging her tightly, she said, "Go wash your face, *ma soeur*. I'll set another place for you at the table. Later we will talk."

But talking to Tillie was no help. Clara felt miserable, knowing that she had behaved badly and that there was nothing to do now but accept the fact that Ray was going to war and he would need her to write to him and pray for him and wait for him. She could not undo what had already been done and, even though she still thought he could have waited to be drafted, or maybe not, she knew that much of what she loved about him was his strength of purpose, his commitment to what was the right thing to do.

The telephone rang just before nine o'clock and Angela answered it. "It's for you, Clara."

"Hello, babe. Are you OK?"

"I'm OK. I'm….I'm sorry I acted like such a ninny."

"Well, you're my ninny and I love you, so let's do a better job of dealing with this, OK? I'll pick you up at six on Friday night and we'll do something special." Both Clara and Ray were well aware that this was a party line, so words were chosen with care and code words meant a lot. "Something special" meant a lovely hotel instead of a roadside cabin. Both of them could look forward to the weekend with particular eagerness.

# CHAPTER 5

## WINTER 1942

January 12 was a grey day, snow was in the forecast, the whole country was anxious with fear of the unknown dangers ahead and Angela woke up at four in the morning, screaming. Pete was alert instantly. "*Merde. Qu'est-ce que c'est?*" He raked his hands through his hair and rubbed the sleep from his eyes as they both stared at the bright red blood spreading on the sheet, soaking the back of Angela's nightgown. She, moaning "*Dio mio*" over and over, tried to stop the flow from her body by holding the pillow tightly between her legs

Tillie knocked and called out, "Angela. Angela, what is it? Are you alright?" Amy was calling, " Mommy, Mommy," and Marie tried to push past her *Memere* to get in the room, only to have her way blocked by

*Memere*'s arm across her chest and to hear her mother call out, "No, darling, don't come in.  Go back to bed." in a voice higher and louder than her usual soft tones.

Pete came out of the room and raced down the front staircase in his bare feet, jumping the banister four steps from the bottom to get to the telephone.  When the operator asked "Number, please," he shouted into the mouthpiece, "This is an emergency.  We need an ambulance at 144 West Street right away.  My wife is pregnant and she's bleeding all over the place."

By then, Edward came up to the closed door of the bedroom Tillie had entered and called out to her, "What can I do?" He got no reply. Clara arrived to lead Marie back to her own bed, murmuring soothing words. "It will be alright.  Don't worry.  Your Mommy will be alright," and then, "I have to get your sister Amy, *chouchou*.  She is frightened, too."

"I want my Mommy" Amy wailed, reverting to her baby habit of sucking her thumb.  "Stop it, Amy."  Marie spoke sharply.  "You're not helping anything."

In just a very short time, minutes only, an ambulance pulled up behind Pete's Studebaker in the driveway and two men in white, carrying a stretcher, rushed up to the front door, held open for them by an agitated (and still barefoot) Pete. Edward, at the top of the stairs, called out, "Up here. Quickly."

While the ambulance attendants strapped a thoroughly frightened Angela, crying piteously, onto the stretcher, Pete shoved his legs into trousers, his feet into shoes and grabbed a sweater from a chair, announcing "I'm coming with you."

When the ambulance raced toward Cooley Dickinson Hospital, siren shattering the quiet of the early morning, Edward and Tillie were following not far behind, leaving Clara to cope with the wide awake and wide-eyed girls. Marie was old enough to realize something had gone wrong with her mother's pregnancy, but Amy, still too young to fully grasp the details of the impending arrival of another sibling, was reacting to the noise and confusion and the palpable emotions of all the adults around her.

Clara gathered the two girls close to her and thought to distract them with promises to make waffles for breakfast, an infrequent luxury. At the table in the warm kitchen, they heard the rattle of the bottles in the milkman's rack as he deposited his delivery on the inside of the back porch, watched their beloved aunt beating eggs into a bowl and they slowly calmed.

Pete sat on the metal chair in the corridor outside the emergency room, his father on his right side, mother on the left. His legs were splayed, knees supporting his elbows as he held his head in his hands. He looked up when his father patted his shoulder. Edward took notice of the bleakness in his son's expression, the redness of his eyes, and evidence of tears streaking his face.

"I sure hope she's going to be all right. That looked like a lot of blood she lost." Pete's voice was ragged.

"God will hear our prayers." Edward said softly.

Two nurses came out of the swinging doors, the rubber soles of their sturdy white shoes squeaking on the worn linoleum floors. They wore the crisp white aprons and distinctive starched caps that marked them as registered nurses. Caught up in their own conversation, they seemed not to notice the trio sitting there, tension radiating from them.

A man came through the doors, carrying a small child, sleeping in his arms. Two ambulance attendants emerged, a guy who looked to be a janitor, carrying a mop and pail and a harried seeming woman with a clipboard tucked under her arm. An hour or so ticked by, mostly in silence and with excruciating slowness.

When Dr. Boucher finally came out, still wearing his white surgical gown, his mask hanging loose below his chin, Pete jumped to his feet. Tillie noted the look on their doctor's face and knew immediately that the news was not good.

Pete blurted out, "Is my wife OK?" and visibly sighed at the nod from the doctor.

"*Oui, oui, mon vieux*, your wife is weak now but she will be fine after she rests and has a chance to recover. I am sorry to say, though, that we lost your son, a terrible tragedy, I know, but there can be other sons later. Angela will still be able to have more children, a miracle in cases like this. We stopped the bleeding without the need to remove any of her organs." Dr. Boucher seemed to rush out the words of his reassurance as he saw Pete's face turn white, watched the father support his son when his body sagged with the weight of his grief.

"A son? It was a son?" Pete's voice was a whisper.

Tillie stepped up beside him and murmured, "It is God's will. We must expect that He has some other purpose for your child. Surely, he will be an angel?" She turned hesitantly toward the doctor, needing to hear that the child was baptized. Dr. Boucher, familiar with the importance of the Catholic sacrament, nodded.

"Jesus, Ma, do you think that's so damned important to me? What the hell kind of god would take a baby boy away from us? What sense does it make? Do I give a shit about God? If He's so hateful, I don't want anything to do with Him." Pete exploded, his voice loud and thick with tears. He pulled his arm away from his mother's touch and turned to the doctor, "Can I see my wife now?"

"She's sleeping, but you can look in on her. Try not to upset her if she wakes up. She's had a tough time of it."

Edward put his arm around his wife's shoulder and led her gently down the hall. "Come, *cherie*, let me take you home now. I'll come back for Pete later."

"I need to call Father Picard and Quinn's to make arrangements for the baby. We should do it right away. Just a private service. That's all." Tillie, in her usual efficient manner began to plan the painful rituals, even through her own tears.

Angela's black curls spilled across the white pillow as she lay there in the iron hospital bed. Her eyes were closed, the blue veins in her eyelids standing out against the stark pallor of her skin. She was in a bed by the window in a room for four, with only one of the other beds occupied. A nurse led Pete in, admonishing him, "Only ten minutes, even if she doesn't wake up," before she pulled the curtains around the bed to afford them a few minutes of privacy.

Pete gazed down at his lovely wife, acutely aware in that moment of how much he loved her and how often he had disappointed her. As bitter as this loss was for him, it would be more so for her, who had carried the child in her body for seven and a half months, suffered the nausea, the swollen ankles, and the awkwardness of her unbalanced body. He lifted her hand in his two, brought it to his mouth and kissed her palm gently. *"Je t'aime, cherie, je t'aime toujours."*

Angela's eyes fluttered, her lips moved, but no words came out. Pete bent his head down close to her. "What is it Angela? Do you need something? Just tell me what you want, sweetheart."

"I'm sorry, Pete. I'm so sorry." She whispered, tears leaking out of her closed eyes.

Pete wept openly, gathering her into his arms. "Don't worry. We'll make another one. We will. Soon as the doc says OK. I love you, babe, and don't forget it. Just get well as fast as you can. Do everything they tell you to do so you can get strong again."

Two days later when Pete came to visit Angela in the late afternoon, he spotted Dr. Boucher crossing the parking lot heading for his white Cadillac. He quickly reversed his direction and loped over to greet Angela's savior. "Hi, Doc, did you go to see Angela today? Is she better?" he asked, a little breathless from his jog.

"*Oui, oui.* She's doing fine, *mon vieux*. I'm very, very sorry about the boy, but you're lucky, anyway. We often lose the mothers when there's so much bleeding."

"I know that. I hope you know how grateful I am and my parents, too. It was your skill that saved her, doc. But now I'm worried about how sad she seems. It's like she blames herself somehow for this happening, especially since it was a boy, *comprenez-vous*?"

"No reason for her to blame herself. We don't understand how these things happen." The doctor shrugged and held up his hands. "Some people would say it's God's will."

Pete privately thought that was a crock of shit, but he didn't voice that thought to Dr. Boucher. "She wants to try again as soon as possible. How long should we wait before we try again?"

Frowning, Dr. Boucher answered, "I was going to talk to you about that. As soon as Angela is feeling strong enough, you should bring her in to the office so I can fit her for a diaphragm. And maybe you should be using rubbers, too, just to be sure. It would be very dangerous for her to get pregnant again for quite a while--at least a year or more."

Pete clenched his fist and fought to control the sudden threat of tears clogging his voice. "I guess you don't know Angela really well, then, do you? She's pretty religious and you know how Father Picard is always going on about what a sin it is to use any kind of birth control." Pete was thinking to himself how, after Marie was born and he couldn't get a steady job for so long, they fought about that a lot. She hated it when he pulled out and he only got away with that by convincing her that the sin was his and not hers. Then, as soon as he did get a steady job and they decided to try again, it didn't take long before she got pregnant with Amy.

"I'm telling you, Pete, it could be very dangerous."

"Doc, Angela is pretty damn near irresistible and she's a passionate woman who's not afraid to get the ball rolling herself, either. I don't know how we're going to do this. It will be really tough. I've got to think about it." Pete looked over the doctor's shoulder at a blue Packard coming into the lot and shifted his feet.

"I'll talk to her, *mon vieux*. She'll understand how important it is to get a diaphragm."

Pete walked into the hospital a troubled man. He loved his wife and kids. He couldn't imagine a life without Angela. It tore him up just to think about her being hurt. He walked into the men's room and stood in front of the mirror, aware he shouldn't visit his darling looking obviously distressed. She'd be sure to think he was still broken up about the loss of the boy. And in truth, he was, but not nearly as much so as the prospect of danger to her. He splashed water on his face, combed his hair and smiled into the mirror. Shit, the smile looked so fake, he was disgusted with himself. He walked back out to the front of the hospital, where the flower lady had her stand, and bought a yellow rose. There, now, he thought, she'll look at the rose and not my face.

It was a short visit. Angela loved the rose and the nurse, a woman Pete's Aunt Clara had gone to school with who was in Angela's room checking her temperature, went out to find a vase to put the flower in. Pete covered Angela's face and hands with little kisses, told her how much better she was looking (a lie, but still--), and smoothed her wild black curls back from her forehead. Tears leaked from her eyes and slid down toward her ears. Pete kissed them away. He felt so helpless. What could he say, except, "I love you. I want you to get well.

The girls miss you." And he kept on stroking her hair, struggling to swallow past the lump in his throat, until her eyelids started to droop and she fell asleep.

When the nurse returned with the rose in a pretty blue vase, she noticed Angela's eyes closed and said to Pete. "It's good for her to sleep. It will help her get her strength back. I'm sure she's glad to see you when you come, but don't expect her to be able to carry on a conversation. She's not up to that yet by a long shot."

"Thanks," he said. "Thanks for taking such good care of her."

It was very dark when he walked out the door of the hospital, and then, reaching in his pocket, he realized he was out of cigarettes, so he headed the car down Main Street to Lizotte's, sure that there'd be some of his friends hanging around there, probably with news from those who had already gone off to Fort Devens in Massachusetts or even Fort Dix in New Jersey for training. The shop was warm and fragrant with the smell of tobacco, the air thick with smoke from the men standing around arguing what the government should or should not be doing to win the war. Most of them were old men who had seen it all up close during their stint in the Great War, who remembered the mud and the stink and the constant itchy feet from socks that never seemed to get really dry. They had sage advice to offer any young men who would listen, not to dissuade them from doing their duty to God and country but to warn them what to expect.

"Too many kids I talk to today think they're going to get a chance to be heroes. Hell, forget heroism and just concentrate on staying alive. Watch your buddy's back and hope to hell he's watching yours." Jim O'Reilly was a big-bellied Irishman who had come back blind in one eye. Other men standing near him nodded in agreement. "Sure, some guys who haven't seen a paycheck in a long time might see this as a chance to get some money, maybe help out their old mothers. But they'll soon find out it's no picnic."

Pete put down his thirty cents for two packs of Lucky Strikes and deftly, with one hand, opened a pack, tapped the bottom smartly and plucked out a cigarette. "Anybody heard from Paulie?" He asked the group standing there, eager to hear about his friend who had enlisted right after Pearl Harbor. "Yeah, I saw his Mom outside the church last Sunday and she said she got a letter. I guess he's doing fine, lost a lot of weight, but told her he's getting big muscles." Everybody standing there broke into laughter. Paulie had always been a little pudgy. "He's supposed to get a leave so he can come home after basic training, before he ships out."

"I never thought he'd go enlist like that. Wasn't he engaged to marry that St. Lawrence girl?"

"Yup, he sure was. And she was pretty broken up about it, too. Say, Pete, I just remembered. I heard about your wife losing your boy. What a shame. My condolences, *mon ami.* You're young, though, and you'll get a boy yet. Already two girls, right? You'll never get drafted. Don't have to worry about that. I guess you get to sit this one out and let the other fellows do the fighting.

Pete brought Angela home from the hospital ten days after she'd gone in an ambulance and ten days after she lost the son they had been hoping for so much. It was early afternoon and so his Pa and his aunt were still at work and Marie was still at school. When they came in the back door, Pete holding Angela like a fragile piece of china, his Ma and Amy were baking cookies in the kitchen.

Immediately Amy launched herself toward her mother with loud, happy cries of "Mommy, Mommy. You're back." And Pete deftly stepped in front of Angela and caught his younger daughter up into his arms, tickling here and kissing her nose at the same time. She giggled and hollered, "Stop that, Daddy. I want to kiss Mommy." Still holding her, he let her lean over and bestow multiple kisses and a hug on her beloved and much missed Mommy. Ten days seems an eternity when you're four years old.

"*Memere*, come and kiss Mommy. She's come home. We missed you, Mommy," Amy's little face took on a look of sadness, her eyes and her mouth turned down. "And I'm so sorry my baby brother died before you could bring him home." Amy felt a little guilty that she was not more sorry about the baby since *Memere* told her that Mommy and Daddy were sad. Still, she didn't see why they needed any more babies.

Angela's mother-in-law came to her with open arms, hugging her fiercely and with more emotion than she had ever before exhibited to Pete's wife. "You must rest, *cherie*. It will take a while for you to get your strength back. Pete can help you up to bed and I'll bring a cup of tea and some cookies up to you in a few minutes. I put a new nightgown out on the bed for you."

Pete grinned at Angela. "Do you think I can carry you up the stairs?" She swatted at him playfully and said, "Don't even think of it. You'd probably drop me or hurt your back doing it. I just need a little help."

When Pete had helped her out of her clothes and into the nightgown, taken her into the bathroom and waited for her just outside the door, he settled her into bed. "I'm going to take Amy out so she won't come looking to bother you right now. You need to rest a little after all the excitement of coming home."

"Don't you have to go back to work?"

"No, I took the whole day off. Everybody understands. I'll bring supper up here on a tray and we'll eat together right here. For now, you should try to sleep." He brushed the black curls from her face and kissed her, carefully keeping the worry off his face and the pain of their loss to himself.

# CHAPTER 6

## WINTER 1942

It started to snow right after lunch. Marie looked out at the big flakes hitting the windows of the classroom. Mrs. Riley rapped the pointer she was holding against the chalkboard. "Never mind the snow. It will still be there when school is out. Right now we are using worksheets to parse sentences. Please raise your hand when you are finished."

Marie was already finished, but she didn't raise her hand. She was thinking. Would Mommy be sad for a long time because the baby she was supposed to bring home from the hospital died as soon as he was born? And how about Aunt Clara's friend Ray in the Army now, training at Fort Dix in New Jersey and *Pepere* signing up to be an air raid warden. Would they be safe? *Memere* told her they would be getting rationing books soon. Was the war going to last a long time? Would Daddy have to go and fight, too?

Henry Frenier poked her in the back. She knew he wanted her to lean over so he could copy off her paper, but she ignored him. When he poked her again, she turned around and gave him a dirty look, hissing, "Stop that."

The coughs and fidgets sounded loud in the room. Gradually hands began to rise and Marie raised hers. Mrs. Riley walked up and down the aisles collecting the papers. The bell rang for fifth period and everybody started for the door. Over the sound of departure, Mrs. Riley called out, "Don't forget to read the chapter on punctuation. There will be a test tomorrow."

"Whew, that was boring." Betsy said as she caught up to Marie. "Did you hear that there's going to be an assembly tomorrow to announce a savings stamp drive? We'll get savings books and every time we buy a stamp it goes in the book. After you put in eighteen dollars and fifty cents worth of stamps, you get a savings bond, then when you cash it in ten years, you get twenty-five dollars."

"That'll be good." Marie answered her in a distracted voice, paying little attention to Betsy's words.

"My Ma isn't going to think it's so good. She's going to say 'Where am I going to come up with the twenty-five cents every week for a stamp?'"

"Can't you take it out of your allowance?"

"Well, maybe you can, but I don't get any allowance. You know that perfectly well, Marie LaPointe. You're not paying any attention to me."

Clara looked out the window next to her work station, her hands automatically moving the silk hose onto the machine, not even seeing the snow.

Her thoughts were all of Ray, training at a camp in New Jersey, suffering tired muscles every night as his beautiful body got used to the rigors of strenuous physical training. She missed that beautiful body, those hands that caressed her with such tenderness, those arms that held her tight and made her feel so safe.

Clara shivered and looked around her, guilty for her wandering thoughts, afraid the super would come by and notice the flush on her cheeks. Thank God nobody seemed to be looking her way.

Later, walking home in the dark winter night, her galoshes covered with slush, the flakes settling on her eyelashes, she allowed herself to return again to thinking of Ray, of his pressing her to get married, of her fears for his safety. When he returns to me after this war, then we'll get married. Not now. It would be bad luck, tempting the fates to do again what they did to her before. She could never survive it a second time.

She passed over the bridge and saw the lights on the porch. There would be a letter waiting for her. There was always a letter. She would wait until after supper to take it to her room and read the words of love that sustained her. And then she would write him back, pouring onto the page a message of her longing.

Tillie called out from the kitchen when she heard the door open. "*Bonsoir, ma soeur.* Come and sit with me and get warm." The smell of warm piecrust reminded Clara she was hungry.

Marie looked up from her book and smiled. "Hi, Aunt Clara. Did your feet get wet coming home?" Amy bumped down the stairs and ran to hug her.

"How lucky I am to have them all here," Clara thought.

Curled up on her bed after dinner, Clara read Ray's letter.

*My dear, darling Clara,*

*Even though I ache in **every** bone and muscle from the grueling training here, I would crawl over broken glass to hold you in my arms tonight. Not that I could do much more than that, because I'd probably fall asleep in a minute. Ha Ha.*

*Seriously, though, even when I sleep, you are in my dreams. Every night. But that's a good thing. It reminds me that the fight I go to is to protect the ones I love.*

*Mostly I don't mind the hard work here*

*because I know how important it is.*

*God, Babe, I love you so much and I miss you, miss you, miss you.*

*Have to go now. Thanks for the cookies and the letters which are so precious to me.*

*Love you with all my heart,*

*Ray*

*P.S. Did my sister call you? She wants you to come to dinner. I hope you'll go.*

Clara folded the letter and put it carefully into the shoe box with the others. Then she went to her little desk by the window and stared out into the night. There had been no phone call from Ray's sister, but she wasn't surprised. She got along with Anna and her husband fine, even liked them. But now Ray's mother was living with them and she knew Mrs. Carpenter didn't approve of her relationship with Ray, didn't like Catholics in general and made no bones about the fact that she wanted Ray to marry a young girl and give her more grandchildren.

Clara sighed and took out the pretty blue stationery to write her nightly letter.

*My darling Ray,*

*I can almost see you lying on your cot in the barracks moaning about your aching body, the body I've loved for so long now. You can be sure it will get better as the days go on and all those beautiful muscles get used to it. When will you get a leave and will it be long enough to come home? I've missed you every day you've been gone. We all listen to the news every night to hear what is going on. I don't know how much to believe and how much is made up or at least exagerated (sp?) Do you know yet what job you'll get?*

*The weather here has been really nasty, lots of snow and cold. I'll be glad to see the spring come and especially glad to see an end to this war.*

*I love you,*

*Clara*

Clara sealed her letter and started to undress for bed. Thinking of Ray, remembering his passion, her hands stroked her body. She was proud that her flesh was still taut, and that her lovely breasts were firm and silky even though she had just turned 44. After so many years of regular, satisfying sex, it felt strange to be celibate. But celibate she would be. No one but Ray would do. She knew she would wait for him to come back to her. With a little sob and a sigh, she realized how very much she loved him. No one else would do.

In the front bedroom, Pete and Angela were getting ready for bed, when Pete asked, "Did Doc Boucher talk to you about getting a diaphragm, Angela?"

"Yes, he did. But I reminded him how the church teaches against that, Pete, and I told him absolutely not. We'll just have to take our chances. God is the one who will decide."

Pete turned to her, fists clenched, jaw tight, "No, godammitt, we will not let God decide. This is your life we're talking about here. You've got two little girls who need a mother. Doc says you could die. There's no way I'm going to let you take a chance of having another baby too soon."

Angela started to cry. She sat down on the little bench in front of the dressing table and covered her face with her hands. "Pete, I don't want to go to Hell, either. We'll have to count the days."

Pete's face got red and he raised his voice. "Don't you understand what Doc told you? How many girls do we know who got pregnant on the rhythm method? How many? It's too risky. If you got pregnant and then died, I'd feel like I was the one who killed you."

"Pete. Stop yelling. You'll wake up the girls."

"Shit, shit, shit. This is stupid. You aren't even listening to me. I'm going down to sleep on the couch."

It was not yet daylight when Angela heard Pete come into the room and go to the closet. It was really too early for him to be going to work. He managed a men's clothing store and the store didn't open until nine. "Where are you going, *caro mio*?" she called out softly to him.

"I couldn't sleep anyway. I'm going down to the diner for some breakfast. I have to think."

Angela rose and put her arms around him. "I do love you and I'm scared, too. But I don't know what to do."

Pete folded her into his arms and kissed the top of her head. "Yeah. Well, I'll figure something out."

Three days later, when they were all together on Sunday around the dinner table, Pete announced that he had enlisted in the Army and would be heading out to boot camp in two weeks. Angela gave a little scream and left the table to run up stairs. His mother covered her face with her hands. His father asked sharply, "Why?" And Aunt Clara and his two daughters looked stunned.

The two weeks went by in a blur for Angela and in agonizing slowness for Pete. He was terrified that he would lose control and leave Angela pregnant. Doc Boucher had him convinced that it would practically be a death sentence for her. He pleaded with her to let him use a rubber and, although she was fearful of the spiritual consequences, she resolved to go to confession after he left and cleanse her soul of the sin. Still, Pete knew rubbers were known to fail and he worried about it constantly. He reasoned that leaving her to serve in the Army would save her life.

His father was torn between distress at Pete for abandoning his family and pride in his son's willingness to serve in a noble cause. Despite Edward's former belief that the country would never enter into this foreign war, he had come to accept that his hero, Roosevelt, had no choice after the country was attacked at Pearl Harbor. The prayers of the whole family would keep Pete safe.

Tillie was heartbroken and very, very fearful, but she carefully put a good face on it, assured Pete that his little family would be well taken care of and consoled Angela as best she could. Privately, she spent many hours praying to every saint and to the Blessed Mother, making promises for lifelong acts of charity.

Clara was shocked that her nephew would do this thing, but felt sure the best thing for her to do was deepen her friendship with Angela, offering love and support and help with the care of the two girls. Some people said the war would be over quickly, but Clara didn't believe that, sure that they were in for at least a couple of years of hard times, painful shortages and many, many sacrifices.

Marie saw her Daddy as a hero and she was bursting with pride at his enlistment. She told everyone who would listen to her that he would be the best soldier in the whole Army, citing his skills as a hunter to assure her friends that he already knew how to shoot a gun and didn't need anyone to teach him how. Amy was too young to have any idea of what Daddy's enlistment meant and so she nodded her head to agree with anything her big sister said and piped up a "Me, too," frequently.

When the day came to leave, there were tears, but no wailing. They had all resolved to see Pete off with a smile, a wish for good luck and promises to write daily. Pete climbed onto the train, conflicting emotions showing in his face. As he walked up the aisle to a seat, he passed a guy he knew from a work gang they had been on together during the worst of the Depression when no one could find a job. Happy to see a familiar face, he said, "Hey, I know you. I can't remember your name, but didn't we work together for a while back about three years ago?"

The guy's face lit up with a smile and he said, "Yeah, I'm Stanley Borowski. I remember you. Aren't you Pete? Here, sit down next to me. Going to Fort Dix?"

Out Route 66, way past the State Hospital, the prison jail was located on a country road, no paving, and not visible from the highway. Charlie Billieux had been there since his sentencing for manslaughter in the accidental killing of his brother Oscar in February of 1938.

That horrible event was the culmination of a simmering anger between the two brothers. Oscar, the oldest son, was striving to become an important man in the community, rejecting much of his French-Canadian roots. He was a foreman in a factory, a member of the Elks Club and a haughty man, who treated all his siblings with an autocratic disdain. For months he had been wooing their *Maman* to be sure she left control of all her worldly possessions to him alone, believing that he was the only member of the family smart enough to manage the income property.

But it was Charlie, the youngest son, who had managed the rental property since it was first built, after the state took their farmland by right of eminent domain. And it was Charlie who cared for the houses and the grounds, collected the rents and mediated the problems with the tenants. Rage at his brother's highhandedness combined with his grief over his beloved *Maman's* death drove Charlie to confront Oscar at their mother's graveside.

After Oscar died from a blow to his chest, Charlie was sentenced to five years in prison for manslaughter. Unable to forgive himself, Charlie imposed a further sentence on himself. He insisted that his family not come to visit or communicate with him while he was incarcerated.

Now, four years after he entered the jail, Charlie was leaving, having gotten time off his sentence for good behavior. The years had aged him. At 55, his hair was completely gray, his face heavily lined, his eyes had lost their former evidence of humor and bonhomie. His body was still strong however, from the labor he did clearing fields, working in the prison garden, chopping wood and also from his own determination to keep it so.

As he collected his meager belongings, the officer handling his discharge asked him, "Do you want a ride to your house, Charlie. George is going that way."

"*Non, merci*, but I'd like a ride to the bus station if he could take me there."

"Aren't you going home?"

Charlie ignored the question and asked, "Do you think he could drop me at the bus station?"

"Yeah, I'm sure he could. He goes right by there on the way home."

When Ray's sister, Anna, called, Clara remembered Ray's letter and she was pleased that Anna had given a lot of thought to how Clara could make the trip down to Hartford on Sunday.

"I called the Greyhound bus station and they told me that a bus leaves Northampton at 10:10 on Sunday morning and makes one stop in Springfield before coming directly to Hartford and getting here at 12:15. We usually have dinner on Sunday at 1:30, so that would work out fine. My husband, Randy, will come meet the bus and get you to our house in about 20 minutes. Please say you'll come."

It would be very rude to decline, Clara knew, so she accepted with good grace, making sure her voice conveyed her pleasure at being invited. Even so, she was sure it would be awkward and painful for Ray's mother and she would get questions she would rather not answer.

When Sunday arrived, she asked Angela to help her pick out a dress that would be appropriate, conservative, not sexy, not dowdy, not offensive, but still pretty enough to show that Ray had good sense in choosing her for a special friendship. Anna, of course, was no fool, and must know that she was more than Ray's friend, but Clara thought his mother was probably from the "old school" and rejected any notion of sex outside marriage, considering it sinful to even have such thoughts in her head.

Angela patted her arm and assured her, "It doesn't make any difference what she thinks, *cara*, she cannot change how you and Ray feel about each other, so don't get upset about it."

The two women agreed that a navy blue serge dress with a white satin collar looked good, fit well and worn with a single strand of pearls, was the perfect outfit for a Sunday dinner. Marie came in while Clara was fixing her hair and said, "Ooh, Aunt Clara, you look beautiful." Amy, right behind her sister, whispered, "You're so pretty."

Edward drove Clara down to the bus terminal and said he'd be there to meet her when she returned on the 6:30 bus.

The ride down was interesting, mostly because Clara studied her fellow passengers and invented little stories in her head for who they were, why they were on the bus and where they were going. No one she knew got on with her in Northampton and, since the bus was not crowded, she sat alone. In Springfield, however, a young man, maybe in his early twenties, joined her and introduced himself immediately. "Hi, I'm Andy Kellog. I'm heading back to New Haven today. I'm in medical school there. My Dad's not been well, so I visited my family this weekend, but I have to be back for classes tomorrow morning." He grinned widely and added, "I thought I'd better tell you so you wouldn't think I was some draft dodger."

Clara laughed at the guy's forthright manner and assured him, "I really didn't give the draft dodger idea a single thought. You're way ahead of me if you're thinking about that. But I'll bet you will be drafted as soon as you finish med school." "Oh, yeah, I'll probably be doing my residency in a military hospital somewhere." he agreed.

The 40-minute ride to Hartford went by quickly as Andy regaled Clara with funny stories of his experiences. He'll be a great doctor, she thought, as he revealed his own fumbling mistakes and spoke ruefully of his inadequacies. He had a wonderful, open personality and an engaging way with a total stranger. She put out her hand to wish him good luck and goodbye as she got off the bus in Hartford. The traveling companion left Clara feeling very upbeat and she smiled widely, genuinely, at Anna's husband, Randy, when she spotted him waiting for her just inside the door of the terminal.

Ray's two nephews had come with their father to pick up Clara. They wanted to know about the bus ride, which they both considered an adventure, so she related the story of the medical student and the trip to the house went by quickly. The two boys, James, 12 and Edward, 15, disappeared as soon as they got in the door and Clara was met by Anna and Mrs. Carpenter.

Unsure about the protocol here, Clara instinctively held out the box of chocolates she had brought to Ray's mother rather than his sister. "They're Fanny Farmer. I hope you like them."

"Well, I have to be careful about sweets, but thank you anyway." Mrs. Carpenter mouth was set in a pinched, downward turn. She was not going to make this easy. Clara caught the look on Anna's face that showed her chagrin and apology. Oh, well, she would do her best to make it a pleasant visit. Nothing could be done about Mrs. Carpenter anyway.

They all sat in the front parlor for a drink before dinner, Anna excusing herself now and then to check on something in the kitchen. Randy carried the burden of keeping the conversation going with his tales of the activity in the Pratt and Whitney plant, his confidence in the superiority of the US soldiers and their equipment to win this war and his own pride in the work he was doing.

Dinner was superb. Anna was a wonderful cook, so Clara's compliments were sincere and lavish. When Mrs. Carpenter asked Clara directly, "How often does my son write to you?" she was startled by the question, but answered truthfully, "Not exactly every day, but several times a week." With a tight face and rapidly blinking eyes, Mrs. Carpenter said, "Well, we're lucky to get a letter a week and sometimes not even that."

Clara was not sure what she could say to that and so said nothing. She was rescued by Ray's 15 year old nephew, Edward, who announced, "I've been reading all about the training soldiers get and I wouldn't be surprised if he was too tired at the end of the day to write anybody."

"Of course, he has time to write somebody, but it's not me." Mrs. Carpenter snapped.

"Now, now, Mother Carpenter, you've gotten lots of letters and two phone calls, too, didn't you?" Randy asked.

Mrs. Carpenter rose from her chair. "He shouldn't even be there. If he'd had a wife and a house full of children, he wouldn't have enlisted, but no, not him. Excuse me, I'm not hungry anymore." She left the table and they all heard her climbing the stairs.

"I'm so sorry, Clara. I thought it would be all right. After all, you both ..." Anna hesitated, "care for him deeply. I really thought it would be helpful to get together."

With great dignity, Clara said, "I appreciate the invitation to dinner, Anna. It's good to see you again. I understand how your mother feels. She had plans for Ray and they didn't include me and she's hurt. I can go to the bus terminal now, if you can drive me there, Randy."

"No, no, of course not.  Mother will stay in her room, reading.  She does that when she's mad at me for something and, believe me, that happens often.  I'm thinking of getting a job myself now.  Mother can watch the boys after school and I'd be doing something to help the war effort.  Randy's none too sure it's a good idea, but he's agreed I could go apply, didn't you, darling?"

"Yes, I did agree, partly because staying home is tough with two women having different ideas on how to do things, but also, I can see that women are beginning to come into the plant and some jobs they do even better than guys.  I think maybe it has something to do with finger dexterity and patience with some tasks."  Randy's tone was thoughtful and understanding. Clara was impressed.

The two women worked together to clean up the kitchen and afterward, Edward played his cello in the front parlor while the adults sipped after dinner liqueurs.  When it was time to leave, Anna hugged Clara and asked, "Could you come down on a Saturday sometime and we could have lunch at a restaurant downtown? Or I could meet you in Springfield?  I really hate to lose touch."

"Of course. I, too, would not want to lose touch. I'm so sorry about your mother. Please tell her so for me. I don't blame her for feeling angry, but the decision to enlist was Ray's. The choices he's made are his. She has no reason to be angry with me."

On the bus ride back to Northampton, Clara replayed the dinner scene in her head, trying to think of how she could have avoided the uncomfortable and ugly results. If she married Ray when he returned from the war, it would still mean estrangement from his mother. She didn't think there was much of a chance of producing children and anyway, Mrs. Carpenter would probably resent any woman who claimed her son's affection. She dozed off in the overheated bus and was jolted awake when they reached the terminal in Northampton.

Edward was waiting for her, as she had known he would be. One look at her face and he knew the visit had not gone well. She told him about it as they drove home and he patted her hand, remarking sagely, "Some things cannot be changed and so, we just must bear them."

# CHAPTER 7

## SUMMER 1942

When Ray called, Clara had already gone upstairs to her room to write her nightly letter to him. Tillie called up the back staircase, "Clara, Clara, come down quick. It's Ray on the telephone. Calling long distance."

Marie, reading in the alcove, jumped up and ran into the parlor, "Mom, did you hear what *Memere* said? Aunt Clara got a long distance call."

"Yes, *cara*, I heard her. Maybe your father will call us long distance if he gets a chance and you can talk to him." The subtle message was not lost on Marie. She went back to her alcove, although she kept her attention turned to the phone, just in case Aunt Clara might call her to say hi to Ray.

Clara was a little breathless when she said, "Hello, Ray. This is Clara."

"I'd know your voice anywhere, babe, and God, it's good to hear it. Now listen, I've got great news. I've got a weekend pass and a guy I know has a brother who can get really terrific hotel rooms in New York City for soldiers on leave. Please, please say you'll take a train down on Friday and meet me in the bar at the Astor Hotel on Times Square at 6 o'clock. I'll get a camp bus that should get in about that time. I have to go back on Sunday afternoon, but we could have almost 48 hours together. I need to see you and hold you....." his voice stopped, caught in a spasm of emotion. Then he remembered he was talking on a party line.

Without a second's thought on the logistics, Clara answered, "Yes, yes, I'll be there. I'm so happy now, just to know I'll see you soon."

"Tell the bartender that you're waiting for me. He'll be sure nobody bothers you until I get there. We'll have a great time, babe, I promise."

"Just to see you will be enough for me. Now we'd better hang up. I'm sure this is costing you a fortune. Don't worry, I'll be there. Bye now." Then, not caring who was listening, she said, "I love you.  Don't ever forget it."

"Clara, sweetheart, I love you, too.  Bye."

Clara put the earpiece in its cradle and stood there for a moment, thinking, before she turned to her waiting sister. "Tillie, *ma cherie*, Ray wants me to meet him in New York City for the weekend. How am I going to do this? I'll have to take Friday off from work. The super's not going to like it.  Maybe he'll fire me.  I don't know what to wear. I haven't got a suitcase. I've never been to New York. It's a lot bigger than Boston. Different, too, I'm sure.  Will I have any trouble getting a train ticket at this late date?  Friday is only three days away."

Edward came in from the kitchen, carrying one of the several newspapers he read every day and announced, "I'll go down to the train station right now and get your ticket.  What time do you want to leave on Friday and when do you want to come back on Sunday?"

"And I've got a suitcase you can use.  Remember the one I got when Pete and I went on our honeymoon to Niagra Falls?  It's only been used that one time.  It's got a red stripe in the middle. It's in the attic, I think." Angela headed up the stairs to retrieve her suitcase.

Tillie said, "Come on. We'll go look in your closet to see what you can take with you." Clara, still in a haze of unreality, followed her sister up to her room. When they got to the top, Tillie turned into her own room, walked over to the big mahogany dresser and pulled open the bottom drawer. "What are you looking for?" Clara was curious at her sister's behavior.

"*C'est la.*" Tillie handed a flat, white box to Clara. "Open it."

Peeling back the pink tissue paper. Clara lifted out a peach satin nightgown, edged with wide ecru lace. "Where did you get this? Why are you giving it to me?"

"I got this gown from my girlfriend, Annamarie, for my honeymoon, but we went to Quebec to visit family and we stayed with Edward's cousins and it didn't seem right to wear this. I wore a flannel gown *Maman* had made for me and I put this away. I've just never had a chance to wear it and now I want you to have it."

"Tillie, I don't know what to say." Clara was a little flustered.

"You think maybe I don't know you sleep with him? Of course I know. I've known for a long time. It's none of my business. Say thank you, take it and enjoy your weekend. You are very dear to me, *ma soeur*."

The two sisters hugged, both a little teary, and headed for Clara's room to inspect the possibilities in her closet.

The next day at work, Clara was surprised at how easily the super allowed her to take Friday off when she told him she was going to New York City to see her fiancé who was a soldier at Fort Dix who had a weekend pass. She thought she ought to add the respectability of designating Ray her fiancé. The super didn't question it.

The girls at work squealed with excitement when they heard her news and many made offers to loan hats, bags, or anything else she needed. Most welcome was the loan of a camera, although Clara could have borrowed one from Edward or Pete. Somebody left a brand new pair of silk stockings at her work station. Clara never did find out who, although she suspected it was one of the few guys who worked on the floor. It made her feel a little wary of such special attention.

The days passed quickly and Friday turned out to be a lovely, sunny Spring day. Edward took a little extra long mid-day meal break from work so he could drive her down to the train station and still have time for something to eat. He hugged her, kissed her cheeks and admonished her to enjoy herself. He'd be there to pick her up on Sunday evening.

It was twelve thirty and the train left at twelve forty-eight. Clara stood on the platform, Angela's suitcase with the red stripe at her feet. She wore her grey spring coat, light weight wool with a black velvet collar and a black velvet hat with a red feather and a small dotted veil. She carried a black handbag and wore black suede sling-backs. Underneath her coat she was wearing a military blue silk crepe dress with a pin-tucked bodice, belted with a soft leather belt borrowed from her friend Marge. The shawl collar was cut low and would have showed a bit of cleavage were it not for the rhinestone brooch that Angela loaned her.

Clara had taken the train to Boston many times and to Quebec, too, but never to New York City. She wanted to meet Ray looking her best and she knew the train might be crowded, smoky and stuffy. It would probably mean she would arrive tired, but she was determined not to be cranky. She sent up a little prayer, "Please God, let this visit be perfect. Let the weather be sunny and warm. I promise to make a Novena when I get back."

The train had come from Quebec with two stops, Burlington and White River Junction in Vermont and, of course, it was quite crowded, but Clara had not walked far down the aisle when a sailor got up and offered her his seat. She took it gratefully and sat next to a very large lady who seemed to be dozing. By the time the train left the station, there were several people standing in the aisle.

The sailor, standing beside her, leaned over and held out a copy of the new Look magazine. "Would you like to read this, ma'am? I'm finished with it."

"Thanks, I would. It's very nice of you to do this. Are you going to New York City?"

"Yes, I've just come from home on leave. I'm shipping out on Saturday."

"Good luck to you and let's hope this war is over soon."

"Well, I don't think so, ma'am.  It doesn't look that way to me."  He stared off into space lost in his own thoughts and Clara opened the magazine.

The run to Hartford went by very fast and when they were on the approach to the station, the conductor called out loudly "Hartford, next station is Hartford." and the woman sitting next to her jolted awake and started pushing on Clara. "*Vite, vite.*  Get up.  I have to get off here."

After the woman left, Clara moved over to the window seat and the sailor sat down beside her.  "My name is Tom Cassidy, ma'am.  I should have introduced myself earlier."  He held out his hand and Clara took it.  "And I'm Clara Pelletier, going down to New York City to see my fiancé."

They chatted for a few minutes but when a very old woman with a cane got on board, Tom again relinquished his seat.  The new arrival did not thank him, nor did she look in Clara's direction at all, but instead, removed a large black rosary from her black tapestry bag  and began to murmur prayers.

By the time she got to Grand Central Station, Clara was tired, but not frazzled and very excited. She touched the sailor on his sleeve and said, "I really appreciated your courtesy. You must be very tired after standing all that way." "Oh, I'm fine, ma'am. My mother would kill me if she thought I might sit while ladies were standing. That's just the way I was brought up." He hoisted a large duffle bag over his shoulder and took Clara's suitcase in his other hand. "I'll just carry this up the ramp for you. Is somebody meeting your train?"

"No. I have to get a taxi, but I'm sure there must be signs."

"Yes, ma'am, you'll have no problem." They parted when they entered the huge lobby of Grand Central.

Clara smiled and repeated again, "Good luck to you. And may the Lord watch over you."

She spotted the Information sign and went to stand in line there, looking around at the sights to be seen in this huge, rococo building. The man at the desk directed her to the taxi stand and she hurried toward it. It was already nearly five thirty and she began to worry about getting to the Astor before Ray got there.

111

She didn't want him to think for a single minute that she might not have come to meet him.

The taxi driver grumbled when she gave him her destination, "You could have walked there, you know." Clara paid no attention. Her focus was on getting there, seeing Ray, holding him. Nothing else mattered.

The bar at the Astor was very crowded, noisy and smoky, but the man who opened the door for her seemed to recognize her and as soon as she said who she was meeting, grinned and led her to a table in a far corner. "Well, your guy did a good job of describing you. You sure are a looker and if you was mine, I'd want somebody to put you someplace where no SOB could bother you."

Clara barely had time to settle herself on the banquette before she saw Ray coming toward her. He looked so handsome in his uniform, she thought, how can he really choose me? He hugged her so tight she squirmed and they sat down side by side all in the first two seconds. "Clara, babe, you look so wonderful to me. I hope to hell this isn't a dream or I won't be able to stand it."

"I'm here. This is real. We're together." Clara was holding back tears, trying to smile. A waiter came over. Ray looked at her and she said, "I'll just have a glass of water right now, please." and Ray said, "A beer for me. No, make that a Seven and Seven."

He took Clara's hand and, reaching into his breast pocket, removed a thin gold ring and slid it on her finger. "There. I don't want some house dick knocking on our door because some nosy guy at the front desk notices you're not wearing a wedding ring."

Clara nodded and Ray continued, "We've got a reservation in this hotel. It's pretty ritzy but this guy who is one of my bunkmates has a brother who's a night manager here and he got me a terrific deal. Also, through some special connection he's got, we have reservations at the Stork Club tonight."

"Ray. I don't have the right clothes to go to the Stork Club. Everybody will think I'm some bumpkin."

"No, they won't. They'll think you're beautiful and I'm the luckiest guy in the whole damn Army to be with you." He kissed her nose and grinned, his eyes telling her all she needed to know.

When the drinks arrived, Ray took a big swallow and asked, "Are you hungry? We could have a bite to eat now, if you like. Our reservations are for nine thirty tonight."

Even though Clara had barely eaten anything all day, she answered, "No, not hungry, but maybe a little tired."

Ray's smile could have lit up all Broadway. He stood, put some money on the table and reached for her hand. "Come on. We'll register and go up to our room right now."

The room was certainly luxurious. Clara was in awe, especially at the bathroom. Ray waited a respectable two minutes for her to inspect the room before he picked Clara up in his arms and sat down in the big arm chair with her in his lap. He took off her shoes, unhooked her belt, undid the long zipper down the back of her dress and unhitched her stockings from her garter belt, all while covering her face and neck with kisses. And while he did this, Clara busied herself with his tie and the buttons of his jacket and shirt.

In no time at all, they were entwined in the bed, eager to reconnect their bodies and reaffirm their commitment to each other. Their first coming together was frantic and left them both exhausted. They dozed for a while, then awakened and made slow, sweet love again before Ray said, "I'd better take a shower and get out a clean shirt to go over to the Stork Club. We'll have fun. Wait and see. Maybe Walter Winchell will be broadcasting from there tonight."

"I've never been anywhere like that. You know, famous, where important movie stars go." Clara was willing to go anywhere to be with Ray, but still apprehensive about a place where she might stick out like a sore thumb.

"I've never done that, either, but so what? We'll go and ogle everybody. That's why they go there, so somebody can see them."

Ray wanted Clara to get in the shower with him, but she worried about getting her hair wet. She had little experience with a bathroom shower, although she liked it on the few occasions when she had a chance to use it. Still, wet hair would be a real problem.

While Ray was in the shower, Clara looked over the choices she had for what to wear tonight, decided not to fret about it and put on the mauve silk with the lace collar she had brought to wear on Saturday night. With luck, the wrinkles would shake out of the blue by tomorrow and she could wear it again.

Ray was feeling proud of himself and he had that all's-right-with-the-world smile in his eyes when they got to the Stork Club. Clara got to ogle stars she knew from reading magazines and even he had recognized some of them. A guy sitting in a booth across from them sent over a bottle of champagne and when the waiter brought it, he just said, "The gentleman over there sends best wishes and good luck, soldier." Both Ray and Clara together said "Thank you" and they waved to their benefactor.

Clara couldn't remember what she ate, although she certainly remembered that it tasted delicious. She was none too sure they belonged in a place like that, but since everybody was so nice, she just ignored that little feeling of being an imposter trespassing far above her station in life. Besides, she was with Ray and that made wherever they were the best place in the world.

On Saturday, they got up early despite their late night and decided to explore what they could of the city. It turned out to be a beautiful spring day, enough of a nip in the air that Clara was glad she had her coat. First, they both agreed, had to be the top of the Empire State Building, (a little scary for Clara) and then the ferry out to the Statue of Liberty, which left them both in awe and then they hurried up to Central Park, to visit the zoo.

They laughed at the antics of the animals, stopped to kiss each other every few minutes and finally decided to skip the Metropolitan Museum in favor of going back to the hotel to make love. Ray was tender and gentle, removing Clara's clothes slowly, rubbing her feet where her shoes had left a red mark, unhooking her stockings from her garter belt and rolling them down her legs, kissing her knees as he did. He pulled her dress over her head and removed the pins from her hair, putting his lips on her nape as he did it. When he slid her slip straps over her shoulders and let the slip fall to the floor, Clara turned in his arms and kissed him with all the emotion that was crowding her senses at the moment. Tears rolled down her cheeks and Ray caught them with his fingers.

"Why are you crying, babe? I thought you were happy."

"I am happy, so happy to be here with you. But I hate to leave you. I don't want you to go and fight. War is such hell."

Ray stroked her back, murmuring, "Shhhh. Shhh. I'll be fine. Let's not think about that now. We're here. We're together. Let's just enjoy this day, this time, right now."

Clara pulled herself together and smiled up at him, caressing the back of his neck, wiggling her hips against him and willing herself back to the moment. Of course, he's right, she thought, we have this weekend. What's done is done. He's in the Army now and nothing can change that.

Later, they got dressed and went out looking for a small, simple restaurant, where they could have a quiet supper. They found one not far from the hotel, one that an Italian buddy of Ray's had mentioned and where they were greeted warmly by a big, effusive Italian man with a large mustache and a smile that demanded a smile in return. They drank Chianti and ate fantastic gnocchi with meat sauce and crisp bread slathered with garlicky butter. Walking back to the hotel, Clara wondered aloud how the restaurant had managed to get butter when it was so scarce at home.

"You're such an innocent, babe. The black market is alive and well right here in New York. And probably everywhere else, too. You can get anything if you're willing to pay the asking price for it." Ray's cynicism was not new to Clara, but still, she thought everybody was ready to sacrifice for the war effort.

"Well, you know, there's sacrifice and then there's sacrifice, not always the same thing to all people and in all situations. Look at the guys who actually injure themselves just so they'll be unfit for combat duty. I've seen a lot of men who take advantage of others, men who are proud of being slackers, some stuff I wouldn't even tell you about, so nothing surprises me anymore."

Clara, horrified, said, "You've seen a lot since you signed up to join the Army, haven't you?"

Ray stopped right there, on the sidewalk, and pulled Clara around to hug her tightly, sighing into her hair, "Oh, yeah, and a lot of it not so good. Mostly, though, I think of you and my family and your family and I remind myself that some of us have to be willing to take on the lousy job of fighting off the really evil stuff in the world. So nothing is perfect or without warts. I can live with that."

"Just be careful, darling and stay safe. Promise me you'll stay safe." Clara whispered into his shoulder.

They stayed in bed late on Sunday morning, making love, reminiscing about events and friends and sharing breakfast in their room. Neither of them wanted to talk about leaving until the last minute, when they both knew they had to scramble, Clara for her train and Ray for the bus back to camp.

Ray took Clara to the train station in a cab. They were quiet during the ride, Clara fervently hoping she could hold her tears until they had parted. When he had settled her in a seat on the train, Ray admonished her, "Don't let any guys get pushy. Call the conductor if somebody is bothering you."

With more control of her emotions than she had ever had to exercise before, Clara smiled at him, put her arms around his neck and said, "Don't worry about me. I know what to do, soldier. Write to me often as you can. I love you very much."

"And I love you, babe. More than I can tell you. More than I ever thought I could love anybody. Don't worry about me. I'll be back." He kissed her very tenderly, hugged her and quickly left the train.

On the train ride home, Clara looked, unseeing, out the window, the new issue of Life magazine in her lap opened but unread. She thought about her marriage at seventeen to Gus Pelletier, a man so full of life and love, so passionate about saving the world from itself. He was her knight, her champion. It had never even crossed her mind that he wouldn't come back to her because she believed him when he promised that no harm would come to him. He thought he was invincible.

They called it the Great War. What a bad joke. How did we get into that fight anyway? It was just a bunch of old men behaving badly. Clara was especially bitter about it because of Gus, but also she had read a lot. Edward knew her interest in books about that war and he brought them home from the library for her. Sometimes they were hard to understand, but she kept reading and thinking and sorting it out in her mind.

When Gus had been killed on the last day of the war, it had been a devastating blow to Clara. She curled up in a ball on her bed and refused to eat anything. She cried constantly and bit her lip until it bled. She wouldn't talk to any of them but only moaned loudly and rocked her body in a violent thrashing. Her mother thought she would never recover. And in some ways, she had not.

Her refusal to marry Ray wasn't because she didn't love him. She did. It wasn't because she was ten years older than he, although she often wondered why that didn't bother him. It wasn't because they were of different religions. Clara believed that it was only important that they both believed in God, not how services were conducted. She did worry that Ray's mother seemed to dislike her a lot. But was that a barrier to marriage? Not really. Lots of women she knew had a big problem with their mothers-in-law.

All the way from New York to Northampton, Clara thought about Gus and Ray, war and marriage, love and loss. Edward was waiting for her at the station and after they had greeted each other and she had assured her brother-in-law that she had a wonderful time, she said, "I've decided that, if Ray asks me again to marry him, I'm going to say yes."

Edward responded with a huge grin, "*Bon*. It's about time."

# CHAPTER 8

## SUMMER 1942

Clara's walk from hosiery to home usually took less than five minutes, just over the bridge and about 100 yards toward Hospital Hill and she was at the door. But today, she was contemplating her life and her pace slowed. She noticed the repairs to the bridge were never finished, the apple tree in front of Wilson's house had lost a limb in the storm last night, and the grass everywhere looked brown and neglected. Would this war never end?

Ray was picked for officers' training and had not yet been sent overseas, for which she was grateful. He had spent a weekend visiting with his family once since their fabulous weekend in New York, getting together with her on Saturday night of that weekend, but unable to get away at all on Sunday. His sister called to ask if she would like to come to Sunday dinner and seemed relieved when Clara declined. Now she was wondering when she might see him again. He wrote every day, or nearly every day, telling her about the other guys, excited about what he was learning, professing his love for her always. And she wrote him back every night. But no more was said about marriage by either of them.

When she entered the house to the aroma of garlic, she knew Angela had had a hand in the cooking. "Welcome home, Clara. Can you smell my vegetable soup? The crops are coming in, so I'm making good use of them. You've got a letter from Ray waiting."

"Thanks, Angela. The soup smells great. I'll go wash up and then come help you serve. Where's Tillie? Where are the girls?"

"They went down to the railway station to a bond rally. Some movie star was on a train stopping at every station from New York up to the Canadian border, trying to get people to buy more war bonds."

"Oh, yes, I remember reading about that in the paper. As much as they love the movies, they'll be thrilled to see a real live movie star. I think it's supposed to be Betty Grable."

Supper was sandwiches of lettuce, tomato and mayonnaise and heaping bowls of vegetable soup, eaten between bursts of excited chatter from the girls about the bond rally. "You should have seen all the flags on the train and Betty Grable was smiling and waving and some people even went up close and touched her hand. *Memere* wouldn't let us get too close, though, because the people were pushing and poking each other and she said it would be easy for Amy to get knocked down." Sometimes Marie seemed to be a little girl still and then she would catch herself and assume her more grown-up manner. "Of course, I thought it was very rude of Eleanor Cooley to push herself up there so she would be noticed. I wouldn't do anything like that."

Tillie smiled at Marie and Amy, her much loved granddaughters. "We had a good time, though, didn't we, *mes petites*?"

After the dishes were done and Angela took the girls out to catch fireflies, Clara brought Ray's letter to her room. She scanned it quickly the first time, looking for any news that he was about to be sent overseas and re-read it several times, trying to gather any meaning between the lines.

*My darling Clara,*

*What a miserable day here. It rained buckets, but we still had maneuvers and artillery practice. I was glad to get into the classroom in the afternoon, although the lights went out once and the thunder was pretty noisy for part of the time. The instructor never stopped with his lesson on strategy and nobody stopped taking notes. All the news we hear is that the war in Europe isn't going well and there have been a lot of losses in the Pacific. I still don't have any idea where I'll be going when I finish here.*

*When I read your letter telling about the vegetable garden, I could just see you and Amy and Marie, all on your knees pulling weeds like they were the enemy. I'd sure like to be eating a big fresh tomato, warm and smelling wonderful right out of the garden. We never had a garden like that at my house, but it seems like a good idea.*

*Don't cut your hair, no matter what
anybody says.  I dream about your hair,
all spread out on the pillow, smelling great.
Those people that tell you to do that are
just jealous they don't have your wonderful
hair.*

*I think about our weekend in New York all
the time.  I keep hoping we can do it again,
but the pressure's on to get trained and get
in there and win this war.  Lots of rumors
around and not much hard information.*

*I love you,*

*Ray*

On the day Pete was due to arrive at the train station, a Saturday, when they were all at breakfast, Angela asked Edward, "Could I borrow the car, Papa Edward, and go meet Pete's train by myself?"

Before Edward could even open his mouth to reply, Amy and Marie protested loudly, "Oh, but we want to come, too."

Edward reached over and patted Angela's hand. "Of course, *cherie*, that's a very good idea. You should go alone. You can drop the girls off at the library on your way. Mrs. Swift is opening the doll cabinets this morning and the storyteller will be there."

Marie felt she was too old to go to story hour, but she said nothing, realizing that she could visit some other part of the library while Amy enjoyed Mrs. Swift. *Pepere* was just being a peacemaker. And anyway, her Dad was going to be home for a whole week. This wasn't a good time to make a fuss.

After breakfast, Tillie shooed Angela upstairs to dress, insisting that she and Clara could clear the table and clean up the kitchen without her help. In the bedroom Angela examined herself in the mirror, wondering if Pete would still think her beautiful. She decided to wear the blue georgette dress that she knew he loved to see on her and she let her hair fall down on her shoulders, something she hadn't done in a long time. She rubbed a little lipstick onto her cheeks as well as her mouth and decided it would have to do. A little splash of Evening in Paris and she was ready to go.

The station platform was crowded with people waiting to greet friends and family getting off in Northampton as well as those waiting to get on to go north. All heads turned right when they heard the train coming down the track, brakes squealing as it pulled to a stop at the station. Most of the folks looking out the windows were dressed in uniforms of the different services, more Army than anything. Angela looked for Pete, but of course he would be standing in the aisle or even in the vestibule, waiting to jump off as soon as the train stopped. Suddenly, he was there, right in front of her, dropping his big duffle bag and hugging her so tight she could hardly breathe. He moved his head and kissed her neck, just below her ear and his first words were, "Oh, God, *ma coeur*, you smell wonderful."

Angela, struggling to hold back her tears, laughed instead and said, "Welcome home, *mi amore*, I'm glad to see you, too, even though you smell like you've been on a packed train for hours."

Pete laughed, too, and kissed her again and again before he raised his head and asked, "Where is everybody?"

"They're home. Except the girls are at the library. I wanted to pick you up myself so we could have a few minutes alone together."

"Did you drive the car down here by yourself?"

"Yup, I did." Angela smirked a little in her pride.

"And you can park it OK?"

In mock outrage, hands on her hips, Angela admonished him. "Of course. I had to take a test to get a license. You know that. And I passed the very first time with a perfect score."

Pete laughed and hugged her again. "You sure are something else, *cherie*."

When they got to the car, Pete maneuvered her around to the passenger side, opened the door and held out his hand for the keys. Angela sighed and slid onto the seat, a little chagrined not to be able to demonstrate her new skill, but glad to have him back and in charge again.

Pete leaned forward to put the key in the ignition and then paused, pulled Angela close to him and, leaning over her to shield her from curious eyes, deftly unbuttoned the front of her dress. When his hand closed over her soft breast, he closed his eyes and inhaled a deep breath. "Oh, Jesus, Angela, I've missed you so much. I don't know how I'm going to wait until tonight. You don't know what it's been like."

Angela whispered, "I've missed you, too, *mi amore.*" The kiss they shared was so passionate, so full of their longing for each other, it bore no resemblance to the kisses of welcome on the station platform.

When they got to the library, Angela convinced Pete he should go in alone and find the girls. Marie, sitting at a long table in the reading room with her head bent over a book, was startled when he came up behind her and kissed the top of her head. "Daddy, Daddy, you're home." She wrapped her arms around his waist and hugged him tight, forgetting for the moment that she had decided to abandon Daddy in favor of the more grown-up sounding Dad. He hugged her back and thought how she had changed in just two months since he left for basic training.

"Come on, *chouchou,* let's go find your sister." People were turning around or raising their heads to see the soldier in uniform following his daughter to the story room.

When Amy saw them come in, she ran to her father, arms outstretched and he caught her up, lifted her for a kiss and a hug and carried her out of the room. He turned back at the door and nodded to Mrs. Swift. "Excuse us, please. I just got home. I'm sorry to disturb you."

"Quite all right, Private Lapointe, we understand, don't we, boys and girls? Say goodbye to Amy." Twenty or so heads had already swiveled to the back of the room to stare at Amy and her father. "Bye, Amy." They sang out in chorus.

At 144 West Street, Pete's mother and father waited in the parlor, Tillie peering out through the lace curtains every few minutes. "What do you suppose is taking so long? Do you think the train might have been late?" She fretted.

"They had to stop and pick up the girls at the library. They'll be here soon." Edward was as eager as Tillie to see their son, but he knew Pete and Angela and the girls would not arrive any sooner if he paced the parlor carpet. When he said that to Tillie, she snapped at him. "How can you sit there so quiet when he's your only child and you haven't seen him in months?" Since there was no acceptable answer to that, Edward didn't respond.

The crunch of the tires on the gravel of the driveway sent Tillie flying out the door and down the front steps. Pete jumped out of the car the minute he set the brake and caught his mother in his embrace. They were both laughing as they hugged, tears running down the grooves in Tillie's face even while she laughed. "Ooh, *mon cher garcon*, how glad I am to see you and don't you look handsome in your uniform. Did they feed you there, at that camp?" They kissed and kissed again and then Pete noticed his father waiting patiently behind his mother. Still holding her, he reached out to include his father in the circle of his arms.

Angela and the girls got out of the car just as Clara came out the front door and called out, "If anybody is hungry, I've got food on the table."

Pete moved away and answered her, "Great. I'm starving. There was nothing fit to eat on that train."

The meal was set in the dining room, with the embroidered linen tablecloth and the best china, silver and crystal in celebration of Pete's homecoming. Ham and sweet potatoes, green beans with crumbled bacon, freshly made buttermilk biscuits and an apple pie with lots of cinnamon. In between bites, Pete answered questions and told edited stories of his adventures. They all smiled when he described how hard it was for many men to get used to waking up at five in the morning and getting onto the training field for calisthenics before breakfast. Angela added, "Especially you." And Pete agreed, "Oh, yeah, especially me."

With no small amount of pride, he told about getting a ribbon for his marksmanship skills and Marie stored up that story in her head to tell everyone at school later. He was careful in the telling of his distaste for the food so that none of them turn that into worrying about him. He never mentioned how difficult it was to get used to sleeping in a barracks with a large group of men of very different backgrounds and personalities, some crying in the night, some cursing, some snoring and some shouting out at the release of sexual energy. He didn't tell of the petty cruelties he had seen inflicted on weaker men, nor did he complain about the lack of privacy and freedom. These things were for him to bear alone.

When they finally pushed back from the table it was mid-afternoon. While the women cleared the table and cleaned up the kitchen, Pete joined his Pa and Amy to inspect the plot they had plowed and raked and made ready for their Victory garden. Of course, *Gran'mere,* when she was living, had designed and tended a sizable kitchen garden, dominated mostly by herbs and tomatoes and Tillie had kept that going after her mother's passing. But Edward and Angela wanted to do more, so they selected a site near the orchard, further from the house, to put in a plot approximately 20' x 20'. Digging up the grass there, getting rid of the weeds, breaking up the earth clods, was a tough job, but with Clara and the girls helping, they had done it.

Amy grabbed her father's hand and pulled him to the end of the plot, "See, Daddy, that string is where I'm going to get to put in the lettuce seeds. All by myself. *Pepere* says so." Her eyes were wide and sparkling, her thrill at being part of the project making her father bend down and lift her up in his arms for a smooch. "You're getting to be a big girl now. I can hardly lift you up anymore." Amy squirmed and giggled in her pleasure.

Edward stood at the edge of the garden plot, smoking his pipe and savoring the sight of his son and grandchild.

How fortunate a man I am, he thought, to have such riches. I pray *le Bon Dieu* will bring him back to enjoy his little family as they grow and to have grandchildren himself one day.

The evening meal was a light one, Amy was sent to bed and Marie joined the adults in a game of cards and soon it was bedtime. Pete congratulated himself that he had been patient and respectful to his parents, mindful that they needed to be with him on his first day of furlough, but now he was eager to be with his lovely wife in their bedroom alone.

Angela was a little nervous. Would Pete still think she was beautiful when she got undressed? Would he still want to kiss and cuddle before sex? Should she be doing something different now that he had been with all those guys for two months and heard all kinds of stories about what other women did?

She need not have worried a bit. Pete was still her darling lover, the rituals they had established in thirteen years of marriage as familiar and comfortable, arousing and satisfying as always. His strokes were sure, his mouth was eager, his words of love as tender and stirring as they had ever been. After their first spectacular climax, Pete held her tight and nuzzled her,

"I've been dreaming of this minute every night since I left here. Promise to take good care of yourself. If I were to come back to find you changed or hurt or gone, it would kill me. I could not bear a life without you."

Angela was shocked. "How can you say that, Pete? You have two little girls who need you. I pray every day that you come back to us and even if the war changes you or hurts you in some way, we will still love you. And if, God forbid, you do not come back, I will need to be strong enough to take care of our girls." She started to pull away from him, but he tightened his hold on her. "I guess I said that wrong. I will come back to you and, no matter what, I will take care of the girls. I was only thinking of what Dr. Boucher said about how hard the miscarriage was on you."

Neither of them mentioned Pete's use of condoms, Angela preferring to ignore it and later take the sin to the confessional and Pete resolute in his intention to avoid impregnating Angela no matter her objections. "I only want to be sure you know how much I love you," Pete said as he started kissing his way down her neck, lavishing his attention on her breasts and her belly until she began to squirm, raising her hips in invitation.

In the days that followed, Pete visited his friends at the Franco-American Club, took Angela dancing at Toto's, used precious rationed gas to go with his father to a favorite fishing hole and played jacks with the girls on the parlor floor. He hugged his mother often, had a serious conversation with his Aunt Clara, giving his hearty approval to her decision to say yes to Ray the next time he asked her to marry, and moderated his drinking so his father had no cause to admonish him.

Then Angela raised the issue of going to work in the defense plant in Florence and Pete's equanimity vanished, all his intentions to have a peaceful and controversy-free furlough out the window in an instant. "What the hell are you thinking of? Working in a plant with a bunch of men with their tongues hanging out every time you walk by? Are you crazy? Men are like mad dogs when they see a woman like you, with a husband away in the service. They think you're ripe for the picking. No, no and no. You are not going to work anywhere."

Since she had been expecting Pete's reaction to be just what it was, Angela stayed calm, keeping her volatile

Italian temper in check. She had all her arguments ready. "Your Aunt Clara has been working in a factory for years and you don't think anything about that. Most of the able-bodied men in town are gone into the service and what's left are either old men or 4Fs. That's why they're recruiting women."

"Yeah, well they can recruit old women, then, not my woman."

"Pete, listen to me. This is not a job for old women. It takes good eyes and steady hands. The International Silver plant in Florence got a contract to make bombs. You wouldn't want to run out of bombs because all you guys are refusing to let your wives do this work, would you? What if every soldier said 'not my wife,' then who would work in the plants? There aren't enough workers unless women work."

"Bullshit. There are plenty of old guys and 4F types to work in the plants."

"No, there are not. For God's sake, don't you read the newspapers?" Angela's voice was starting to rise, the hold on her temper slipping.

"And when do you think I get a chance to read newspapers? In my sleep?" Pete's voice rose in response.

"Ask your father, then. He reads at least three newspapers a day. He agrees that I ought to go work in the plant, but he told me I should get your OK before I do it."

"So, you've decided to do this whether I like it or not? Jesus, that's great."

"No, I won't if you're dead set against it, but you'd be making a mistake. Besides giving me a chance to make a contribution to the war effort, I could put every dime I make into the bank and then, after the war is over, we'd have the money for a down payment on a house of our own."

Surprised by that part of Angela's argument and aware of how much they would both love to have a home of their own, his obstinate refusal to his wife working alongside men in a defense plant started to soften. "I still don't like the idea, but I'll give it some more thought and talk to you later. I've got to meet the guys for a poker game right now, but I'll think about it. Yeah, I'll do that."

When Pete left to go back to camp at the end of the week's furlough, he went with the prayers of the whole family. No one spoke of his expected shipment overseas or their fears for his survival. He felt reasonably sure that he hadn't gotten Angela pregnant. He knew he didn't want to leave her with another child to care for if he didn't come back or maybe, God forbid, leaving his mother to care for all his children if she didn't survive a pregnancy. He made Angela promise to write him as soon as she knew for sure, one way or the other. They took lots of pictures of all of them together, of Pete with his little family, of Pete and his parents and Pete alone and promised to send them to him as soon as they were developed. He carried Aunt Clara's brownies in a sack, along with the cookies the girls had made to feast on during the train ride back. And he had agreed that Angela could get a job in the defense plant. Not, however, without giving her demonstrated lectures on how to defend herself from predatory males.

# CHAPTER 9

## SUMMER 1942

Angela was feeling excited the morning she decided to go apply for a job at the defense plant in a little town just two or three miles north called Florence. Papa Edward had gotten Pete's car tuned up before Pete came home and Pete had agreed she could drive it, so no problems with transportation, although with gas rationed, she was sure she'd get into a car pool if she got the job. She wore a dress that was very modest, but attractive, and she pinned up her hair in a tight roll in the back, making a fat pompadour in the front because she had heard that keeping hair out of the machinery was important.

The plant was on Chestnut Street, right off Main Street in Florence. It was a cluster of brick buildings that belonged to International Silver and they were now dedicated to this special defense contract. As she approached, she saw that it was surrounded by a tall link fence and that armed guards stood at the gate. Geeze, she thought, do they need guns?

A large sign right on the fence said NOW HIRING, with an arrow and underneath in smaller letters, employment office. Angela parked the car across the street on the shoulder and approached the guard. "I've come to apply for a job." He jerked his thumb in the direction of the arrow.

Inside, Angela saw a small office and one desk where a skinny young man with Coke bottle-thick glasses was handing out forms to the people in line. All along the walls were wooden chairs with right arms shaped like fat paddles. There were two men and one woman sitting there with their heads bent over, pencils gripped in their hands, bodies radiating tension. Angela took her form and sat down.

The form was simple, questions easy to answer, but as she contemplated it, Angela reflected on her path in life. She had been an exceptional student. She skipped grade five in elementary school and was encouraged by her teachers to think she might be able to go to college, but in the summer when she turned fifteen, her mother died of a stroke.

Angela was the youngest child of five and the only girl. Her father, a mason and a hard man, had decreed that she leave school to stay at home and take her mother's place, cooking, cleaning, and doing the wash for all of them. She loved her family and grieved for the loss of her mother, but still, she felt cheated that she never made it past the ninth grade.

She had few opportunities for recreation, but now and then she did go with some of her friends to the dances at Roseland Ballroom in Holyoke. It was there she met Pete LaPointe, handsome, charming, and happy-go-lucky and a great dancer. It was love at first sight for both of them. He was an only child who had been away at a private school. He was expelled before he graduated after one too many outrageous pranks, the last straw being an effigy of a much-despised teacher being strung up on a tree in front of the administration building.

When they had a pregnancy scare, Pete drove them down to Elkton, Maryland, where they were married by a justice of the peace and no waiting requirements to a legal union there. Returning to Northampton late the next day, Angela told her father, who disowned her and threw her out of his house, giving her only a few minutes to gather up some of her possessions in a pillowcase before he pushed her out the door. Angela and Pete spent the night in a motel cabin and in the morning, Pete took her to the Forbes Library where his father worked and left her out in the car crying while he went inside.

Of course Pete's mother and father were not happy about the elopement, but they immediately began planning a small church wedding, which was held the following week at the Sacred Heart Church. All Pete's aunts and uncles as well as cousins attended. Afterward there was breakfast where the whole family pretended this was a joyous occasion. Truly, only Pete's mother seemed to be unhappy about it, maintaining a look of grim resignation throughout the day. And, although Pete's father had gone over to Angela's father's house to invite her family, the door was slammed in his face.

Since it was accepted practice in the community for young people newly married to live with parents, Pete moved out of his small boyhood bedroom in the back of the house. They were given a larger room formerly used for storage to make into a nest of their own. It was a big house, after all. The very next week the pregnancy scare proved to be a false alarm. Pete had not told his family about that part and so no one ever knew. It was fifteen months later that Marie was born.

Angela filled in the birthdates for herself and her children and amount of education as having completed the ninth grade. When she handed the clerk her questionnaire, she stood there waiting to find out what next. He read through all her answers and sent her to another office for a simple eye test and a test of her finger dexterity. When she was finished, another man explained the work, the shifts and the rules (no high heels, tie up your hair in a net or a snood, cut your fingernails short, and be on time). He admonished her sternly, "You must not talk about what you do or see in the plant. This is important work that could affect the outcome of the war." He told her to report to work at 7 AM the next day.

It was impossible to contain her excitement as she told about her experience at the supper table that night. Marie was proud of her mother. She said "Wow, Mom, you'll be helping to win the war." Amy, a little confused about what this meant, asked, "Can I come help, too?" *Memere* answered her, "You have to stay here and help me, *ma petite*."

Clara asked for details on what she would be doing, but Angela frowned and said, "You know, I'm really not sure, but the man there told me I mustn't talk about it anyway, so when I do know, I can't tell." And when Papa Edward asked her how much money they were paying, she told him it depended on how much you got done and he nodded, "Ah, *oui*, piece work."

It took less than a week for Angela to become comfortable with the noise of the machinery and the repetitive nature of the work. Trays of bomb casings came down the line and she positioned them exactly before pulling the lever that sent the right amount of powder into them. She thought often of the men who needed these bombs to win the war, resolutely ignoring the reality that other men would be killed by the same bombs.

She met some girls who had been in school with her and some from the old neighborhood. Most were friendly; a few were not. She was surprised one day to see her brother Salvatore coming into the plant when she was going out. He must be working the late shift, she thought. At the same time she opened her mouth to hail him, he saw her and turned his head down, stared at his boots and walked away. Sal was the slow one in her family of brothers. He had been in a special class at school and quit when he was thirteen to work with their father. She was a little saddened but not surprised that he ignored her. He had always done whatever their father told him to do, just as she had. It was painful to remember all the clothes she had hung on the line, all the dishes she had washed, without question, because their father told her she must.

Three girls who lived out on Route 66 past the Hospital Hill School offered to include her in their car pool. They had to go past her home anyway. She paid Hilda, whose husband was in the Navy on a ship in the Pacific Ocean and who had a big, comfortable Packard, two dollars a week and one ration coupon. Besides being a convenience, it was fun to share experiences with the others. She heard stories about some of the guys there who hassled the women and how to avoid them. One story was of an attempted rape of one of the younger girls who worked in the packing room by a man in the molding department. A group of guys got together and beat the shit out of the would-be rapist. There'd been no more incidents of that kind of stuff after that, at least none that got to be stories going around the plant.

Most of the girls there had started wearing slacks and blouses to work, although the older women frowned on it and called the girls hussies. Mama Tillie raised her eyebrows the first time she saw Angela in slacks. But then, when Angela explained that there were times when she had to climb up to unhitch a stuck gear or climb over boxes to get to some supplies she needed, Mama Tillie nodded her agreement and said, "Well, maybe that is a good idea. Better than people seeing your underpants."

Angela wrote Pete every night, even though she was bone weary and bleary-eyed from work, telling him upbeat stories.

*Dear Pete,*

*Today I increased my production again and the supervisor came by to tell me I'm a good worker. She's really kind of a sourpuss and hardly anybody hangs around with her, but I think she's tough because she has to be and anyway she's always fair. Hilda says it's because I haven't felt the sting of her tongue and I guess that's true enough. I put my paycheck in the bank today. $35.00. It's adding up fast. Just think, mi* amore, when you come home we'll be able to get a home of our own, maybe over off Bridge Street. That's a really good school over there, only a few years old, not falling apart like Hawley Grammar.

Amy is going to be in a dance recital at the People's Institute. Your mother made her costume and Clara gave her a rhinestone bobby pin to wear in her hair. She's so excited. I hope she won't throw up on her big day.

I know Marie wrote to you herself, so I'll let her tell you her own news. She's growing up fast. Now that summer is here I have to watch that she doesn't get into trouble with some of the boys from the alley. She still seems so young to me, it's hard to believe how fast kids grow up.

Be careful, Pete. We love you and want you back with us. I hope this war ends soon. I can't tell anything from your letters. The censor makes big black marks through whole sentences sometimes. Are you getting your packages? Clara thought *they might not ever get to you.*

*All my love,*

*Angela xxxxxxxxxxxx*

A week later, while Angela was waiting for the rest of her car pool after work, Tony Scarlotti came up behind her and whispered in her ear, "Hey, Angela, *bambino*, are you waiting for a man now that your frog of a husband is off playing soldier?"

She ducked her head and lashed out with her elbow aimed at his middle, but his belly was hard as a rock and he just laughed at her. "Whoa, there, who taught you that trick? You have to do better than that to scare me off, *mi amore*."

Just then, Hilda, Sara and Dotty came out of the plant and hurried to her side. "What happened? Did that creep try anything?" Hilda was indignant. "I've heard stories about him. Somebody told me he damaged his own eardrum to get a 4F."

Angela shuddered and wiped at the tears she tried to stop. "He was always a bully, even when he was a little kid. He used to tease my brother Sal, calling him a dummy and worse stuff, too. I wish he wasn't working here."

"They're so desperate for workers, though, they'll take anybody."

Later that night, Angela thought about the incident and decided not to tell Pete. No need to worry him. She'd just have to be extra careful not to be caught alone and to keep an eye out for the slimy creep.

The day was hot already; tar coating some driveways was already turned soft and Amy started to get very cranky. Marie pulled the red wagon with a load of scrap metal they had collected. "OK, Amy, you can get in and ride, but hold the big pans in your lap so they don't fall out."

Marie started to climb the porch steps at O'Houlihan's when she noticed the gold star in the window. "I didn't know Jack O'Houlihan had been killed." She muttered to herself as she stepped back and turned the red wagon around.

"Why aren't we going to knock on the door, Marie?" Amy asked.

"Because Mrs. O'Houlihan's son was killed in the war, Amy, and we don't want to bother her right now." Marie sighed and wiped the sweat from her upper lip on the shoulder of her white cotton blouse.

The door opened and Mrs. O"Houlihan came out on the porch. "I saw you girls coming down the street. Are you collecting for the school scrap drive?"

"Yes, we are, Mrs. O'Houlihan, but we saw the star and we didn't want to disturb you. I'm sorry about Jack." Marie was polite and really mortified that she had disturbed this neighbor.

"It's OK. Wait right there. I've got some things to contribute. I'll do anything to help win the war. Jack was proud to serve his country. He'd want me to do whatever it takes." She disappeared into the house and came out with a big paper bag, the handle of a pot, a metal ruler and a spoon sticking out. She set the bag in the red wagon. "And I brought each of you a cookie, too. You are such good girls to be doing this in the heat. God bless you and God bless all of the boys over there."

The sisters went on down the street, stopping at each house to collect scrap until the wagon was full to overflowing. Amy picked up a much-dented soup pot as it fell off and put it back in as best she could. When the noon whistle sounded from the State Hospital laundry on Earle Street, it was the signal for them to head back home for the mid-day meal and both of them were grateful to be finished with their collection chore. Later, *Pepere* would put the stuff in his car and take it down to the schoolyard where a giant pile was growing.

Just as they came in through the back porch, they heard Memere and Aunt Clara through the screen door. "I heard that the Delaney boy is Missing In Action. They say his ship was hit by one of those Kamikaze planes and they were only able to rescue some of the men from the water. I guess he wasn't one of the rescued." Aunt Clara sounded sad.

"*Mon Dieu*, when will it end? So many good boys lost already and sure to be more to come." *Memere* said. Then she noticed the girls coming in to eat and she brightened her voice. "Well, there you are. Did you get a wagon full of scrap this morning?"

Amy ran over to her grandmother and put her face up for a kiss. "*Oui*, lots of scrap and guess what, Mrs. O'Houlihan gave us a cookie, but she's sad because Jack was killed."

Aunt Clara looked over at *Memere* and sighed, "Another one."

*Pepere* came in with the paper in his hand, gave each of the women and the girls a kiss on the cheek and sat in his seat at the table. "Did the morning mail come yet? Any letter from Pete?" *Memere* answered, "*Oui, Oui*. One for us and one for Angela. No letter from Ray for you this morning, Clara, and nothing for you either, Marie, but maybe there'll be one in the afternoon delivery.

They ate their meal of fried ham steaks and mashed potatoes, fresh from the garden carrots with maple syrup and bright red sliced tomatoes. Even with meat rationed, they managed to have it on the table at least four days a week, sometimes five. Fortunately, Mrs. Galusha had taken over her husband's butchering and made meat available to customers who had faithfully made their way to her farm down in the Meadows, willing to by-pass the store-front butcher shops downtown. The Galusha family had raised livestock and butchered it for many years, selling their meats to a small clientele. She often added a pound of bacon to an order without taking coupons for it, and took the money to pay for it "under the table."

When *Pepere* and Aunt Clara left to go back to work, Amy went upstairs for a nap and Marie sat down in the little alcove to write a letter to her father.

*Dear Dad,*

*Today Amy came with me and we took the red wagon around to ask for scrap metal for the war effort. We got a lot. Our vegetable garden is doing swell. We had carrots and tomatoes from it today. I hate weeding, though. So does Amy. But we do it anyway. Mom says we all have to do things we don't like to do to help win the war.*

*I went swimming at Look Park with Mrs. Larson and some other girls from my class. It was very crowded, but we had a good time. We ate peanut butter sandwiches at a picnic bench in the park and Mrs. Larson brought lemonade and chocolate cookies, too. It was very nice of her to ask me to go and I was very polite because I'd like to be asked again.*

*I'm writing a poem for you, but it's not finished. I'll send it to you when it's done. I'm glad there isn't any fighting where you are now. Do you know when you will have to go to a place where the fighting is? Be careful.*

*Love,*

*Marie*
*xxxxxxxxxx*
*P.S. Amy loves you, too*

Marie walked across the street to the green mailbox and dropped in her finished letter. With some reluctance she headed for the vegetable garden to do her share of the weeding.

# CHAPTER 10

## FALL 1942

When Clara got home from work, she was disappointed to find no letter from Ray, but she knew that sometimes she got two in one day, so she thought no more about it. Then, as she was finishing up the dishes, the phone rang. Angela called her, "Clara, it's for you. Ray calling long distance."

"Hello, Ray, this is Clara."

"I'd know your voice anywhere, babe."

"Are you getting another weekend pass?" Clara's voice was a little bit breathless as she remembered the weekend in New York.

"Well, it's more than that. I'm finished here and I'm getting a furlough for a week before I ship out, so," Ray hesitated, took a deep breath and blurted out, "I want to come home and marry you before I go. Please don't say no, Clara. I need to do this. It's important."

"Yes."

"Did you say yes?" he shouted into the phone. "Omigod, did you really say yes?"

"Yes, I really did say yes." Clara's hands were wet, gripping the neck of the phone and the earpiece. "When will you get here?"

"A week from Saturday. Oh, God, I love you so much. You've made me so happy. I was afraid to ask again, but I had to because I love you and I want you to be my wife. Tell me you want me, too."

"Yes, Ray, I love you and I want you, too. I already decided that, if you asked me again, I would say yes, so I was waiting for you to ask me."

"This is so great. I'll get the papers we need and we'll just go to a justice of the peace, soon as I get there."

"I don't think my family will want me to do that, Ray, but, we'll see."

"OK, my darling, whatever you want to do is OK with me. I'll be there soon. I love you so much. Goodbye for now. Good night."

Clara hung up the phone, in some confusion and slightly disoriented. When she turned around, her whole family was standing in the parlor looking at her, waiting to hear her news. "Ray asked me to marry him and I said yes."

Tillie, asked, "When is this to happen and where?"

"He's coming home a week from Saturday and he says we can go to a justice of the peace."

"Oh, no, no, no. You'll be married in the church and the whole family will be there and then we'll have a celebration right here. I'll ask everybody to give me some of their coupons so I can make a proper cake." Tillie was horrified at the idea that her sister even thought of being married by a justice of the peace.

"Ray's not a Catholic, Tillie. There's no time for instructions and all that." Clara's answer was automatic. She was still shaken by what she had just done.

Angela hugged her and kissed her cheeks, "It will be wonderful. You'll be so glad you did this, I just know it. And Ray is a wonderful man. He'll make you so happy."

"Oh, Angela, he already makes me very happy. I don't know why he wants this so badly, but he does and I can't deny him any more."

Marie hugged her and asked, "Can I be a bridesmaid, Aunt Clara?"

"Well, we'll see." Clara's mind was racing with thoughts of the enormous step she had taken. Was this the right thing to do? Had she been foolish? What was Ray's mother going to say?

Tillie and Angela took over all the planning for the wedding, which would take place in the rectory of the Church of the Sacred Heart. Clara would wear a pale blue dress of Angela's that had to be taken in at the waist and let down at the hem, a chore Angela undertook happily. Her sister Tillie found a lovely hat in her closet that only needed a new veil and some flowers. Clara would wear freshly polished white shoes and brand new white gloves.

Tillie called all the family, except for Oscar's widow. She called Ray's sister and invited her and her family as well as Ray's mother to join them at the wedding celebration at the house on 144 West Street. As she had expected, Alphonse's wife declined in a voice as frosty as the coils on the Frigidaire, but the rest would be there. And Tillie collected enough rationing coupons to make a splendid wedding cake, three layers and butter cream frosting.

On Friday night when Ray called, it was an excited and happy Clara who answered the phone." Hello, Ray, wait until you see how Tillie and Angela have been planning our wedding. You'll be surprised."

"Clara, sweetheart. God, I don't know how to tell you this." Ray's voice was choked with emotion. "All leaves have been canceled. We're shipping out tomorrow."

"*Mon Dieu*, no, no,no." Clara felt herself sliding down the wall, sitting on the floor. Her ears were ringing and her vision blurred. She touched the little champagne glass charm hanging on its long chain underneath her clothes, a talisman that Ray had given her years ago. "How can this be happening?"

"It's some bullshit about space on a troop ship being available. They didn't tell us much."

Tillie came running at the sound of Clara's pain. She took the phone from her sister's hand and asked, "Ray, what is it? This is Tillie."

"Tillie, I'm so sorry to tell you there will be no wedding until I get back. All leaves are canceled. We're leaving here for overseas tomorrow."

*"Jesu, Marie et Joseph, aidez-moi."* Tillie looked up to the ceiling. Her prayer for divine help was automatic, but no divine intervention would be forthcoming. Clara stirred and reached for the phone in Tillie's hand.

"Ray, I love you. We'll get married as soon as you get back. Take care of yourself and come back to me. I'll write every day."

"Goodbye for now, my darling Clara, my beautiful babe. I love you forever." There was no more to say. Ray hung up the phone.

The undoing of all the plans took place without Clara, who stayed in her room and wept bitter tears, railing against the war, the fates, generals who took men away from their families. When Tillie looked in on her Friday afternoon, it was to bring her a tray with cucumber soup, a slice of warm pumpernickel bread and freshly cut very ripe, red tomatoes sprinkled with salt and pepper. "You must eat something, Clara, *ma soeur*. You promised to write and to marry him later. It will do no good to ruin your health."

On Saturday, Clara came down to breakfast wearing a navy blue sundress and carrying a straw hat. *"Bonjour, ma soeur.* Good morning, Angela. Do you think you girls might like to go with me to Look Park today?" She asked Marie and Amy who were sitting at the table eating scrambled eggs.

Angela looked up over her cup of coffee and said, "What a great idea. I'd like to come, too. How about if I make some sandwiches and lemonade and we'll have a picnic?" Marie and Amy were already out of their chairs and running up the back staircase to get dressed.

The first week back to school the weather was very hot. All the kids in school complained about it as they sweated through the days, lethargic in the heat. Very little breeze came through the open windows. Mrs. Cooley's temper was quick to flare at the slightest infraction of the rules. Marie, who usually loved going back to school and relished every new challenge, became cranky at home and even surly to her little sister.

In the kitchen at 144 West Street, Tillie chopped onions and peppers and green tomatoes, measured out the vinegar and spices and watched the droplets of sweat from her rosy red face drip onto the hot stove. She was determined to get this job done before the vegetables began to soften in the heat. They'd all be glad to have the piccalilli this winter and some jars could be decorated and given as gifts at Christmas. Amy sat on the floor with a box of paper dolls and was a willing helper when her *Memere* needed something from the pantry.

At her window station in the hosiery, Clara felt some slight breeze coming in from the street and was grateful that she worked in the lowest level of the building where it was the coolest, well aware that the girls on the third floor were really sweltering. While her hands moved mechanically over the leg forms on her machine and her eyes searched for imperfections in the stockings she inspected, her mind imagined what Ray was doing today, where he might be and how soon he would come back to her.

At the munitions factory in Florence, Angela's hair was damp from sweat, her blouse was stuck to her back and her face was flushed a bright pink. Everybody was suffering from the heat of the day added to the heat of the machines banging and clacking away endlessly in the frantic effort to keep up with production goals.

Walking back from the restroom, through the shipping department crowded with crates, she rounded a corner into a long, dim passageway and saw Tony Scarlotti. Right away, she suspected he'd been watching for her to be alone and had waited for her to come back from the restroom. Her breath caught in her chest and she fought a moment of nausea. Oh, please God, she thought, knowing intuitively that Tony was trouble, don't let this happen, and she said angrily, "Get out of the way. Let me pass."

"Well, well, well. Look what I caught." He grasped her around the shoulders with her back to his chest and pulled her away from the open corridor behind a stack of large crates. "Now I've got you." He pulled at the waistband of her slacks and thrust his hand down the front. Angela heard the button roll on the floor and opened her mouth to scream. Her voice came out in a squeak an instant before he tightened his grip on her chest with his powerful forearm, squeezing her shoulder, an elbow bruising her breast and thrust his big hand over her mouth. She kicked and flailed and struggled, angry, frightened and frustrated that she could not seem to connect any blows. She tried to bite his hand, twisted her head from side to side in an effort to free her mouth, threw her head back violently trying to connect with his jaw, but nothing loosened his grip.

"Wait a minute. Wait a minute. Relax. You're going to enjoy this." His hand was inside her panties. "I've been wanting to do this for a long time." He laughed as his slid his fingers further in. With a burst of strength, Angela surged forward, straining against the arm that pinioned her to his chest in an attempt to dislodge his hand. "Want to play rough, do you?" He pulled his hand out of her pants, spun her around with one hand and slapped her with the other. In that instant, with his hand away from her mouth, Angela screamed and drove her knee upward. She missed and tried again.

Suddenly, he let go and she fell to the floor. Then she heard her slow-witted brother Sal say, "You bastard! I saw what you was doing. You slapped my sister." She got up off the floor, started to adjust her clothes and realized she was shaking so hard, she couldn't do it. Tony was sprawled on his back between the aisles of crates. "Angela, are you OK?" Sal cradled her face in his enormous hands, saw her tears and gathered her to him in a gentle hug. He sighed deeply. "He hurt you. I'm going to hurt him." Tony rolled to his side quickly to evade Sal's big boots kicking at him.

"Oh, *Dio Mio*, don't do anything, Sal. I don't want any trouble. Don't tell anybody about this, OK? I don't want anybody to know. Promise me you won't tell. Promise me."

"Ok, Angela. If you say so, I won't tell. But I'm going to watch him now. If he comes anywhere near you again, I'm going to kill him. Not here, though. They wouldn't like it if I kill him here."

Tony was still lying on the floor, his hand on his head. "You stupid son of a bitch dumbbell, what did you do that for? I was just having a little fun. I didn't really hurt her. Just a little tap. She's the one that wanted to play rough."

Sal shook his fist in Tony's face. "You stay away from her, you hear me? I mean it. I'm going to be watching you." Since Sal was at least four inches taller and thirty pounds heavier than Tony, he was a menacing sight as he leaned over him.

"OK, OK, you big ox. I thought your father disowned her when she married that frog. And your brother says she's nothing but a slut. What do you care about her?" For an answer he got a swift kick in his ribs.

Angela went back to the restroom, while Sal waited outside of the door. She threw up her lunch and still kept heaving. Grateful that no one had come in while she was sick in the stall, she washed her face and pulled herself together. When the supervisor made a comment on how long she'd been gone, Angela said, "Must have been something I had for lunch didn't agree with me. I tossed my cookies. I think I'll be fine now, though."

"Well, I hope so. We can't afford to fall behind our production goals. You do look a little flushed. Better take it easy tonight."

When she joined her car pool at the end of her shift, Hilda reported that she'd heard there had been a fight between Tony Scarlotti and Angela's brother, Sal. "I don't know what it was about, but somebody says Tony has a big bruise on his jaw and he's walking around with a limp. And when people asked him what happened, he said it was the dummy Sal who hit him for nothing. Of course, Tony is such a shmuck, everybody figures he deserved it."

Dotty asked, "Do you think Sal will get fired for that?"

"Oh, no, I don't think so. The supervisors like Sal. He's a good worker, even if he is slow-witted. Sorry, Angela, but that's what everybody says. And most people know Tony teases him a lot, too, so nobody would stick up for Tony."

Angela had a moment of panic before she chimed in, "Sal is harmless. He'd never hurt anybody unless they had it coming."

The other girls all agreed.

Amy was sniffling when Angela walked in from the back porch, where the smell of piccalilli curing in the crocks was almost overwhelming. "What's the matter, *cara mia*?" Angela picked up her little daughter and kissed her tears away.

"Marie is mad at me because I stepped on her book. But I didn't mean it. The book was on the floor and I tripped." Amy hiccuped. "She's the one who left the book there. And it only tore a little bit."

"Well, never mind. Let's go talk to her now. You can stop crying. That won't help anything."

Marie knew the book tear was an accident. She even knew she was being unfair because she was the one who left the book on the floor. But still, she was in a bad mood and she scowled when she saw her mother approaching with Amy.

" OK, girls, kiss and make up.  It's too hot to stay angry.  Let's put our bathing suits on and go take a dip in the river.  I'm hot myself and it will be cool under the trees there."

The Mill River ran past the fields on the side of the house and the girls were forbidden to go there without an adult because the bank was steep and, depending on the amount of rainfall, the water could be deep.  There were large trees that grew out over the water, providing shade and privacy.  Sometimes boys from the alley went skinny dipping there.  They even had a rope that hung from one of the branches so they could swing out over the water and cannonball in.  Soft moss covered the ground under the trees and watercress grew there.  As soon as she thought of it, Angela realized how much she needed to wash away the events of the day.

Carrying their towels and a pitcher of lemonade, Angela and her two daughters made their way to the spot everyone called the "swimming place."  There were two boys in the water when they arrived, splashing, shouting at each other and having fun.  Angela knew them to be O'Malley boys, nice kids from the alley houses, maybe ten or eleven years old. They waved and hollered, "Come on in."

The water was cool and reviving for all of them. After a little splashing in it, they stretched out under the trees on their towels and listened to the rustling of the leaves, the hum of insects and the rippling noise as the water moved over the rocks in the middle of the river. The smell of green things growing, new cut grass and the faint tang of the manure spread in the garden not very far away contributed to the peace of the place. All three of them were dozing when Clara came looking for them. It was time for supper already.

Later that night, after the girls were in bed, Angela picked up her pen to write to Pete. She had decided from the time he entered the service that she would never tell him anything that would make him worry about them. And of course, she had no intention of telling him about the incident in the afternoon. She wondered if she would ever tell him. Or, for that matter, whether she would ever tell anybody. It felt strange, though, not to tell Pete. He was her best friend as well as her husband and he would know what to say to make her feel better about it. Mostly, she worried that she might have said or done something that would make Tony think it was OK to do such a thing to her. Maybe she should stop wearing lipstick. Maybe she should wear baggier pants. She rejected that thought immediately. She didn't want to make it any easier for somebody to put his hands down her pants.

*Dear Pete,*

*The girls and I went swimming today at the swimming place on the Mill River. It's been so hot here that everybody is a little bit cranky and that seemed like a great way to cool off. All of us enjoyed it. The girls ate watercress and we picked some to bring back to the house. Amy spotted a yellow bird that none of us had ever seen before. I think it was a parakeet that escaped from his cage, but Amy was sure it was a magic bird because we were having a magic afternoon. Maybe she's right.*

*I keep depositing more money in our bank account all the time. With what I've saved from the allotment they send from the Army and what I've made, we're up over $500.00* now. Aren't you surprised? It will be so wonderful to have our own house. Not that I'm not very grateful to your parents for helping us out, but still, we need to be on our own. I know you want that, too.

From your letter, even with the black marks of the censor, I've figured out that you must be in England. Your father got a big map so we could see where England is. The girls have enjoyed his little geography lessons. And we all listen to the news every night, especially Gabriel Heatter and Edward R. Murrow.

Did you get the package of cookies and the magazines we sent? The girls helped with the cookies. I guess you can tell from the decoration on some of them. I hope they didn't all get broken. Somebody at work told me about putting the popcorn in with the cookies, although I'm sure the popcorn must have been stale by the time it got to you and, anyway, without butter or salt it doesn't taste very good.

Stay safe, caro mio. I love you very much.

## *Angela xxxxxxxxxxxxx*

Lying in bed, listening to the insects hit the window screen, Angela stared at the ceiling lit by moonlight and let the tears seep from her eyes.  She thought of how hard it was to sleep alone, without her darling Pete to hold her, comfort her, and assure her that all would be well.  Would she ever be able to forget Tony's hand in her panties?  Would she ever get over her shame that for a minute there her body had responded to that awful touch?

# CHAPTER 11

## FALL 1942

Outside a little village in southern England, not far from the coast, in a Quonset hut that was one in a long row of Quonset huts, Pete LaPointe sat on his bunk and read the letter from Angela. He thought about how much he would have enjoyed jumping into the water at the swimming place with his wife and girls, then feeling the soft moss of the bank under him, hearing them laughing and splashing. *Mon Dieu*, he was glad they were safe.

Like every other guy he talked to in the Army, he knew that their safety was the reason he was here, doing what had to be done to win this war. When Pete enlisted, he didn't have any idea what to expect and he wasn't even sure he knew why he was doing it. His reasoning was complicated by his fear of getting his wife pregnant and the possibility of losing her to an untimely pregnancy after her frightening miscarriage, and the patriotic fervor that had gripped the whole community. It was probably a mixture of these things and a lifetime of seeking excitement, too.

Once he began his basic training at Fort Dix, though, the atmosphere of shared purpose among the men he met there solidified his thinking into a clear belief that the most important thing he would ever do in his life was to help win the war over the evil that had been let loose. Sure, there were some jerks and deadbeats and con artists in the Army, but that was to be expected when they came from everywhere. Most of the guys he met were honest, solid, hard working people who saw this as a job that had to be done. And, despite the physical pain from muscles never before put to the test, the demands of military discipline, the chickenshit everybody had to take from some of the junior officers, they all pushed on and did what had to be done.

Like a lot of others, he had been hunting with a rifle since he was a kid, so learning to use the weapons of war was not a big stretch. He won a medal for marksmanship early in his training. After a few weeks of pain and suffering from the long hikes, burdened down with nearly 50 pounds of equipment, his body responded and he was able to perform the physical feats required with hardly a twinge. Still, he was older than most of the guys in his unit and one of the few married.

Most of his buddies wrote to their girlfriends or their mothers. He was almost embarrassed at mail call when he got more letters than anybody. And he got teased a lot, called "Old Guy" and "Pops" by some of them.

He was a little surprised when the results of the Army Qualifications Test showed him to be well suited to vehicle repair. When he thought of it, he'd learned a lot from hanging out with his Uncle Charlie, who could fix anything, especially anything with a motor. He got some extra training after basic and made Private First Class before he even shipped out.

Now he was on a post in England, doing maintenance on a whole fleet of vehicles, keeping up with the drills and the target shooting and the demands of military discipline while he waited for the push they all knew would come sooner or later. The scuttlebutt was that an invasion was being planned, but nobody knew when or where. Some people said it was supposed to happen right away, but the Brits didn't want another Dunkirk and they didn't think the Allies were ready. He guessed that was true because they sure didn't have enough of anything to launch a major push across the Channel any time soon. If he was making a bet, he'd bet the build-up to it was going to take a long time. Meanwhile he missed his family every day.

"Hey, Pete, any cookies left?"

Pete looked up from his letter to see Stanley Borowski and George Corelli standing there. He and Stanley had been buddies since they both left for Fort Dix from the train station in Northampton on the same day and then they met George Corelli when they first got to this post and it turned out he came from Easthampton, a small town just a couple of miles from home. The three of them started to hang out together, share their miseries, laugh at the absurdities and enjoy themselves.

"Not even a crumb. And no popcorn left either, so don't ask."

"I just heard that we're going to get a whole shipload of tanks next week if the ship they're on doesn't get sunk before it gets here." George was a clerk for the commanding officer, so he heard rumors before anyone else. He hated his assignment but he was a fast typist and they were hard to come by in the Army. The colonel kept telling him to keep up with his weapons and physical training, because when the big push came on, he'd get his turn at fighting the bad guys.

"Great. I've been hearing about these tanks for a while. Supposed to be the best ever. I hope I get to work on them." Pete's natural ability with motor repair made it likely he would be picked to work on the new Sherman tanks.

"Hey, we're thinking of going into town to get laid. Want to come?"

"Not today, I've got to write my letters. You know, I don't get all this mail unless I write back." Not exactly true, but Pete was still wrestling with his guilt over the last time he had sex with a girl in the village. He knew most guys who were married rationalized the infidelity with the excuse of the special circumstances of war, but he still didn't feel right about it.

"OK, but you'll be sorry when we come back and tell you how we scored." Both guys walked off, laughing.

Pete took out a sheet of the tissue thin paper called V-mail and started to write. His pen paused after Dear Angela and he closed his eyes and imagined himself home, sitting down to dinner with the whole family around the table, eating roast beef and mashed potatoes whipped with cream and butter and green beans from one of the jars in the cellar. Amy was fidgeting, Marie was talking, his father was reaching for something and across the table, his eyes met Angela's and he knew, he just knew how much she loved him.

His eyes popped open and he resolutely refused to think about sex with his wife right now because he'd never get the letters written and he'd be miserable with the pain of his loneliness and his need for her soft, beautiful body. Oh, shit, he thought, I'll go walk over to the PX and get some cigars. Then, when I come back, I'll write the letters.

When Charlie went north on the bus from Northampton after he was released from prison, one of the first things he did was go to the convent in *Trois Rivieres* where he asked if he could visit with Annamarie Labeque, the sweetheart of his youth, the love of his life. There he learned that she had died in an outbreak of measles that had sent four other nuns in that little convent to their deaths. She was buried in the cemetery behind the church. He wept bitter tears at her gravesite, falling to his knees on the damp grass, shattered at the loss of what might have been. He stayed there a long time, reluctant to leave his beloved. It seemed to him then that his life had been a total waste. For a few days he thought about killing himself, but then he decided that would be too easy. He didn't deserve to end his pain before God decided.

He knew from talking to another inmate at the prison that there were jobs that paid good money in the logging camps in Maine, more money than he could earn anywhere else. He would save his money and give it away to people who needed it.

When he went to one of the camps, the boss said to him, "You're a pretty old guy for this kind of work. Think you can keep up?"

And Charlie answered him, "*Oui*, I can do it if you give me a chance to try."

"You're going to be hurting for quite a while until you get used to it, you know." The foreman warned.

"That's OK. I'll do the job. You'll see."

And he had done the job, working on a two-man team loading fresh cut logs onto a chute that would take them to the river and earning a lot of respect for his hard work, his willingness to help anybody who needed help and his tight control on his temper. He never allowed anything to ruffle him.

One of the men, married with a family and a little house in the village close by the logging camp, invited him to come for Thanksgiving dinner, but Charlie turned him down, claiming he needed to go into Old Town, the largest city nearby. He didn't say for what, but he took the battered old truck he had bought with his first month's paycheck, drove the eighty miles or so to the city and presented himself at the rectory of the French church there. When a nun answered his knock on the back door, he asked, "Do you have any jobs that need to be done, Sister? I would like to offer my help by doing any repairs to the house or the church as a gift."

"Do you know anything about plumbing?"

"*Oui, oui.* I can do anything you need done if I have the right tools. Or maybe you have some tools I could use?"

So it began. Charlie spent his weekends and holidays as the unpaid handyman at the little French church to the relief and delight of the two priests and the nuns in the convent there.

Tillie, Angela and Clara were cleaning up the kitchen, putting platters and silver away after the Thanksgiving feast. They were unusually quiet, each caught up in their own thoughts about the absent members of their family. As always, Tillie thought of her brother Charlie and wondered where he was today. Hard to swallow the news they'd gotten that he left town on the first bus out of here after he was released from jail. And both Tillie and Angela were thinking of Pete, Clara of Ray. Tillie and Clara's brother Maurice, his wife, Simone, and their son Bobby moved to Connecticut, where Maurice went to work in a defense plant there. They had one son in the Navy and their youngest, Bobby was about to turn 17. If the war went on another year he would surely be drafted. They knew of friends and relatives who had lost sons and husbands and brothers. Every street had some houses with gold stars in the windows.

Tillie was putting the remains of the feast in wax paper. "Look at all this turkey we have left over. I'll have to make a fricassee."

"We could share it with some of the tenants in the alley." Clara said, "Everybody loves fricassee."

Angela held out a platter of sliced turkey. "We'll have plenty of breast meat for sandwiches on Sunday night."

"Maybe you shouldn't have gotten such a big turkey, Tillie, *ma soeur*." Clara remarked.

"*Alors*, I don't like to see a small turkey on the table. It doesn't look nice. And anyway, it will all get eaten up, don't worry." Tillie wiped her hands. "There, we're all done. Does anybody want to play pinochle?"

"I'm so stuffed, I need a walk," Angela stretched her arms over her head. "Anybody want to come with me?"

"I do," Clara answered, "And why don't we see if Amy and Marie want to come, too?"

"Well, I'll go see if Edward wants to play some rummy." Tillie was an avid card player.

☆ ☆ ☆ ☆ ☆

Outside, the sidewalk had been mostly cleared, but there was a lot of slush at the cross streets. Amy and Marie walked ahead of Angela and Clara. When Angela pulled a pack of cigarettes out of her pocket, Clara looked at her in surprise. "When did you start smoking, *cherie?*"

"Everybody at the plant smokes, you know. They give us smoke breaks. I was sort of sticking out like a sore thumb. Hilda told me I should try it, that it's relaxing. At first I didn't like it and it made me cough, but after a few smokes, I realized it does relax me. Is that so terrible?"

Clara shrugged, "I guess not, but I think it makes your clothes smell bad and I wonder if it's good for you."

"Well, Ray smokes. Pete smokes. Papa Edward smokes his pipe. And anyway, I only smoke a few a day. I'll quit when this war is over."

"Yeah, everything will be different when this war is over."

Ray Carpenter was hot and dirty and tired. There'd been a skirmish with a small group of Italians this morning and he could still smell the cordite and the blood from it. He hated Africa. The heat and the sand and the flies were bad enough, but the dunes and the bright sun that distorted vision and hid the enemy were a painful challenge. He'd already lost four of the men in his platoon and they hadn't been there three weeks yet. All of them were untried in battle and there would be heavy casualties until they learned how to deal with the realities of war. Most guys showed up thinking this was like a game, where the play was understood by everybody and everybody played fair. What a crock. Hard to learn that it's messy and chaotic and nobody, absolutely nobody played fair, unless they wanted to die quick.

Ray had been sent to OCS, officer candidate school, and done well there, learning the awesome responsibility of leading other men into battle. He had a natural ability to inspire because he led by example. Never would he ask anybody to do what he would not do. Of course, he knew that was expected of all officers, but many interpreted it as, "Never ask anybody to do what you could not do." Big difference.

He flopped down on his camp bed and closed his eyes. Thanksgiving Day in the US of A. He pictured his lovely Clara, her cheeks flushed from the stove, carrying a big turkey to the table, her whole family sitting around. Oh, God, how much he wished they could have gotten married before he left. Then he'd know she was really his and some day they'd have a home of their own. He'd come home at the end of the day and she'd be waiting.

Gene Barlow came through the tent flap and threw a package on his chest. Ray sat up and rubbed his eyes, always red and gritty from the damned sand and said, "What the hell is this?"

"What does it look like, buddy? I passed by that big Noo Yawker's tent and he gave it to me to give to you. He got it by mistake. How could two guys named Carpenter be any more different than the two of you, I don't know. Open it. It's from your girl. Maybe it's cookies."

"Well, if it is, they will certainly be in crumbs. It looks like somebody dropped this package from a crane. And it's got stains, too. Probably sea water." Still, Ray opened it eagerly. "Wow, brownies. With walnuts."

He took a bite. "A little hard. Let's go get a cup of java to dunk 'em in."

Ray had met Gene on the ship that took them from Norfolk, Virginia to Portsmouth in England. They thought they were on their way to join a force that would invade the European continent very soon, at least that was what everybody said. It was an unpleasant surprise to learn, after they were sent to a base in Scotland, doing not much more than keeping up with target practice and daily drills, that they would be heading out for Africa. The big brass had decided, for who knew what reason, that the target would be the German and Vichy French forces in northern Africa.

Like Ray, Gene was just out of OCS, a newly minted Second Lieutenant and a little older than the rest of the guys, but at 28 quite a bit younger than Ray, who was almost 35. He had one year of college at Princeton before his mother and father were both killed in an auto accident and he left school to take responsibility for his father's dry cleaning business and watch out for his two younger brothers. When the two boys were drafted, he enlisted. Gene and Ray became close buddies very quickly, sharing whatever they had, watching out for each other. The ship had a fair share of card sharks and hustlers to watch out for, too. Both men were of the opinion that it would be a miracle if this bunch of guys could win a war.

All those movies he had seen about war, all the books he'd read about heroic acts, spectacular rescues, all that was just so much bullshit. The noise and the smells and the gore were bad enough, but the worst were the guys who risked their fellow soldiers by their cowardice and venality, stealing, cheating, and hustling whenever they could get away with it. We'll win this war in spite of those assholes, Ray thought, just because there's more good guys than bad guys, but it won't be easy.

When Gene and Ray got to the mess tent, they heard that General Eisenhower had been there earlier in the day. "Too bad we missed him." Gene grinned at Ray. Gene was always glad to avoid big brass.

"I like him and I respect him a lot. He may not be a blazing star in this man's Army, but he knows what it's going to take to win here and he tells it straight. I give him a lot of credit for that." Ray sipped his coffee, dunked the brownie in it and savored the rich chocolate treat. It made him think of Clara again and he said to Gene, "I'm going back and write a letter. I better do it now. I've got a patrol to take out tonight."

# CHAPTER 12
## CHRISTMAS 1942

Edward LaPointe stamped his feet to shake the snow off his galoshes and climbed the stairs to the back porch. As soon as he opened the door, the smell of penuche made him grin. *"Ma chere* Tillie, I can tell you've been cooking something other than my supper, eh?"

"Well, of course, I had to get started making the things that are going into the Christmas boxes for Pete and Ray. Clara says they have to be in the mail this week. And we're going to make *tire lire* tonight."

*Tire lire*, a taffy made from white and brown sugar, corn syrup, molasses, vinegar and baking soda, was a favorite treat. After it was cooked, it was poured into greased pie pans to cool until it was lukewarm. Then, with buttered hands, it was pulled and stretched into long ropes, cut into small pieces and wrapped.

Marie was coming down the back stairs and she whooped, "Fabulous! Ooh, that's fabulous. I love to make *tire lire*. Will we wrap the pieces in waxed paper or Christmas wrapping?"

"Both. First the waxed paper and then the Christmas paper."

Everybody in the house got involved in the making of the several different treats that would be sent to Ray and Pete. Added to the brownies and cookies, penuche and *tire lire* would be jars of jam and jelly, pictures drawn by Amy, a poem for Pete written by Marie, photos they had taken of each other and, in Ray's box, a gold St.Christopher medal on a chain that Clara had gotten at Gare's jewelry store. Everything would be wrapped carefully, cushioned with copies of the Daily Gazette, covered with popcorn, then mailed to the APO in hopes that the boxes would arrive in time for Christmas.

Every year since Marie had become a Girl Scout, the troop went to The Lathrop Home to sing Christmas carols to the aged ladies living there. The girls met with the Scout leaders in the basement of the Edward's church on the corner of State and Main Streets and, unless the weather was really very bad, they walked in a group the half mile or so to the Home on South Street.

Uniforms freshly washed and pressed, sashes covered with hard-won badges, the girls greeted one another, gossiped about school matters and jiggled in nervous anticipation of their yearly performance. Marie was proud of every badge she earned, especially the citizenship one, because that's how she won the essay contest, working on required activities for that badge.

"Where's Irene Frenier?" Marie asked a couple of girls standing near her. "I didn't see her at recess today. Is she sick?"

Mrs. Newton, the young assistant leader answered. "I'm sorry to have to tell you girls that Irene's uncle, who was in the RAF, was shot down over the English Channel. Her family just heard and they've gone up to Quebec to be with her aunt and her grandmother. We should remember him in our prayers."

Many of the girls in this troop had brothers or uncles in the service and the distress on their faces was evidence of their awareness of the dangers facing them. Marie was the only one whose father was overseas, although some of the girls had fathers who had been pressed into serving in non-combat roles, working on getting supplies to the troops like Joan's father or training new recruits at Fort Dix, as Patty's father was doing. She felt a clog in her throat and tears in her eyes, but she managed to say, "Could we say a little prayer for him now, Mrs. Newton?"

"Why, yes, Marie, that's a good idea. Why don't we bow our heads for a minute and each of us can say a private prayer?"

Sixteen heads bowed; some girls reached out to hold hands with special friends. Marie was grateful that the prayer was silent, since her version of The Lord's Prayer was a bit different than most of the girls in the troop and sometimes it was awkward when they prayed out loud together.

Poor Irene, she thought, how proud of her uncle she was. And how much she will miss him. Then she turned her thoughts to her father, praying that he be safe and come back to them soon.

Amy was excited, her cheeks rosy and her eyes wide. Mommy was taking both her girls Christmas shopping and they were going to see Santa at McCallum's Department Store. She had a whole dollar to buy presents, which she could pick out herself. Marie said she'd help with counting the money and *Memere* said she'd help her wrap them. Amy was five years old now and she could do lots of things by herself, but sometimes she needed a little help. She could count just fine, but counting money was a little different. She hadn't mastered that yet.

*Pepere* dropped them off in front of the store and promised to return for them at four o'clock, so they had two hours of gawking and shopping and seeing Santa, of course.

"Let's go visit Santa first." Mommy smiled and tugged at Amy's hand. They first stopped to admire the beautifully decorated windows with a tall fir tree covered in red, white and blue. There was a tiny train running around the tree. Some cars had little flags attached to them. Amy could read the big sign in the window. It said "God Bless Us All." And another one said "Merry Christmas and Happy New Year." There were dolls and coloring books and little army trucks and tanks and a battleship, skates and mittens and sweaters, all spilling out of boxes under the tree.

Marie grabbed Amy's other hand and tugged her toward the front door. Inside there were wreaths and ribbons decorating the cross beams of the ceiling and a long rope of wonderful smelling greenery twined around the balustrade in the back of the store where the stairs led upstairs or downstairs. A big sign with an arrow pointing up announced that Santa was on the second floor. Amy's head was swiveling around trying to see everywhere at once.

When they got upstairs, there was a line of children waiting to see Santa, but it wasn't a long one and Mommy bent down and asked Amy, "Do you want to get in line, *cara*? Do you want me to stay with you?"

"I can go by myself. Aren't you going to talk to Santa, Marie?"

"No, I'm too old to talk to him now. He only needs to talk to you."

Marie and her Mom waited a little distance away while Amy moved forward. A few times she turned to look at them and waved, but there were no signs that she was nervous or frightened in any way, even though some of the children cried or refused to get on Santa's lap. With supreme confidence, Amy climbed onto Santa's lap, smiling broadly. When Santa asked her name, she answered, "You met me before. Don't you remember my name?"

Santa laughed a big booming laugh and tweaked Amy's nose. "You'll have to tell me again. I'm getting old so I forget sometimes."

"I'm Amy LaPointe and I hope you don't forget to bring me a new Betsy-wetsy doll because the last one broke and she doesn't do her pee-pee anymore."

All those people waiting close enough to hear her words as well as Santa himself started laughing. Amy looked out at the crowd and said, "It's not funny. She doesn't work anymore."

Santa lifted her off his lap and gave her a little kiss on the cheek. "Amy, I promise you a new Betsy-wetsy and Merry Christmas."

Mommy and Marie managed to suppress their laughter and commended Amy on her meeting with Santa, then they headed down Main Street to Kresge's Five and Ten Cents Store. Marie and Amy went in while Mommy waited outside so Amy could pick out Mommy's present first. They browsed the aisles looking at tins of talcum powder, shiny lipsticks, handkerchiefs, hair clips, cardboard papers of shiny bobby pins and jars of cold cream. They admired the goldfish in the murky tank, but Marie thought Mommy didn't have time to take care of goldfish. Finally they settled on a special present and Marie assisted in the transaction with the money. When they came out of the store, Amy was clutching a paper bag, her tiny purse dangling on her arm with the precious change from her dollar inside. More shopping had to be done, but with less drama, except when she was selecting a gift for Marie. Amy was a veteran shopper now. She knew how to do it.

Marie checked the clock in front of Gare's Jewelry store and noticed they had about half an hour before *Pepere* would be coming to pick them up. "Can we get a soda at Beckman's, Mom?"

"Yes, sure, that's a good idea." They hurried up the street and were lucky to find a booth near the front of the restaurant, where both girls ordered cherry Cokes and Mommy got a cup of coffee, savoring every swallow as both coffee and sugar were now being rationed.

Preparations for Christmas were certainly not the same this year, but still the holiday would be honored. Edward went out to buy a Christmas tree, since he didn't relish the idea of tramping through the snowy woods looking for an appropriate tree to cut down. That task had been Charlie's specialty and then, after Charlie went to jail, it was taken over by Pete. Edward found a lovely tree in a lot run by the Boy Scouts and with some fumbling and much muttering, (Edward never used curse words) the tree was set in its stand.

They all participated in trimming the tree, Amy now old enough to hang the glass balls as well as drape the branches with tinsel. When they sang French Christmas carols, it was without accompaniment, although Tillie and Clara both had tears in their eyes as they remembered all the Christmases when Charlie played the piano as they sang.

Angela and Clara and the girls walked down to the Calvin Theatre, stopping to watch the WAVES in their dark blue uniforms marching from the Hotel Northampton, where they had all their meals, to classes at Smith College. They were in training to become commissioned officers in the Navy, to be sent all over the country, relieving men to be sent to war zones. Smith was the designated headquarters for the Naval Reserve Midshipmen's School. Marie watched them, starry-eyed, wishing she were old enough to be among them.

Main Street was decorated as it had always been, with swags of greenery from one lamppost to another; store windows were festive with decorations of the season. But here and there, posters reminded shoppers of the troops and the long line at the tobacco store on the corner of King and Main attested to the shortage of cigarettes. Nearly every store had music playing from the popular new film "Holiday Inn," including a song called "White Christmas" that reminded everyone of the men who would not be home for Christmas.

On Christmas Eve, Franklin Delano Roosevelt spoke to the nation and the world in one of his fireside chats. "I cannot say 'Merry Christmas,' for I think constantly of those thousands of soldiers and sailors who are in actual combat throughout the world, but I can express to you my thought that this is a happier Christmas than last year, happier in the sense that the forces of darkness stand against us with less confidence in the success of their evil ways."

Edward, who was a great admirer of the president, nodded his head vigorously as he listened to the message of inspiration and hope. Angela left the room, unable to control her strong emotional reaction to the speech, but well aware that Edward was enthralled. What crap, she thought, to make nice speeches when our guys are suffering every day. Really, it made no sense to her for pretty speeches to be made. Even though she knew they had no choice but to go to war after the Japanese bombed Pearl Harbor, she couldn't understand why Americans had to be fighting Europe's war with Hitler. While she simmered with her private anger, she didn't speak of it publicly, afraid to be thought a traitor, the worse thing anyone could be thought to be.

It was raining on the day before Christmas when Pete got his package from home. When he heard his name at mail call, he let out a loud whoop, so pleased that it had arrived, when he had begun to feel sorry for himself that there would be no goodies from home for him. Other guys in his Quonset hut had been getting packages for the last two weeks and every day he showed up at mail call and came back with only letters, he scoffed at himself to be so damned ungrateful. Plenty of guys got nothing at all, except for letters school kids sent to "Any Soldier."

He opened his package eagerly, knowing it would contain brownies, some kind of fudge and jams and jellies. He was surprised by the *tire lire*, though. He wasn't known to be all that crazy about *tire lire*, so he wondered why he found himself swallowing fast to contain the emotion that the sight of the wrapped candy brought up. It was the sudden sharp memory of his girls sitting at the kitchen table cutting the long ropes into bite-size pieces and wrapping them carefully in waxed paper, laughing and chewing at the same time.

He hung up the pictures Angela had taken with her Kodak Brownie camera right away and glanced quickly at the poem Marie wrote for him before he shoved it in his pocket. He'd save that to read later when he was somewhere a little less public than the barracks. George came in holding a package of his own and said,

"Goddam, I was glad to get a package today. I was thinking they forgot me."

"Yeah, well, me too. I should have known better. My family is really great about sending stuff. Of course, some gets lost on ships that go down, but mostly they get here sooner or later." Pete's grin was wide, his manner easy.

"I hear we're going to get a feast tomorrow. Turkey and all the trimmings and even cranberry sauce. Pie, too." George did love food.

Pete's grin faded. "We should be damned grateful we aren't in Africa fighting those slimy French bastards who surrendered to the Germans. My friend Ray Carpenter is a new looey running a patrol in the desert. I bet they don't get any feast. They're probably lucky to eat C rations in between skirmishes."

"I'm guessing we'll get our turn in the barrel one of these days. There's supposed to be a troop ship coming in next week, and another one right behind it. Got to stay sharp so when we do go, we don't get killed." George ambled off in the direction of his own bunk and Pete headed for the latrines so he could read Marie's poem.

Ray's Christmas package had arrived, but he had not yet had time to open it. The fighting was fierce so he led his platoon out every day, confronting the enemy directly, cutting communications lines, disrupting transport by blowing up roads, doing his job. He'd lost two more men and he felt it keenly. At least he didn't have to write the letters to their parents. The Captain did that duty.

One of the men in his platoon got hit today and the medics brought him to that tent hospital everybody talked about. They told him it was incredible how fast the damn thing got set up and working. Fifty nurses and fifty doctors, mostly surgeons. Some guys laughed when they saw them arrive, most of them with the accents of the South, bright-eyed and bushy-tailed. Some SOB was making book on how long it would take for them to start running and hiding when a barrage came. But everybody was impressed as hell when they all adapted to living in tents, washing in cold water, even using open ditches for latrines when they first got set up. And they took in anybody—civilians, enemy, whoever showed up and needed help.

Ray set his package aside and went over to the tent hospital to see how Corporal Kelly was doing. When he drove the Jeep toward the place where the hospital was supposed to be, he didn't even see the damn place until he was almost on top of it. The green tents blended into the landscape of low brush and hills perfectly. He was amazed at how huge it was. Laid out in streets with rock borders, it was as big as a small city. Shit, he thought, how am I ever going to find him? But right then, he saw a big sign that read Headquarters. With startling efficiency, he was given the location of his man and made his way to the right tent.

A nurse in khaki coveralls came up to him as soon as he entered the tent and led him over to the bed where Corporal Kelly lay, his leg in a cast, fast asleep.

"How's he doing?" Ray asked.

"He'll be fine. Good thing you gave him that morphine shot, though. He could have done more damage thrashing around in pain if you hadn't done that." She smiled at Ray.

"That's the first time I ever did it. I was hoping I got it right."

"Oh, yes, Lieutenant, you did it right. And the sulfa powder prevented any infection from developing. He'll be good as new in about six weeks."

As Ray was leaving, he heard the sounds of Christmas carols being played on a guitar and then, passing another tent, some guys were singing "Silent Night." He'd forgotten it was Christmas Eve. If he hurried, he could get back and open his package before the chaplain started services.

Clara and Angela decided to go to midnight Mass at the Sacred Heart Church so that they could get Christmas dinner started while Tillie and Edward took the girls to Mass in the morning. The fragrant smell of pine filled the air and mingled with the ever present smell of incense and lemon furniture polish. Red poinsettias, donated to the church in memory of some loved one, were everywhere. The manger and creche scene with its life size plaster figures took up a large space inside the communion rail.

Both Clara and Angela knelt down in front of the bank of candles on the left of the altar, put their dimes in the slot and selected candles to light. They prayed silently and intensely to Holy Mary, Mother of God that she might intercede on behalf of Pete and Ray keeping them safe from harm.

In the U.S. Army post outside of the village of Trowbridge in the southern part of England, Pete and his two buddies, Stan Borowski and George Corelli, went to the midnight Mass being offered by the chaplain, Father McConnell. There were no fir boughs, no creche, no organ music, just a portable altar in a Quonset hut, full to bursting, with men standing all along the sides. Father had recruited four former altar boys to help him with his duties. Well over half the men took communion and there were many with tears in their eyes as they walked back to their places with the wafer on their tongue. Hundreds of prayers were said to bring this war to an end and to protect loved ones left at home.

When Ray slipped in to the back of the bomb damaged building that had been converted to a temporary church, the service had already begun. There were no seats that he could see and so he joined the many men who were standing in the back. The service was said to be interdenominational, but Ray knew this chaplain to be Baptist. Still, what difference did it make? The purpose here was to remind them of God, of the birth of His Son and of the importance of faith. Cynic he may be, but he was here and he was wearing the medal his beautiful babe, Clara, had sent in his Christmas package. If I live through this goddam war, he thought, I'll marry her right away and we'll go to church every Sunday to thank God for our survival.

# CHAPTER 13

## SPRING 1943

Marie had been surly all day, snapping at Betsy and Esther, refusing to join the usual group at recess, scowling at everyone. Then, when she yanked Amy's braids and made her cry for no reason other than that she was standing too close while Marie read in the little alcove off the living room, Mommy sent her to her room "to think about her misbehavior."

When she came down to supper in response to *Memere* calling up the stairs, she was subdued, picking at her food. *Pepere* asked if she was feeling well and she shrugged her shoulders and said, "I'm OK."

"Maybe you should get to bed a little early, *cara*," her mother said, "You look a little pale. Maybe you are coming down with something."

210

Amy kissed her sister sweetly before going up to bed and then when Marie followed her into their bedroom not more than half an hour later, asked, "Are you sick, Marie?"

"No, but I'm really, really tired." Marie answered in a voice that conveyed no doubt about her weariness.

Marie woke to the smell of something she didn't recognize. She made a grimace of distaste then, with a jolt of pain in her belly, she realized that she was wet and sticky down there, in her private place. The place *Memere* called her fess.

"*Mon Dieu, mon Dieu*, I think it's started." Her thoughts raced wildly from elation to fear. She had read the little blue booklet from the Kotex Company that Mommy had given her last summer and the girls at school talked about getting "the curse" often enough so it was no surprise. But right now she didn't know exactly what to do, so she called out to Amy in the other bed, "Amy, are you awake?" and when Amy raised her head from the pillow, sleepy-eyed and tousled, Marie told her, "Go get Mommy and hurry up."

"Why, are you going to throw up?"

"No, I don't think so, but I need you to go get Mommy right now. Stop asking questions and just do it."

When Mommy came in clutching her pink chenille bathrobe tight around her, she knew right away what had happened. The silent communication that took place between mother and daughter was an expression of compassion and sadness, mystery and acceptance. Amy was hustled into her robe and slippers, sent down the stairs to breakfast with a few soothing words and a little pat on the rump.

Marie threw back the covers and looked wide-eyed and scared at the dark red, sticky yuck staining the sheets and her favorite yellow flowered pajama bottom. With Mommy's arm around her, Marie went into the bathroom, stripped off the sticky, smelly pajama bottom and swayed, somewhat light-headed as Mommy washed her legs gently and made soothing noises.

"Sit here while I get the things you need. Will you be OK for a few minutes?"

Mommy returned with a pad and a belt made of elastic with little tabs hanging down the front and back and demonstrated how to thread the long tails on the ends of the thick white pad into the metal piece with the teeth. The pad felt very strange between Marie's legs, bulky and awkward.

"How can I go anywhere?" Marie whimpered. "Everyone will know. It's so big it will show."

"No, *cara*, it will be fine when you put your panties over it."

"It smells funny." An edge of panic came into Marie's voice.

"Well, you'll have to remember to change it often. What you're smelling now is the PJ bottom. Don't worry, it will be all right. Now I'm going to change the bed and then I'll get you a hot water bottle."

Marie was listless. She was aching and tired and just wanted to lie down again. Slightly nauseous and a little dizzy, she worried about fainting almost as much as she worried about the blood seeping through the pad and announcing her condition to everybody. It felt like it ought to be secret, this thing that was happening to her body.

When the bed was ready with fresh and wonderful smelling sheets, Mommy helped her get in and covered her tenderly. "Why don't you rest for a while? I'll bring up a tray with some breakfast a little later. Wouldn't you like a nice cup of tea with plenty of milk and sugar?"

"Yes, please." Marie's voice was small and quivering.

She lay back against the pillows and thought about how she had wanted this day to come and how she would tell Betsy and Esther about it and how they would be jealous that she was the first of them to reach this milestone.

Later in the day, Angela sat at the kitchen table writing her daily letter to Pete.

*Well, Pete, mi amore, when you left you had two little girls and now one of them has become a woman. Marie took it pretty well, although she was feeling a little poorly all day today. It's a big change in her life. I've been expecting it mostly because of her moodiness the last month or so. Now I'll have to watch her with the boys around here even more carefully. Oh, how I wish you were here to help me, so I do the right thing. She seems so young to me sometimes. And then other times, she seems so –I don't know what to call it.*

*Stay safe. We need you to come back to us.*

*I love you. Always remember that.*

*Angela*

It was only a week later that Marie came home from school to find a letter lying on the table next to the door, addressed just to her. It was the first time she had ever gotten a letter all her own, instead of a note inside a letter to her Mom. She took it to the little alcove between the parlor and the dining room and opened it very carefully.

*Dear Marie,*

*I was sure happy to get your last letter with the very good news about your grades. Winning The Kiwanis prize for your essay on freedom was terrific. Good for you. You make me so proud of you. You know I expect you to go to college. Education is*

215

*so important, sweetheart. Promise me that
you will do what it takes to get into Smith
College. Mom tells me you are a young lady
now. Be sure to pay attention to what she
tells you. You have to be careful. You are
very precious to us.*

*Keep up the good work and keep writing
me letters.*

*Love,*

*Dad*

Spring was late coming and when it did, it seemed to
Clara that it rained more than any other spring she
remembered. There was even talk of flooding in some
places. Clara and Tillie recalled the old days when the
Mill River overflowed its banks every spring. There
were those who thought the state project to divert
the river that took the Billieux farmlands by right of
eminent domain wouldn't work and would just be a
big scar on the land. They were wrong. That hadn't
happened and the Mill River never flooded again.

Clara read every newspaper Edward rescued from the trash and brought home from the library and she listened to news of the war on the radio every night. Edward R. Murrow, Eric Severeid and Gabriel Heatter were her favorites. Reading Ray's letters didn't tell her much, but she knew enough from clues he gave her that he was still in Africa.

Edward bought a big map, big enough to cover the whole kitchen table and they used it to find places mentioned by the radio commentators. Who had ever heard of Tunisia before this? Why did it all sound so confusing?

Clara worried. She worried about her nephew Pete as well as Ray, although Pete was not yet into any fighting. He seemed to be waiting for something, probably the order to cross the channel and invade the continent. The Pathe newsreels at the movies showed Roosevelt in his flowing cape and Churchill with his big cigar and it also showed grim faces of Brits sitting in air raid shelters while the bombs landed nearby. At least we don't have to deal with that, she thought.

One day Clara came home and dropped into a chair, sighing loudly and looking exasperated. "I hate this new supervisor. He is driving me crazy, leaning over me all the time, touching me, leering at me. I can't stand it anymore. I am going to have to find another job."

"I wouldn't worry about that, *ma cherie*. There are plenty of jobs now." Tillie answered her.

"Maybe now, but what about when the war is over and the men come back? Will they still hire women? I doubt it."

"Maybe you should look to do something that men will not want to do. Maybe you should do something you would really enjoy."

"Oh, Tillie, I've worked at the hosiery for so long I'm not sure I can do anything else."

Angela came down the stairs, carrying a pile of dirty clothes. "What's going on? You look so sad. Is there bad news?" Angela's voice took on a tinge of panic. She was ever alert to the possibility of a telegram announcing bad news about Pete or Ray.

"This new supervisor I told you about is such a pest, Angela, I need to find a new job."

"That's no problem, Clara. The defense plant is always looking to hire. You can come and work with me."

"I don't want to do that because I think women in plants will be let go as soon as the men return. I'm still going to need a job."

"Won't Ray want you to stay at home?" Angela knew Pete would expect her to give up her job and stay home as soon as he returned and she felt sure Ray would feel the same.

In that moment, Clara realized that she had been thinking of being alone for the rest of her life. She had really never believed Ray would return and they would be married. The thought was buried deep in her subconscious but it was there all right. Her fears had never left her. She just knew that Ray would be killed, just as Gus had been killed. But she swallowed hard, smiled at Angela and said, "Well, I'm sure you're right. Still, I think I'll look for some other kind of a job."

That night, lying in her bed, wide awake and shivering, she realized how little she believed in fairy tale endings, how unlikely she thought it would be that Ray would return.

In Africa, Ray sloughed through a heavy rain storm to reach the radioman. "Call back and tell them we need reinforcements. Those bastards out there are fresher than we are. My men are pinned down and too tired out. They haven't had a break for days. We need a little support here."

The noise of the shelling was deafening. He could see the fear and the fatigue in the faces of all the guys around him. They'd better get a break soon or they'd start dying for no reason other than just giving up to it. Christ, he thought, this is so royally fucked up. There are plenty of troops in England sitting on their asses waiting for the big push into Europe and we need them desperately here. Now.

Just then a shell burst within a few yards and he dove into a slit trench, not a moment too soon. So far he'd managed to stay whole, but many of the men in his platoon had been wounded, been patched up by a medic and gone right back into the fray.

Were they going to win this war? Some days he wondered. But then he remembered that he had arrived in this pissant country only five months ago. He and his men were raw recruits then without real experience in combat and thinking of this as a gentleman's game. Well, it wasn't. It was a no holds barred, messy, dirty business and they were learning every day to be just as ruthless as the enemy. The idea was to win, yes, but also to live to tell about it.

"Hey, Lieutenant, I just got word we can expect a new bunch of guys in a day or so. Of course, they'll need to learn the ropes, but at least they'll be warm bodies."

It was Angela who came up with the idea that Clara might like working at McCallum's Department store. "You like talking to people, you're used to being on your feet all day and you've always been good at keeping track of things. I think you'd make a great saleslady."

Clara thought it over and decided she might like it, but she was used to working piecework, working as fast as she could to earn the most money. Would she be able to make enough to pay her share to Tillie? To buy a few pretty things? Well, you never know unless you ask.

On Saturday afternoon, she dressed carefully in a navy blue voile dress with a white collar and cuffs, navy sling backs, a little pearl necklace and a navy blue spring coat she borrowed from Angela. McCallum's was the only department store in town. It had beautiful mahogany and glass cases to display merchandise, the air was always perfumed with the scent of furniture polish, exotic odors from the cosmetic counter and the rich aroma of leather goods. Except at Christmastime, the music in the background was soothing and hushed. The tearoom was an elegant affair, a place where ladies of leisure went in their fur stoles and nibbled on little tiny sandwiches while sipping their tea from bone china cups. The brass fittings on doors and cabinets were polished to a high shine.

Clara pushed the elevator button and when the door opened a small man in a brown uniform with gold braid on the collar and sleeves smiled and asked her "Floor, please?" She smiled at him and replied, "I want to go to the personnel department."

"Yes, ma'am, third floor. Watch your step, please."

The third floor offices were a lot different than the elegant atmosphere on the shopping floors. Each office had a door with frosted glass panels and a painted sign. Personnel was right in front of the elevator. She knocked on the door. A female voice called, "Come in."

A scarred wooden desk faced the door, a large woman behind it, a straight-backed wooden chair in front. The side walls were lined with gray steel filing cabinets and in the corner a wooden coat rack. The woman looked up at Clara. "I'm Mrs. Corrigan. Are you here to apply for a job?"

Clara took a deep breath and returned the woman's frank look. "I'd like to ask some questions, please. I've been working at the McCallum's Silk Hosiery Plant on West Street for twenty-five years and I've been making good money so I need to know if I can earn as much working here. There's no sense in my applying until I know that."

Mrs. Corrigan looked a little surprised but she gestured to the chair and said, "Well, sit down and tell me what you think you can do. We have some jobs that pay a small salary plus commissions on sales and maybe that's what you are interested in doing."

The interview lasted over half an hour with Clara asking as many questions as Mrs. Corrigan and at the end Clara rose from her chair and said, "Thank you. You've given me a lot to think about. I need to talk this over with my family. Is there an application form I need to fill out? I could do that now and you could keep it until I can come back. Is that OK?"

Mrs. Corrigan smiled warmly. She had quickly realized what an asset Clara would be in the men's department. When all those soldiers and sailors came home, they'd most likely be needing some new clothes. They'd have mustering out money in their pockets and some would find their sizes had changed from what they were when they left home. A beautiful woman like Clara could be a big draw, especially to the younger men. "Yes," she said, "please do fill out the application and leave it with me. Then that will be done when you come back." She didn't say "and I hope you will," but the thought was there.

When Clara walked in the back door, Amy was sitting on the floor with her paper dolls and Tillie was making soup, the big kettle on the front burner of the stove bubbling and the steam giving off the rich smell of pea soup with ham.

"That smells delicious, *ma soeur*." Clara kissed her sister's cheek and gave her a little hug.

"*Eh bien*, tell me how your meeting went with the people at McCallum's. What did they ask you? Will you be going to work there?"

Clara reached for the coffee pot and poured a cup for herself, then leaned back against the sink. "I'm pretty sure they'll take me if I want to go there. A woman named Mrs. Corrigan talked to me and said there were commissions in some departments, so I suppose if I work hard, I'll make as much as I make at the hosiery. And even though it's a longer walk to work, I don't have to get there until 8:45 because they don't open until 9. And I don't think I could make it home for the midday dinner. Maybe I could bring a lunch like Angela does when she works the early shift."

"You know we could change and have our big meal at night. I don't think Edward would care, especially with both of you needing to eat sandwiches in the middle of the day. Lots of people have been doing that. I heard about it from some of the women I talk to."

"I still haven't decided but I'm going to have to do that pretty soon. When will Angela be home?"

Tillie turned back to her soup and started stirring it vigorously. "Oh, pretty soon, I think. She was going to get dropped off by her driver at Main Street so she could stop and buy Amy some new underwear. That girl is growing so fast she hasn't got any decent panties to wear," Tillie was a little flustered. She was ashamed of her jealousy, because it was so petty, but the relationship between Clara and Angela had made Tillie feel like an outsider. It had always been Clara and Tillie who were as close as peas in a pod, but with Angela and Clara both working and both missing their men, Tillie felt she had lost something. She didn't have the same kinds of things to talk about as those two.

"I'm going up to change. Then, Amy, *ma petite*, how would you like to go pick a bunch of violets with me?" Clara headed for the back staircase.

"Oh, yes, Aunt Clara. I love violets. I'll put away my paper dolls right now."

When Edward walked into Lisotte's Tobacco store, the men hanging around there greeted him and all wanted to know how Pete was doing in the Army. Some of them were veterans of The Great War, the "war to end all wars." They were cynical and contemptuous of all politicians. But they put great faith in the words of the radio commentators. Everybody listened to the news and almost all had seen the newsreels at the movies.

"*Bon soir*, Edward, what's the news from Pete? Is the big push coming soon?"

Edward asked for his pipe tobacco and learned that he could get only half what he ordered. He turned to the men lounging there. "Pete is still in England and I suppose that's where the attack will have to come from, but I don't know any more than you do. If Pete says anything in a letter that the censor thinks might be dangerous, it gets marked out with big black ink marks."

"But he's OK, right?"

"Yes, he seems to be OK, *merci le bon Dieux*." Edward handed his money to Lisotte and took his bag of tobacco.

"Did you hear that the one of the Poudrier boys was killed on some island nobody ever heard of? They say that his mother fainted right there on her porch when they got the telegram. And you know his wife just had another baby, a boy this time."

The group of men all stood silent, their eyes downcast for a few seconds.

"If I was a betting man, I'd bet they're going to end it soon, cross that English Channel with everything we've got and smash that son-of-a-bitch to smithereens." Ernie St. Lawrence smacked his fist into his other hand, teeth clenched, his lips in a snarl.

"Yeah, well, the weather will be getting better now. It will probably be pretty soon."

# CHAPTER 14

## SUMMER 1943

Ray got the word about the convoy right after the major told him he's been promoted to captain. The promotion was a surprise and a welcome one. More money to be sent home and more clout when it came to getting scarce supplies for his men. He wondered what Clara would say. Probably tell him to keep his head down, so as not to be a target.

The convoy would be going across the desert and over the mountainous terrain of Tunisia, driving all night to avoid attack from German planes. And it would go in as near total blackout as they could manage, on pitted and scarred roads. The troops took the news with resignation when Ray gathered them together to give the orders. Everybody knew how cold it gets in the desert at night, especially in the mountain crossings and a moving vehicle, often open to the elements, just made it worse.

It took hours to get ready to leave, pulling out of battle stations, taking down a command post, dismantling communications, and there was a lot of sweating and swearing. They set out right after dusk, Ray's company near the tail end, over two hundred vehicles ahead of them. It was a tension-filled journey, all of them aware of the risks. Roads in the mountains they would have to cross included some very steep grades, switchbacks and narrow passes. Occasionally they passed other vehicles and that presented a problem, especially in the dark. The moon kept disappearing in a cloudbank and when it did, the challenges were multiplied.

Except for the frequent soft cursing of the drivers, the troops were mostly silent. But the grinding of gears and the clanking of tanks could not be helped. All through the night, Ray stayed awake and alert. At one point, when the moon lit the desert, he saw a camel ridden by a man wrapped in his red and white checkered headgear, loping alongside the convoy. What a contrast, he thought, these behemoths of war and that slim-legged beast.

As daylight approached, the tension rose another notch. Everybody began a lookout for planes. A machine gun was unwrapped and mounted on a Jeep. The line of vehicles slowed to create more distance between them. Cold, tired men shook off their blankets and picked up their weaponry.

A squadron of German planes came out of nowhere and started strafing the convoy. The troops jumped out of whatever vehicle they were in and ran into the desert, diving into any available cover. Ray was out of his Jeep, guiding the men in his company to a rocky outcropping that looked like it would provide some shelter from the hail of bullets when he felt a sharp sting in his thigh. Ignoring it, he continued to assist others who were hit, some seriously wounded. A machine gun made a direct hit on the fuel tank of a low flying German Messerschmitt, the resulting explosion sending bits of shrapnel flying all over the area where the men had taken cover.

When the attack ended, Ray limped around to all of his troops, assessing damage, helping the too few medics pour sulfa powder into wounds, giving shots of morphine where it was needed. It was only when one of the medical corpsmen noticed Ray's pants leg soaked in blood that he let the guy minister to him.

"Will this little bee bite keep me out of commission for long?" Ray asked.

"Probably not," the medic answered, cutting away his pants and marveling how the captain had kept going when his pants were soaked in blood. "You've lost a lot of blood, sir, so that's a factor. It doesn't look like any bone was hit. They'll take out the bullet at the field hospital and dope you up for a day or so. But my guess is it won't take more than a few weeks before you're back with your unit."

"Shit. I wish I could get the major to stop the telegram letting my family know. My mother will be hysterical." Ray sighed and surrendered to the morphine.

Clara answered the phone with shaking hands. All day she'd had a feeling of unease, certain that something bad had happened to Ray. Her head was pounding and she felt nauseous as she answered, "Hello" in a tentative tone not at all her usual speaking voice.

"Could I please speak to Clara Pelletier?" Clara recognized Ray's sister right away.

"What's happened?" She whispered into the phone.

"Oh, Clara, I didn't know it was you. We got a telegram that says Ray was wounded, but not seriously. A report is supposed to come directly from the field hospital. When the Western Union guy came to the door, my mother became hysterical. It took a while to calm her down and repeat over and over that it was not serious or I would have called you earlier."

"I'm so glad you called. All day I've had a feeling something awful had happened. Is his wound enough to bring him home, do you think? Clara's voice was so full of hope that Angela, listening from the kitchen felt her heart lurch.

"It doesn't say. But I doubt it. I heard from one of those radio commentators that they just patch up these guys and then send them back to fight some more. Disgusting, isn't it? Especially when you see some of the soldiers still here in this country doing not much of anything, stationed in some cushy job that doesn't amount to much. Why don't they take a turn fighting?"

"I know. I feel the same way. Nothing we can do about it, though. Thanks for calling me. Let me know if you hear any more. If I get a letter I'll call you. I know how expensive the call is, Anna, and I'll be happy to pay you back."

"No, no, that's not necessary. It's important to stay in touch. Take care of yourself. Bye, now."

As Clara hung up the phone, she realized that she owed Anna a letter, telling about her new job. Since Ray's mother blamed Clara for the fact that Ray had not married some younger woman and spawned a bunch of kids, which would have kept him out of the service, the only contact Clara had with Ray's family was through letters and an occasional phone call from his sister.

Angela came in from the kitchen. "I heard a little of that conversation. I guess Ray was wounded, but not seriously, right?"

"Not bad enough to get him sent home, anyway. *Mon Dieux*, I hate to think of him hurt." Suddenly Clara dropped into a chair and covered her face with her hands, crying softly.

Angela got down on her knees and put her arms around her aunt-by-marriage, her best friend, and hugging her tightly she crooned, "It's OK, it's OK."

Later in the week, the postman delivered a letter from Ray, which Clara tore open immediately when she came home from work, although usually she saved the letters to read and savor in the privacy of her own bedroom after they had finished supper.

*My darling Clara,*

*If she's done as she promised me before I left home, my sister has already called you with the news that I got hit. Please don't worry about it, sweetheart. It was hardly more than a bee sting and quick treatment in the field prevented infection, so there's nothing to worry about.*

*Better news is that I've been promoted to captain, which means more money for my brother-in-law Randy to put into an investment for our future. I keep dreaming about the pretty little house we are going to buy when I get home, in a nice neighborhood, with a lot of flowers and trees. And when I get home from work, you'll be there in the kitchen with dinner cooking on the stove* and the place smelling wonderful. And at Christmas, we'll put up a tree and invite all the family and all the neighbors and we'll sing Christmas carols.

I'm in a field hospital temporarily, but I expect they'll decide soon that I'm healed well enough to go back to my unit. I took a bullet in my right thigh. It really wasn't much of a wound, nothing vital damaged at all. I was sure lucky. It must be the medal you sent me last Christmas that kept me safe.

I need you so very much. You are in my thoughts every day. War is hell, dirty, noisy, evil. I hate the fact that I've become hardened to some really gruesome sights and I hope it doesn't change me in ways that will make you love me less. Oh, Babe, I wish you were here to hold me close tonight.

I love you, now and forever.

Ray

Clara's tears, falling on the page, made the ink run, blurred her vision and made her get up to find a handkerchief. Conscious that her sister Tillie could hear her crying, she walked into the kitchen and reported, "Ray got promoted to captain and his wound is not bad. He's in a field hospital."

"*Merci le bon Dieux.* Is he still where there's fighting? Will he have to go back? I'm so glad Pete is still on that post in England. Maybe the war will be over before he has to get into the fighting."

Amy, sitting in Gran'mere's old rocker with her Betsy-wetsy doll on her lap, looked up and said, "Why are you crying, Aunt Clara? Did you get a boo-boo?"

"No, *cherie,* I got a letter from my friend, Ray. He's fighting in the war, remember?"

"My daddy is fighting in the war, too. Mommy says he'll keep us safe." Amy was solemn, her big brown eyes wide.

"Oh, *chouchou,* I hope you're right."

Clara started her new job in the men's department at McCallum's with a little trepidation and a lot of excitement. She would be doing something very different from the work she had been doing for over twenty years in the hosiery factory. Warned by Mrs. Corrigan in the Personnel office that she would have to get used to standing on her feet all day, Clara had laughed and told her not unkindly that she was used to it already. In fact, it turned out that there was a little stool in back of the counter where it was permitted to take short breaks when the store was not busy and some other salesclerk was available.

At first, Clara was a bit wary of Mr. Barron, the buyer and head clerk. He seemed to be impatient, fussy, annoyed and cranky with his small staff. Always dressed in impeccable taste, his ties matched to his neat pocket squares, shoes polished to a high shine and hair brushed just so, he provided customers with an excellent example of how a man could look elegant. Women who came in to shop for their husbands tended to simper when they approached him.

Clara was a quick study, learning the stock easily, smiling often, never complaining about rude customers or sore feet. She voluntarily cleaned the glass countertops when they got smudged with fingerprints, re-folded the white tennis sweaters on the sale table when customers left them in a jumbled heap, and generally made herself useful. Mr. Barron had been quite negative when he was told his new clerk was a woman, but after a few weeks, he changed his mind, finding that Mrs. Pelletier was an asset to the Men's Department it was his privilege to manage. And in a month, he was singing her praises to anyone who would listen when the department heads had their weekly meetings.

On her part, Clara learned that she loved coming to work every day. The sight of the beautiful chandeliers, the polished mahogany cases, the neatly stacked linen handkerchiefs and rows of gorgeous silk ties was a treat. The air smelled of lemon furniture polish and lingering aftershave. She enjoyed the touch of fine cloth and the sound of the brass cylinders whizzing along the cables that carried the money up to the accounting office. All of it appealed to her and made her wonder why she had spent so many years working in the Hosiery when she could have been doing something else.

It took only a few weeks before she met some of the other women working in the store and made new friends. One special friend was Ruth Goldberg, who worked in Ladies Lingerie and whose husband was in the Navy on a destroyer in the Pacific. Ruth was a tiny woman in her twenties with very black, very curly hair, cut in a short bob. She had been a student at Hunter College in New York City when she met her husband-to-be, who was then a student at Columbia University. Since he was a gentile and she was a Jew, neither his father nor her mother was thrilled when they announced their intention to marry.

Her husband's father was a Professor of Ancient History at Smith College, a widower and a man who thought he was enlightened, liberal and worldly. Still, when his son announced his intention to marry Ruth Goldberg, he was unexpectedly distressed and reminded his son that mixed marriages placed a heavy burden on both parties. "Better to marry someone who has the same background, I think, and a lot easier on children, too." he said.

His son countered with, "But you're the one who taught me to be tolerant, to respect all cultures, to broaden my understanding of the world."

Ruth's mother, also widowed, who worked as a salesclerk at Bergdorf Goodman on Fifth Avenue, warned Ruth that her life would be hard because both the Jewish and the gentile communities would judge her harshly wherever they might live. She urged Ruth to keep her family name rather than take her new husband's so she could retain her own identity. She reminded Ruth that education was power and encouraged her to finish her degree at Hunter.

They were married at a justice of the peace in Duchess County in the State of New York in 1940 right after Ruth finished her Bachelor of Arts degree with a major in art history. Bob had a job at an up and coming company called International Business Machines and he could only get a few days off, so they drove up into the Adirondacks for a long weekend and called it their honeymoon. He had no problem with Ruth keeping her family name. He admired her independence.

Ruth looked for a job in every museum and gallery in New York City, but, unable to find one after a month of looking, took her mother's advice and went to work at Saks. The young couple lived in a tiny apartment in the area known as Greenwich Village and quickly found a community that was compatible and welcoming. Friends gathered frequently to discuss politics and the state of the world with passion and considerable knowledge. Many of their neighbors were young Europeans who had fled their countries; some people were committed to Socialism or Communism. All believed that the United States would be brought into the war soon, although none of them anticipated the Pearl Harbor attack.

 It was no surprise to Ruth when Bob told her he intended to enlist in the Navy as they sat listening to the radio reports of the destruction in Honolulu on December 7. His engineering degree being a major asset, he was sent to Officers' Candidate School immediately.  Ruth could no longer afford to live in the Village, nor could she move back in with her mother, who had taken in two refugees, natives of Austria, distant family connections, who had barely escaped with their lives.

It was Bob's father, Professor Rhoades, who suggested Ruth move to Northampton, claiming she would be safer than in New York City which would be overrun with refugees and that it would be a likely target for an enemy attack. He cited the cultural advantages of a college town and the opportunity to audit classes at the college.  What he never said, but Ruth was astute enough to recognize, was that he was lonely and worried about his only child so far away and so at risk.  So here she was for the duration, happy to have found work she liked and a friend in Clara.

"Come with me to John M. Greene Hall tonight. It's a chamber music concert by the Juilliard String Quartet. You'll like it." Ruth urged Clara.

Clara laughed, "I don't even know what chamber music sounds like. I've never been to hear any of that kind of music. You know I never went to college."

"That doesn't make any difference. Everybody has a first time. How can you find out if you like something if you've never tried it?"

"I thought the college was closed for the summer."

"No, the WAVES are here and there are some graduate students in botany that come in the summer to take courses because Smith has such a great plant collection, not to mention the wonderful botany faculty."

"Will your father-in-law be there, too?"

"Oh, yes. He wouldn't ever miss a concert like this. And I know he wants to meet you, so don't worry about that."

"Do we have to get tickets?"

"No, no. And it's free, too. Meet me there at 7:30. And wear something cool, because it gets hot in there, even when the place isn't full."

"Well, OK, I'll come, Ruth, but remember I'm not an educated person. I might not understand it."

Ruth squeezed Clara's arm. "I'm so glad you said yes. And you don't, maybe even shouldn't, try to understand music. You should just feel it with your heart."

The evening was a huge success. Clara was overwhelmed by the beauty of the music. Professor Rhoades was a surprise, handsome, elderly, with a mass of white hair, white beard and stooped posture, he bounced on the balls of his feet when he got excited. That night began Clara's love affair with classical music.

Amy had a summer cold, so Angela decided to stay home from church and tend her cranky, feverish younger daughter. It turned out to be a good thing she did or she might have committed murder right there on the steps of the church.

Tillie and Edward, Clara and Marie suffered in the heat through a long sermon, fanning themselves with their gloves and wiggling surreptitiously to unstick their dresses from thighs and back. When the priest announced the wounding of Private First Class Oscar Billieux, Junior, they were all shocked, having heard nothing about that previously. Since Junior was Tillie and Clara's nephew, they were distressed to learn of his wounding and annoyed that their sister-in-law had not contacted them to let them know.

It was common knowledge that the family of the late Rose Billieux had become estranged when Charlie accidentally killed his brother, Oscar, at their mother's gravesite with a blow to his chest, the incident a culmination of years of bitterness between the two brothers. Oscar's widow claimed it was murder and she was enraged at Tillie and Clara and another brother, Maurice, for supporting Charlie. And then she was apoplectic when she learned that Rose Billieux had written her will to guarantee that Tillie, Charlie and Clara would have a home for the rest of their lives, denying Flora the pleasure of throwing them out of the family home on West Street. As if that wasn't insult enough, they also were bequeathed the income from the tenant houses on their land that Charlie had managed and cared for ever since they were built.

Some members of the congregation lingered on the portico and the steps to see what might happen when the two sides met.

As they were leaving the church, Tillie reached out to her brother's widow and patted her arm, attempting to comfort her. Flora slapped Tillie's hand away and screamed at her. "Don't you touch me. I don't want anything to do with you. You cheated me of what should have been mine and I'll never forgive you. I heard that murderer Charlie is out of jail already and gone, too. He didn't dare to show his face around here, did he?"

"What does that have to do with your son's wounding? We just wanted to say we are sorry about Junior."

"I don't need your sympathy. I don't need anything from you now. I hope God punishes you for what you did to me. I hope your son dies over there. It would serve you right. Yes, that would be a good punishment. Then you'll see. You'll see what pain is like when you lose someone you love." Flora was screeching now and crying and hitting Tillie's arm with her fists.

Edward, who had been speaking with the priest, hurried over and intervened, holding tight to Flora's hands to stop her attack and pushing Tillie behind him. The priest led Flora away while Edward, his arm firmly around Tillie's waist, urged her down the walk toward the car. Marie was horrified, still standing in the portico, watching the priest talking to her Aunt Flora and the congregation buzzing about what they had just witnessed.

"Come on, *chouchou*, let's go to the car." Clara tugged on Marie's arm.

"Did you hear what she said, Aunt Clara? She's talking about my Daddy. How could she wish anybody dead? That's a sin."

"I'm so glad your mother wasn't here. She would have torn that woman's hair out by the roots. But I would have been glad to see it."

Pete was having a good day in spite of the heat and the persistent smell of gasoline in the big shed where he was working on two M4 tanks that needed some repairs.

He turned to his helper, an older man (as was he in this young man's army). They both were enlistees rather than draftees and both were excellent mechanics. The challenge of working on these behemoths of war was a satisfying occupation. Pete, however, had a special reason for being so cheerful and upbeat today.

"Did you hear what the Major said to me, Joe?"

"No, I was trying to stay far away just in case it was something you wouldn't want anyone to know." Joe was a sensitive guy, aware that it was unusual for a major to come into the shed, much less to single out a corporal for a talk.

"I don't know who told him I speak French, because I didn't tell them that when I enlisted. Hell, I don't even know if those people in France speak the same French as Canucks. But anyway, he said he wanted me to make sure I talked to local farmers in France when we invaded that country and report back to him on anything I could learn."

Joe was puzzled. "I thought they had special intelligence guys that do that."

"Yeah, I said that to him myself. But he said some of those reports came too late to be useful and sometimes these college boys don't get as much cooperation from the farmers as I might be able to get. And anyway, he wants me to come directly to him to tell him what I know."

"How can you be doing that when it's our job to keep these tanks rolling?"

"Oh, I don't think he's talking about making a big deal out of it, just a kind of casual thing. And you know what else he said? He said I could probably look to being made Sergeant after we get over there. How about that?"

Joe smiled. "I'm glad it's you and not me. Now tell me how the hell these young guys who think they're such hotshots can strip the gears on these machines? Don't they teach them anything in Tank School?"

Captain Ray Carpenter was hot and sticky and annoyed. He was sitting on a cot in a field hospital where he'd been recovering from a thigh wound that he felt sure was healed sufficiently to go back to his unit when Major Breen came in through the tent flap and he jumped to his feet and saluted smartly.

"Can that crap, Ray. I know you want to demonstrate how fit you are. You don't fool me, buddy."

Ray continued to stand at attention but he spoiled the military discipline act with a huge grin. "Glad to see you, sir. Does this mean you've got my orders to return to my unit?"

"Sit down, Ray. I want to talk." The major drew up a footstool and Ray sat back on his cot.

"You've probably heard the scuttlebutt that we're about to invade Sicily, right?" Ray nodded in answer. "Well, it's true. Your old unit isn't going but you are. You've demonstrated the kind of leadership qualities that the Army is always looking for and you're being transferred to lead a different unit into Sicily."

Ray was stunned. He'd been looking forward to getting back to the guys he knew, to finding out what had become of those who had been wounded during the same attack where he caught it. "Why, sir? Are we done here?"

The Regular Army frowned on junior officers questioning orders, but this seemed to be a special circumstance. He didn't see any written orders in the Major's hand and besides, he and Harold Breen had met during the one year when Ray had been a student at Harvard, although Breen was two years ahead of him. They had become friendlier than was usual during the hard fought months in Africa, during which Ray distinguished himself leading a unit that took risks and fought well.

"The fact is that you're needed to do your job somewhere else, leading a rifle platoon taking on the Italians and the Germans there. We expect a lot of German bunkers full of machine guns and it will take good riflemen to take them down with a minimum loss of our guys. I know you can provide the kind of leadership it will take. I've got in mind a unit that lost their Captain in the same attack where you got hit, so they'll take to you right away."

Major Breen reached under his shirt and handed written orders to Ray. "I wanted to tell you a little about why you got the job before I handed this to you." They both stood.

"Thanks, I appreciate that." Ray reached out his left hand for the orders and his right to clasp the hand that the Major put out there for him to take.

"Good luck, guy. Keep your head down and your powder dry."

# CHAPTER 15

## FALL 1943

Marie was excited about going to Esther's birthday party. Instead of having it after school as most people did, this was to be a supper and then afterwards they were going on a scavenger hunt. Marie had never been on a scavenger hunt, although of course she knew what it was. There would be eight girls at the party, including Marie and her special friend, Betsy.

All the girls were around thirteen, students in junior high school and Girl Scouts together and all were just becoming aware of their changing bodies, the awkward feeling of budding breasts poking out. Boys began to look different to them and at them and friends became competition. It was a confusing, aggravating, challenging, heady time for them all.

Marie was in a tizzy over what to wear, vacillating from one skirt to another, throwing sweaters on the bed. Amy sat on the floor, watching her big sister and making unwanted observations. "That skirt is wrinkled," or "Ugh, I don't like that color."

"Oh, shut up, Amy, will you please." Marie ordered, irritated that her sister was there at all. She would have ordered her to get out of the room, but it was Amy's room too and Marie knew that if Amy appealed to their Mom, she'd be reminded of that fact.

Finally she chose a grey flannel skirt and a navy blue sweater over a white dickey with navy blue knee socks and penny loafers. Mom brushed her hair until it gleamed and caught the long fall of her waves with a silver barrette to keep it off of her face and out of her eyes. Marie would have preferred to let that wave fall over her eye like Veronica Lake's on the Modern Screen Magazine cover, but said nothing to her mother, who thought movie magazines a waste of time and money. Marie had to read them at Betsy's house. Betsy's mother loved them and always had several lying around their living room.

*Pepere* drove Marie and Betsy, too, over to Esther's house. It wasn't far, but it had started to get dark early and her Mom and her *Memere* had both protested when she said she would walk. Marie thought that was ridiculous, but she said nothing. No need to start an argument over something that wasn't important.

They arrived at the same time as two other guests and found that the rest were already there. Supper was macaroni and cheese, green beans and big sliced tomatoes from Esther's mom's garden. Mrs. Freedman told them the cake would be served after the scavenger hunt. She divided the girls into two teams and handed them a neatly typed list of the items they were to bring back and gave them an hour to find it all, then she handed each team a canvas knitting bag to carry the stuff. "But there's one thing on the list that won't fit in the bag. Let's see who can bring it back," she laughed.

Each team huddled at one end of the living room to read the list. A leaf from a gingko tree, an empty Coke bottle, yesterday's newspaper, a rusty nail, a real live serviceman in uniform. There was a squeal of surprise from both ends of the room as the teams read the last item. What an exciting idea! Which team would find somebody willing to come back with them for birthday cake? All eight girls were flushed and chattering as they got ready to go out seeking the items on the list.

Only Esther owned a watch, so Mrs. Freedman loaned her own watch to the other team.

"One hour, girls. Everybody to be back here by seven o'clock sharp," Mrs. Freedman admonished them, raising her voice to be heard over the din.

Marie was in the team with Esther; Betsy went with the other group, proud to be wearing the borrowed watch. Marie mused as to how strange it was to be going out into the gathering dusk now when her Mom had fussed so about her walking over to Esther's an hour ago.

"Let's get the easy stuff right away. Who knows where there's a ginkgo tree?" Esther was jiggling up and down in her enthusiasm for the task.

"I do. It's right inside the gates of the college. It has a little metal sign stuck into the grass." Marie answered and they all raced off to find it.

One of the other girls had some money in her pocket and said they could buy a Coke at the Liggett's drug store on Main Street and pass it around so it would get empty quickly. Another suggested they go down to Lizotte's and see if he had any newspapers left over from yesterday. He didn't but they were close to the office of the Daily Hampshire Gazette, so they started to rush down there when Marie spotted a sailor in his uniform coming across Main Street from Pleasant Street.

Esther announced she was going down to the Gazette to see about getting a paper and she took Barbara Weinberg with her. "You talk to the sailor, Marie, and we'll meet you right here."

Marie walked right up to the sailor as soon as he had crossed the street. "Excuse me, Mister, but would you do us a favor, please?"

The young man was dressed in the standard uniform of the enlisted Navy man consisting of navy blue wool bell bottom trousers, blouse with square collar hanging in the back, black tie, black shoes and white canvas sailor hat, an outfit very different than any other clothing worn by men. He had wavy black hair under his sailor hat and very long black eyelashes. He looked truly exotic to the girls.

His smile was a mile wide. "What can I do for you, ladies?"

Almost breathless, Marie explained about the party and the scavenger hunt, adding, "It wouldn't take very long. Esther lives up the hill near the college and we'll have cake and punch."

"Sure. That would be fun." He surprised them with his quick answer.

When Esther and Barbara joined them carrying a newspaper, Marie said, "Here comes the birthday girl now. Oh, I forgot to ask you, what's your name? I'm Marie LaPointe, this is Isabel Cohen, the birthday girl is Esther Freedman and with her is Barbara Weinberg."

"My name is Tom Finkelstein. Mazeltov, Esther." He bent over and quickly pecked her cheek.

Esther's face turned bright crimson and she mumbled, "Thank you." Then her eyes widened, her head snapped up and she said, "Are you a Jew?"

"Yup, I sure am. I come from New Rochelle and I enlisted in the Navy as soon as I could after Pearl Harbor. I've been training at New London, Connecticut. I'm a submariner."

Marie broke in and declared they needed to get going if they were to be back at Esther's house before seven o'clock. Hurrying up Main Street and up the hill to West Street, they chattered excitedly, asking questions so fast, Tom could not answer them all.

It turned out he had come to Northampton to visit his sister who was in the WAVES. She had desk duty tonight so he was on his own, looking for a place to get a bite to eat. He and his sister both joined the Navy because their grandfather was an admiral working in Washington. His sister was older and finished with college, so she went directly to Officers' Candidate School at Smith College. He was a senior in high school when war was declared and he decided to enlist as soon as he graduated, even though his parents, especially his father, objected strenuously.

When they got back to Esther's house, the other team had not yet arrived. Marie was eager to hear if another serviceman was going to join them. Mrs. Freedman was very pleased with the sailor they brought home and Mr. Freedman came up from his basement workroom to greet the young man.

"Omigosh, we forgot to get the rusty nail," Barbara Weinberg burst out, "Our team will lose if they got everything."

259

Everybody laughed. Barbara was so competitive. The thrill of the found sailor eclipsed the winning of the game for the rest of the girls. And when Team Two arrived with no serviceman and no empty coke bottle either, nobody talked about winning and losing because they got so caught up in talking to Tom.

When Mrs. Freedman learned that Tom had not had his supper yet, she quickly fixed him a plate so he could "have some real food in him before eating cake." Between bites he talked about submarines and the training he received and how important it was to use submarines in warfare. He knew all about the U-boat attacks that had caused such devastation to the Allies already and he answered questions from the girls and Mr. Freedman, too, on how efficiently the inside of a submarine was set up to accommodate a crew living underwater.

He also talked about relatives who had escaped from Germany and who told frightening stories of the treatment of Jews by the Nazis. He voice turned very sober as he recounted some dreadful experiences his relatives had. Some of the girls had tears rolling down their cheeks. When he noticed, he smiled and suggested that they should tell him something about themselves.

Marie was surprised when *Pepere* rang the doorbell. The time had gone so fast! As the party broke up, each of the girls promised to write to Tom and he promised to write back. "But sometimes, I'll have to write just one letter because I'll be so busy and you'll just have to pass it around to all of you. Will that be OK?"

Marie and Betsy told *Pepere* all about the best birthday party they ever went to and Marie proudly recounted her role in approaching Tom to ask a favor. *Pepere* frowned a little at that part of the story and admonished them that not all sailors you see on the street are as nice as Tom seemed to be. He warned them that they could get hurt. Privately, he questioned Mrs. Freedman's judgment at sending the girls out into the night without an adult escort, but since all had ended well, he decided not to make an issue of it, at least not now.

When Clara read her letter from Ray, she was both pleased and scared. Pleased that he agreed she would continue to work after they were married and scared when she figured out, despite the censor's black marks, that Ray was again in mortal danger.

*My darling Clara,*

*I got four of your letters today, all at once. I don't know why some of them got held up because I've been in this damned field hospital for three weeks. The really good news in that I leave in four days for a new assignment, going (here the censor's black line covered several words.) One of these days I expect to run into Pete. I got a letter from him last week and was pleased to hear of his promotion. I guess none of us ever expected that he could become such an expert as a mechanic. Of course I know he learned a lot from your brother Charlie, but those big tanks are (more black marks from the censor.)*

*I'm getting a new group of guys to work with. I sure hope somebody in the unit can speak (another black line). I think this is the beginning of the end. By the time I meet up with Pete, it'll be almost over. Not that there won't be a lot to do before that happens, but at least the end will be in sight. When I was fighting in (black line) I wondered if I would ever say that. I got pretty discouraged there for a while. One thing you have to say for our troops, they all see this as a job that has to be done and they're determined to do it. Maybe in the beginning we had a lot to learn, but boy oh boy, did we learn fast.*

*I'm so glad you like your new job. It does seem like a better place for you to be. I always knew you'd be great at salesmanship. And, to answer your question, of course you should keep on working after we get married if that is what you want to do. Maybe you could cut back to part time, though. We'll see. I was thinking we could find a house somewhere between Hartford and Northampton if you want to stay at that department store. With two of us working, we might even be able to afford two cars. Or you could get a job in one of the department stores in Hartford or Springfield maybe. I'm not sure if I'll go back to Fix-it Tools, although I know they'll take me back if I want to do that.*

*Anyway, these are things we'll have to work out when I get home. Not a bad idea to be thinking about them now, though. I think about how it's going to be when this is all over every chance I get, and I dream about it, too. You know I dream about you every night. Sometimes I wake up and I swear I can smell your hair. You'd know how funny that is if you could smell what it's really like around here. Phew. I'm laughing.*

*Oh, God, Babe, I love you so much.*

*Ray*

Clara read the letter for the fifth time and, noting that it had been written in July. She decided she had pretty much figured out that Ray had already left Africa and gone to Sicily, since she'd read about the invasion there and seen the storming of the beaches in a newsreel at the movies and, of course, Pete was almost certainly going into Europe with the big push to defeat the Germans. She shivered, thinking about how fierce that fighting would be, about how fierce it had been in the Great War when her husband Gus was killed. The prospect of what was to happen next scared her. It scared her a lot.

It snowed in the morning of Thanksgiving Day, but not enough to keep the occupants of 144 West Street from going to church nor for Maurice and Simone from driving up from Connecticut to share the Thanksgiving Feast. This year they were not to be accompanied by their son, Bobby, who was going to his girlfriend's house for the celebration.

Maurice and Simone (Bobby, as well) were grateful that Bobby had failed the draft board's physical exam because of his poor eyesight. For most of his life Bobby had bitterly resented his hated eyeglasses and been mortified at the casually flung taunt of "four-eyes." Funny how he now embraced the designation "4F," although he would discover there were those who disdained anyone who didn't measure up to the standards required to serve in the Army.

Simone was especially proud that her son would be the first and only one of her children to go to college. With the extra money Maurice was earning in a defense plant they could afford the luxury of foregoing Bobby's potential as a wage earner and contributor to household expenses. Bobby had been encouraged by his teachers to finish high school and then apply for admittance to Springfield College with the hope of becoming a physical education teacher. He had just started on this adventure in September past and had taken to it with determination and even pleasure. Since there were few male students in the freshman class, he had his pick of pretty women. What bliss. His confidence rose with the attention and his academic performance rose with it.

Edward and Maurice sat in the front parlor with Amy on Edward's lap and talked of the war, the news from Pete, the story of the church steps confrontation with Oscar's widow, Flora. They were both avid readers of newspapers and liked to listen to the radio commentators in the evening. Maurice had a special perspective because of his defense plant work, building airplane engines. It never occurred to either of them to ask Angela to join their discussions, even though she, too, must have heard interesting bits of information in her defense work.

"I keep expecting any day to hear about the big invasion of Europe. I thought it would be last summer, when the weather would be better for it." Edward said, thoughtfully.

"Oh, I'm sure it's coming, but not now. Maybe as soon as the spring. I hear the English Channel is very cold water. Remember when that woman swam across? All they talked about was how cold it was. I can tell you, though, that a big push is coming. They're really cracking the whip at the plant. We're turning out engine parts faster than ever, going around the clock. I was lucky to get today off."

"*Oui, oui.* Angela traded with some other woman so she could have the morning off, but she's going to work at 4 o'clock today. Usually she works from 7 to 4."

In the kitchen, Tillie was muttering her frustration with the need to adjust to all the shortages and rationing restrictions in the preparation for the traditional Thanksgiving dinner. "Good thing we've been saving ration coupons or we'd never have been able to make three pies."

"You know, *ma soeur*, we really don't need three pies. Without Pete and Ray and Charlie, we could have made do with one." Clara observed softly.

"Don't remind me of Charlie. He could have been here. Why did he leave Northampton? I don't understand that. Why? Why? Why? And of course we need three pies. We have to have mincemeat, pumpkin and lemon meringue. It wouldn't be right to cut out one of them. We've always had all three so everybody gets their favorite." Tillie was annoyed that anyone would question these verities.

"Wait a minute. We didn't always have lemon meringue. When we were kids *Maman* never made that. She always made apple for the third pie. It was only when you married Edward and he loved your lemon meringue that you started making such a fuss that we changed. You may have forgotten that, but I remember." Clara was laughing and didn't notice Tillie's scowl, but Angela did.

"Come on. What difference does it make? We're here together to enjoy each others' company and thank God for what we have, especially to thank Him that our men are still alive, even though they're in harm's way." Angela's admonition gave them all pause, including Simone, who had been silent during this exchange between her sisters-in-law.

"Has Marie set the table yet?" Clara asked, "Maybe I should go help her. My biscuits are all ready to go in the oven." She walked into the dining room to see that all was ready and Marie had her nose in a book over in the little alcove. Silver gleamed, crystal sparkled, the lace tablecloth and embroidered napkins were in place and the proud silver peacocks decorated the center of the table.

When they all came to the table, they responded with a vigorous "Amen" to Edward's lengthy prayer of thanks for the food and his entreaty to the Almighty for the safe and speedy return of Pete and Ray and all the men serving their country around the world. Conversation was much more subdued than usual. Each of them was caught up in private thoughts of loved ones not present at the feast. Marie's thoughts were not just for her Dad and Aunt Clara's friend Ray but also now included Tom Finkelstein.

The turkey was delicious even though it had been rubbed with margarine instead of butter; the stuffing was almost as tasty as ever with less sausage and more sliced onion and smashed potatoes. If anyone noticed the necessary substitutions, they didn't mention it. The pies were made with no less sugar because Tillie had carefully saved enough for the occasion (and also given up putting sugar in her coffee or on her cereal in the morning).

At 3:15, Angela excused herself from the table to go get changed for work. They were finished eating anyway, Marie and Amy had already been excused, and Edward used the moment to commend his daughter-in-law for her contribution to the war effort. Tillie, Clara and Simone cleaned up the dishes, shooing Marie away when she offered to help. It had been a fairly somber Thanksgiving, all of them aware that it was two years since Pearl Harbor and the war was going on a lot longer than anybody expected.

# CHAPTER 16

## CHRISTMAS 1943

Preparations for Christmas didn't begin until Amy's birthday had been celebrated on the Saturday after Thanksgiving with paper hats made by Marie for all to wear at the dinner table. It was a mystery to Angela and Clara how Tillie had acquired enough sugar for a birthday cake, although they did note the peach jam from the supplies on the shelves in the basement was used to separate the layers in place of frosting. Thank God they had put up so many jars of jam the year before the war. Tillie remembered how the peach crop was so big that year; there were those who suggested they should be getting rid of some rather than making so many batches of jam. Vindicated now, she kept her thoughts to herself and privately congratulated her farsightedness.

Amy got paper dolls and coloring books and hair ribbons, as well as a hand knit sweater from her *Memere* and a red tricycle which *Pepere* had bought from a co-worker at the library and restored to glory with red paint and a steel wool pad he found in Charlie's workshop. From Mommy and Daddy she got a blue velvet dress with a lace collar, the most beautiful dress she had ever owned.

This was the year Angela had decided she must tell Amy that Santa was not a real person and that the story was a part of the Christmas tradition. She was surprised when Amy solemnly nodded her head and said, "I know, Mommy. Isn't it sad that it's not true? Irene Flanagan told me already."

Christmas gifts were bought and wrapped in secret and stashed all over the house as they had always been. Edward bought a tree from the Boy Scout lot up on Hospital Hill. He saw his brother-in-law Alphonse there and they greeted one another with some measure of reserve, having been estranged since the accidental death of Oscar after Charlie hit him with a shovel and Alphonse's wife chose to side with Oscar's widow in believing that Charlie had deliberately murdered his brother. Alphonse had always been a little slow-witted and was what Edward always thought of as hen-pecked.

The tree trimmings were brought down from the attic; the tree was decorated; carols were sung and Tillie made penuche, but it was not the same. This was the second Christmas without Pete and Ray and they were feeling it keenly. When Clara went to confession preparatory to taking communion on Christmas day, she reflected ruefully that the war had forced her to abstain from the sin of fornication where admonitions from the priest for the danger to her soul had not. She shared the irony with Angela, but didn't mention it to Tillie.

It was a very gray day in the south of England and Pete's mood matched it. He had received his Christmas packages last week and intended to save them for opening on Christmas Eve, but early in the day when his shoulder was aching from muscle strain and the damp weather, he remembered that he had asked Angela to send him some liniment and he opened the package to look for it. It was there with a little note wrapped around the box that read, "I wish I was there to rub this into your sore shoulder. I love you." Pete had a fierce struggle to contain his tears.

Tomorrow would be his second Christmas away from home. Christ Almighty, when would this war be over? All anyone talked about was the coming invasion. Everybody at the post was tense, preparing for it, wanting it to happen soon, yet scared of it at the same time. He'd heard about a fake air base that was going to be built to fool the Nazis into thinking they were coming in from one place when really they were going ashore at another.

Pete knew he'd be in one of the forward waves, but probably not the first, since he'd go in with the tanks and it would be mostly infantry that would be sent in to take down the Nazis in the gun bunkers. He was as scared as the next guy, but he wanted to go and get it over with so he could go home. Very few of the guys he knew had any doubts about eventual victory. The Allies were the good guys and the Nazis were evil, period. God would be on their side.

Funny how easy it was to believe that, even though Pete was a pretty much indifferent Catholic. He never went to confession unless his mother prodded him unmercifully. He hardly ever went to Sunday Mass except for Easter and Christmas. And even then, he got bent out of shape by some of the sanctimonious drivel in the sermons.

"Hey, Pete, are you going to midnight Mass?" Stanley was wrapped in layers of clothes and rubbing his arms against the damp cold of December in southern England.

"Yeah, sure, why not? It'll be something to do." Pete shrugged.

"Well, then, let's go. If you want a seat you gotta get there early. George's gone already. He says he's not standing against the wall for Mass any more. His ass is going to be in a chair surrounded by other guys to keep him warm."

Pete laughed, grabbed his heavy jacket and they took off for the big hangar where midnight Mass would not begin for an hour. It was no surprise that the place was half full already. There was less talk about sex than usual, almost nobody was telling dirty jokes and the din of voices was more subdued. Never mind that they were in a bare hangar filled with folding chairs and a utilitarian portable altar. They ignored the smell of airplane fuel and grease and male bodies packed tightly together. For the moment, they were all in church.

Pete automatically followed the rituals of the Mass and joined in with the singing of Christmas carols, but his mind was full of thoughts of Angela and his girls. He prayed for them and also for the little boy they had lost and for his mother and father, too. And then he asked God to give him courage for what he knew was to come and to let him live to return to his family. Later, he was surprised to realize his bleak mood had lifted and he was looking forward to the Christmas dinner they had been promised.

In the logging camp west of Old Town in Maine, Charlie Billieux shaved carefully before attaching the white beard to his face, He pulled the suspenders up that would hold his padding in place and adjusted the white wig. When he was all ready with jacket, black belt and red hat in place, he came out of the bathroom, braced to endure the teasing from the men who shared his bunkhouse.

"*Eh, bien*, Charlie. Going to make a fool of yourself again this Christmas?"

"*Qu'est-ce qui ce passé?*"

"Where did you get that outfit, Charlie?"

He paid them no attention, going out the door to his battered old truck. He was headed into Old Town to the convent there where the nuns would gather up all the orphan children in their care and herd them into a neat line, so each one could sit on his lap for a minute. Charlie carried a burlap sack full of dolls and cars and animals he had carved from soft pine wood, working at it all year, whenever he had a chance. And each child also got a little paper sack full of penny candy which Charlie bought with his own money. Licorice laces and bubble gum and sugar babies, root beer barrels and lemon drops and peanut melts. Charlie picked it out carefully at the little store in Old Town that reminded him of the store his brother Alphonse had on Hospital Hill.

The nuns gathered around him when he arrived at the convent. They introduced any new arrivals to the order he had not yet had a chance to meet and they told him of a few children who had left, usually to go out into the world on their own, rarely adopted. He greeted each of the shyly smiling novitiates with a special tenderness, recalling to mind his sweet Annamarie, the memory of her beautiful smile ever with him.

As always, they invited him to stay for midnight Mass and, as always, he declined. Charlie continued to believe his sin was so great, it would be sacrilegious for him to attend Mass.

When he had finished distributing the gifts to the children, listened to their voices sing for him, thanked the nuns for the bread and cookies they made for him, he got in his truck and headed back to the logging camp.

Every year he thought about joining some of the men he knew at a local bar where they would be drinking their sorrows away and every year he reminded himself that he didn't deserve the pleasure.

In the house on West Street, the family was getting ready to sit down around the table for a simple supper on this Christmas Eve. Angela made the waffles, Tillie fried apple rings. Clara was on the phone talking to

Maurice who had decided the weather was too bad for Simone and himself to drive up from Connecticut for Christmas dinner. "We'll hope it's nice so we can be there for New Year's Day," he said.

"How's Bobby doing?" Clara asked, eager to hear whether her nephew was doing well in college, the first one in their extended family to go.

"*Bien, bien, merci le bon Dieu.* He's a very good student. He knows how lucky he is that his eyesight made him 4F and that he is having this chance to get an education. You know, some people make fun of him because he didn't get into the Army, but he says he expected that. He's gotten used to it when they call him names. He'll be fine."

"*Au revoir*, Maurice. *Je t'aime. Joyeux Noel* from all of us here to you and all your family." Clara hung up. Long distance phone calls were necessarily short because of the great expense, even from Massachusetts to Connecticut.

Sitting around the table, drinking precious coffee after their meal, Angela and Clara announced that they wanted to go to midnight Mass again this year. Tillie and Edward could take the girls to Mass tomorrow.

Angela was a little surprised when Tillie suggested they go through the charade of waking the girls up in the night with bells ringing and cries of "Santa was here. Come see what he brought you."

"Why do you want to do that, Mama Tillie? Both Marie and Amy understand about Santa."

"Maybe because it's a tradition and I don't want to change it. I don't know. Maybe because I feel sad that they are growing up so fast and I want to pretend they're babies a little longer. What's wrong with that?"

Angela shrugged. "OK, I'll tell them we're going to do that. I'm sure they'll see it as fun." She went off to the front parlor where Marie and Amy were playing checkers on a board set up on top of a hassock, the two of them sprawled on the floor.

To Angela's relief, both of her daughters saw the waking up to Santa ritual as just what they expected to happen. "We don't want to wait until morning to open our presents, do we, Amy?" Marie was a little indignant. So that settled that and without argument, they both went up to bed at 7:30.

Edward put on the red Santa hat and the fake beard, but not the suit stuffed with pillows that had been the costume for years worn by Charlie for the task he had loved best. Tillie rang the bell and Angela ran up the stairs to wake her girls. But underneath the laughter and the gifts, they all were acutely aware of the absence of Charlie as well as Ray and Pete so far from home.

Ray was weary, filthy, hungry and disheartened. He and his unit had arrived after the first wave hit the beaches in Sicily. From everything he heard, it was brutal. The concrete bunkers called pillboxes were filled with Italian and German ordinance men equipped with long range guns and plenty of ammunition trained on the invaders. Subduing the enemy in those concrete hidey holes had taken a hell of a lot of courage and skill.

Now the fighting was moving up the boot of Italy, one little village at a time, villages full of frightened old ladies and children, unbelievable carnage, hunger and despair visible everywhere. His men were very tired. Seldom did they get more than an hour or so of sleep. When they all needed to keep their wits about them in order to avoid the constant threat of sniper fire, being tired was a very big threat.

Ray's voice was not much louder than a whisper as he spoke to the man at his side. "Move forward with caution. No heroics, please. We're in no hurry. We'll clean the bad guys out of here very slowly. Pass the word."

They were a close knit unit, every man had a buddy that had been killed or wounded. They knew to watch out for each other. Ray was a good leader, keeping tabs on all of them. He took it hard when any of his men went down. And he knew he was a changed man, hardened, cynical, always alert for disaster. Would Clara still love him? Had he lost his capacity for joy?

One of the guys came over to him, offering a cigarette and remarked, "Do you realize it's Christmas tomorrow?"

"Yes, but we'll have to postpone the celebration. No lights and tinsel for us. We're too far ahead of the rest of the brigade. C rations again tonight." Ray smiled at the guy and accepted a cigarette.

A few minutes later, they were startled to hear the sound of an organ and a chorus of voices singing familiar

Christmas carols in Italian. They crept along the vacant street ahead, rifles at the ready, heads swiveling, alert to possible sniper traps. The sound came from an ancient church, its roof half gone, windows blown out. They looked in and saw that it was full of people. A young woman played the organ for a chorus of children, directing the singing from her seat. The priest at the altar wore robes of gold cloth as he moved solemnly through the rituals of the mass. The rest of the men in the platoon straggled up, some dropping to their knees in the rubble filled ground outside the church, bowing their heads, making the sign of the cross on their heads and hearts and shoulders. Those who were familiar with the choreography of the Catholic Mass responded to the Latin phrases. Even in the midst of hell on earth, they celebrated the birth of Christ.

# CHAPTER 17

## WINTER 1944

In the beginning of 1944 the heads of the Allied Forces held several conferences in order to make key decisions about a move that had been in the planning for nearly two years. Critical to their hopes for a successful end to the war was secrecy about the time and place of Operation Overlord, the cross-channel invasion of the continent. Rumors about this operation had been surfacing among the armed forces stationed in England for over a year. Pete was disgusted with some of the tales that were passed around, especially those that suggested hundreds of ships carrying thousands of men would go over there all in one day. He felt sure that was an exaggeration.

"Hey, Pete, did you hear we're getting another load of tanks tomorrow?"

"Yeah. I guess the factories back in the U S of A are really cranking this stuff out. Maybe that means the invasion date is getting closer."

"I can hardly wait for it to come. We've got to go over there and finish this soon or I'm going to go crazy."

Men and equipment began to pile up all over the post; bunks were crowded together to accommodate more soldiers into every Quonset hut. Every G.I. there knew something big was happening, but exactly what and exactly when, were still a mystery for most of them.

At the International Silver defense plant in Florence where Angela worked, rumors of a visit from some Army brass had all the workers anxious about what it might mean. Did it mean new management? Were they behind on fulfilling orders?

"Goddammit, we've been working our asses off to meet production goals. I sure as hell hope somebody isn't coming here to chew us out for something." Angela overheard an angry co-worker blustering on her way to the time clock. She had worked ten hours overtime this last week and she was really exhausted. The money was great and she loved looking at the growing numbers in the bank book, but it was tough to stay on her feet for such long hours. Clara had spoken to her about it. "Angela, I can't help but notice the dark patches under your eyes, *cherie*. You are losing a lot of weight. Are you ill? Have you been working too hard? I'm worried about you."

Tillie said nothing to her, of course, but she, too, noticed the changes. Between working too many hours and worrying about Pete's safety, Angela was risking her health and Tillie knew it, but she was afraid to say anything that might be taken as a rebuke by her daughter-in-law. Their relationship was one of cautious courtesy, each of them aware of the need to tread with care.

All the workers in the plant were assembled in the shipping department at noon, large crates having been pushed back to the walls to make room. Angela shuddered as she always did when she entered there, remembering her frightening encounter with Tony Scarlotti. As she maneuvered to the front so she could see, she noticed her brother Sal position himself right behind Tony.

A guy in a uniform, his chest covered in medals, climbed up on a makeshift platform and raised a bullhorn to his face. "Good morning to all of you. I'm General Slade and I'm here first of all to congratulate this plant, its supervisors and all the people working hard around the clock here to make bombs that will win this war." A loud cheering and foot stomping interrupted the speech. "You have consistently met your production goals with a commitment to quality as well as quantity. All of us fighting this war against the evil of the Axis powers are grateful that the people here at home have stepped up to the plate and given their all to provide the men who are out there risking their lives every day with the equipment and the material needed to win. And we will win." Another wave of cheering and clapping interrupted the General. "All over these United States, people like you have heard the call to come to the aid of your country. It makes me very proud to be an American." He raised his arms in the air. "Most of you here today have someone in your family or your neighborhood out there fighting for freedom. You know as well as anybody how important it is that they have what they need and we're going to see that they get it." Again, the crowd cheered and then the General's voice lowered. "Now we are on the verge of bringing this war to a successful end, we need you to push a little harder, give a little more. The need is great. We know you will do your best. Thank you and God bless."

There was a dignified amount of applause, but some grumbling could be heard also. Nobody was fooled by the praise. All knew that the production goals would be raised and they would be pushed to more overtime in order to meet them. Angela, heading back to her machine, thought about the General, in his neatly pressed uniform, probably returning home to his wife in a day or two after giving a similar speech at a few other defense plants. Well, she reminded herself, Pete was always saying there's no such thing as fair; there's only the luck of the draw.

The weather had been very cold in the last week, which probably meant that Paradise Pond was frozen solid. Clara thought it would be fun to teach Amy how to skate. She remembered teaching Marie years ago and how much they had both enjoyed it.

"Amy, *ma petite chouchou*, would you like to learn how to skate on the ice?"

Tillie, overhearing, asked, "Will she fit in Marie's old skates, do you think?"

Amy jumped up from her place on the floor where she was surrounded by paper dolls and announced, "Yes, Marie's skates fit me. I tried them on last week. Oh, I really want to go, Aunt Clara."

"Which skates did you try on, *chouchou*? The ones that fit over your boots with the double blades or the white ones with the one runner?" Clara asked.

"The white ones, just like Sonja Henie, and they fit good."

"OK, we'll try it. Get your snow pants on and wear a heavy sweater under your jacket. It's going to be cold." Clara went to get her own warm things.

Marie came down the back stairs and noticed Amy getting into her outdoor clothes. "Where are you going, Amy?"

"I'm going skating on Paradise Pond with your old skates. Aunt Clara is going to teach me. Do you want to come too?"

Marie gave her little sister a look of exasperation. "Amy, you know nobody can get new skates now. Not until the war is over. They can't waste steel on skate blades, dummy."

"*Memere*, Marie called me a dummy." Amy's voice rose in a cross between indignation and outrage.

"Apologize to your sister. That wasn't nice. If you really want to go skating, borrow a pair from somebody. It's not Amy's fault you'd rather have your nose in a book all winter."

"It's not my fault my feet got bigger."

Clara, coming into the room dressed in her gray wool coat that had survived four winters already and a red tam Maurice's wife Simone had knitted for her, asked, "What's all the fussing about?"

"Marie called me a dummy." Amy pouted.

"Oh, for crying out loud, forget it, will you? I'm going to read my book while you go freeze on the ice." Marie walked out of the room with a quick toss of her hair.

"You come right back here and apologize to your sister."
Tillie rarely raised her voice to either of the girls. "And
while you're at it, to me, too."

Marie turned back to the room. "I apologize for
calling you a dummy, Amy. I apologize for being rude,
*Memere.*"

"Thank you. I accept your apology." Tillie's voice
softened. "Me, too," echoed Amy.

"Are you ready, Amy? I've got the skates. Better bring an
extra pair of mittens in case those get wet."

An ocean and a sea away, Ray was rubbing his cold feet
vigorously, examining them for blisters and foot rot
that could cause bigger problems than some weapons'
wounds. He pulled out clean socks from where he was
keeping them warm inside his woolen blouse next to
his chest. He sighed with pleasure as he pulled them
on his feet, the heat in them giving him an involuntary
shiver of sensual delight.

"I just heard that we're being moved out, going up to Anzio on the coast." Sergeant Klein came up to Ray carrying his Bazooka. "Do you think we're going to get some new troops coming in there?"

"Probably. I hope so. Most of the men are tired as hell. They haven't had a break in a damned long while." Ray knew that the German units in the Italian mountains were well supplied and fierce fighters. If the troops that were here now didn't get some help there wasn't a prayer that they could ever take Rome and Rome was the key.

Just then, he heard the mail call. He felt sure there would be a letter from Clara and probably one from his sister Anna, too. He needed to be reminded that there was a world going on somewhere that wasn't filled with terror and the smell of blood, the chaos of battle and the pitiful lives of the civilians in these little Italian towns. Every day, no matter how miserable he was, no matter how tired he got, he remembered that he was doing this job so the people he loved would be safe.

Clara's letter, written on V-mail in tiny script read:

*My darling Ray,*

*When we gathered around the table for Christmas dinner, everybody held hands and we prayed for you and Pete. Tillie worked hard to make a feast, even though lots of stuff like butter and sugar is rationed. Angela is still working at the plant that makes bombs, doing a lot of overtime. Marie is growing up so fast now, it scares Angela sometimes. Amy was in a Christmas pageant at school, playing the role of Mary and you would have laughed at how she put on diva airs and went around claiming she's going to be an actress.*

*We did all the things we've always done at Christmas, but without you and Pete it wasn't the same. I took Marie and Amy to the movies on Christmas Day. We saw a Walt Disney film, not your kind of thing. Angela had to go to work. Can you imagine, working on Christmas Day?*

*I miss you so much. I got invited to a New Year's Eve party by some girls in the store. They're calling it a Hen Party because all of them have husbands or boyfriends in the service. But I said no, I'm going to sit here and listen to the radio and remember the last New Year's Eve we were together. All my thoughts will be of you. Have you heard the song, "I'll Be Seeing You?" Every time I hear it, I think of all the places where we've been together and how I see you in my mind's eye everyday.*

*I love you very much. Be careful and come home to me.*

*All my love.*

*Clara*

Ray tucked the fragile paper in his pocket, knowing he would re-read it until it fell apart. This is what kept him going from one day to the next. Having the letters is what kept the dream of the future alive, even when it seemed that this hell would go on forever. He stood up, shouldered his pack and his rifle and shouted for the sergeant to assemble the men.

Edward walked up on the back porch, stamping his feet to remove the snow. He had long since given up the luxury of driving back and forth to work, since he didn't get enough gas with his A sticker and what he did get barely made it possible to drive everyone to church and take Tillie to the grocery store. Sometimes Angela used her ration coupons to help out since most of the time she went to work with a car pool. But lately, she was doing so much overtime she needed her own car. He just hoped the tires on both cars would hold up until this war was over, because it was impossible to get tires, even if he was willing to pay the black market prices, which he wasn't.

"Halloo, halloo, I'm home." He looked for Amy who usually heard him on the porch and came running, "Where's my girl?"

"Amy's gone skating with Clara, but I'm here." Tillie came out of the pantry, her apron dusted with flour. Edward swiftly crossed the room and kissed her rosy cheek.

"*Alors, ma coeur*, you've been baking today?"

"*Oui*. Just a batch of chocolate cupcakes. They'll be hungry when they come back from Paradise Pond. I thought they'd be here by now. Maybe I'll save the cupcakes for dessert. It's too late for a snack. I don't want to ruin supper."

Edward took Tillie by the hand and led her to one of the kitchen chairs. He sat and pulled her into his lap. She frowned, aware that he still had his coat on. "Bad news today. Oscar's son died of his wounds. Flora got the telegram this morning. I heard about it from John O'Brien when he stopped to pick up one of his kids at the library just as I was coming out. He told me he sent a priest with the delivery boy and Flora hit the priest with her fists, telling him he was a liar, that all her prayers were useless. You remember John O'Brien? He runs the Western Union."

"*Mon Dieu*, when will it end?" Tillie laid her head on Edward's shoulder and wept quiet tears. "Do you think we should go and comfort her?"

Edward pulled Tillie's chin up and frowned, "*Non*, I don't think she'd want us to do that. We can order a Mass card and light some candles at the church. That will be enough. I was sure you'd want to know, though. Better for me to tell you than hear it from one of the church ladies as a surprise."

Just then, the door opened and Amy rushed in, cheeks flushed from the cold, and threw herself at her *Memere* and *Pepere* sitting in the chair. "I did it. I did it. I skated by myself."

# CHAPTER 18

## SPRING, 1944

By late March, the post where Pete was stationed was bursting with men and materials. Rows and rows of tents covered every available inch. Camouflage nets were strung over trees and wires to conceal the post, but very few German aircraft were coming over now, anyway. There was, however, a constant drone of Allied Forces aircraft in motion over their heads, pounding strategic targets in France constantly.

Every man there could feel the tension, knowing that the invasion was going to come soon, although the date and the landing site were secrets kept for only the highest brass. By now, Pete had accepted that this event would be a massive movement of men and equipment.

"I just heard they've started to surround the whole post with wire fences. Did you know that?" Stanley asked Pete.

"Nope. Only thing I know is I was told to be sure every tank was ready to roll when the word comes down. Some of these guys are getting to be a pain in the ass asking me a hundred times if I checked this or that. I keep telling them I'll be right there to fix anything that needs fixing. Did they think I'd be sitting here jacking off while they went without me?" Pete was irritated that anybody would consider him less than competent at his job. The pressure and the boredom were getting to him no less than anybody else. And he was worried about Angela. She loved to tell him about the growing numbers in the bank account and he knew that must mean she was working too many hours overtime. Forget the money for a house. He wanted her to be healthy and rested when he got home.

"I saw daffodils blooming over in somebody's yard across the road from the gates today." Stanley mused. "Do you think we'll still be here this summer?"

"My God, I hope not. There'll be riots here if we are. Who could stand this overcrowding that long?" Pete was shocked that Stanley would even suggest such a thing.

"Let's go into the village tonight, while we still can. I have a feeling they're going to close this post in pretty soon. Why else would they be tightening up fencing?"

"OK, that's a good idea. Will we have any trouble getting passes, do you think?"

"No, not us. We've been here a damn long time. Those new guys might not be able to get off post, but I'm sure we'll be able to go."

"Where's George? Maybe he'll want to go, too."

"The Colonel keeps him pretty busy with message traffic and reports. Besides, he has a Secret Clearance. I don't think they'll let him off the post anyway."

Pete and Stanley walked into a crowded noisy pub, full of boisterous Brits, Canadians, Irishmen and plenty of locals. All of the Allied Forces guys were in uniform, most with their ties pulled down and their collars open, some with their jackets off. The town was full to bursting with troops and the pub was no more than a hundred yards from the gates of the post. Pete caught the eye of the florid-faced, sweating bartender and ordered two beers. "I'll be so glad to get home to cold beer." Stanley sighed, resigned to drinking the warm, frothy stuff served in every pub.

Pete leaned back on his elbows against the bar and looked around at the crowd. There were twenty or so folks around the dartboard, loudly cheering and groaning at each throw of a dart. Two old men sat at a small table playing checkers and smoking pipes. He noticed one guy slide his arm down from a girl's shoulder to pat her ass. Another group of guys and girls were looking at some photos one of them was passing around. Stanley had left his side and was prowling around the perimeter. Out of the corner of his eye Pete noticed a cute blonde come up to stand beside him.

"Are you alone tonight, Yank?" She was wearing bright red lipstick and smelled like gardenias. It reminded Pete of the gardenias he always bought for all his girls back home at Easter.

"No, my friend is over there." He pointed with his beer mug to where Stanley was talking to a girl in the crowd.

"Do you want some company?" Her smile was more seductive than friendly.

Pete removed his elbows from the bar and shifted his body around toward her. "Can I buy you a beer?"

"No, I don't drink. But I do live only a few blocks from here. We could go to my place. I've got a lot of great records. We could dance. It's too crowded in here."

Pete sipped his beer and looked at her, thinking she looked like a nice local girl who was probably feeling patriotic and would tell herself that comforting a lonely soldier was a contribution to the war effort. God, he would love to get laid. If only he could do it without going nuts with guilt. How would he feel if Angela was doing it with some 4F guy and thinking it didn't count because there was a war on?

"Thanks, sweetheart, but I have to get back to the post early tonight. I just stopped in for a quick beer." He set his empty glass on the bar, waved to Stanley and left, walking quickly in the heavy mist.

Clara and Angela sat in the front parlor sipping hot cocoa and chatting. They'd declined to play cards tonight and left Tillie and Edward in the kitchen with their gin rummy.

Angela sighed and shifted her legs up under her in the big Morris chair. "I just found out that Hilda is having an affair with Bill Connelly. You know him. He was a big shot football player at Mass. State until he tore his knee up. He walks with a limp. She told us on the way to work this morning, bold as brass. She said he took her to Toto's and then they went to some cabin out on the Mt.Tom Road. I asked her how she could do that with her husband on a war ship out in the Pacific and she said he didn't need to know. I was shocked."

Clara set her cup down and said, "She's probably very lonely. No kids, no family. And she lives by herself, doesn't she?"

"Is that any excuse? I get lonely, too. Especially at night in that big bed with nobody to hold me. That doesn't mean I can cheat." She paused, "Clara, do you think the guys cheat?"

"I don't know, *cherie*, it's different for guys. You know, painful. I think this war is changing a lot of things.

People are doing stuff they would never think of doing before. I've decided I'm never going to ask Ray anything about it. Whether he did or he didn't has more to do with what was happening over there and nothing to do with me. My guess is that there's a lot about this war that we'll never know. Many men will come back and never, ever talk about it, just like in the Great War. They see some things that are so gruesome they don't want to remember so they bottle it up inside. All that ugliness will change some guys, make them bitter. I just pray it doesn't do that to either Ray or Pete."

"You really think Ray and Pete will be OK?" Angela looked doubtful.

Clara nodded and said, "Don't get yourself all worked up about it, though. All I care about is that both Ray and Pete come home alive and in one piece. I know that the doctors have better ways to treat soldiers who get wounded than they did for the last war, but still, it's not like they make it look in the movies."

"Yeah. Well, in the movies they make it seem like a lot of guys get mixed up with some nurse or ambulance driver and it's OK because they're all fighting the war and who knows what tomorrow will bring. Well, I'm doing my part, too." Angela was frowning and biting her thumbnail.

"Stop it, *cherie*. You're getting yourself all upset for nothing. You love Pete, yes? He loves you. I know that. You have to trust each other, that's all there is to it. Let it go. You're not Hilda and Pete's not anybody but himself. Forget the movies. That's all a bunch of *merde* anyway. Come on, let's have another cup of cocoa." Clara got up and headed for the kitchen.

Upstairs, in the big bed normally shared by Pete and Angela, Marie and her friend Betsy lay in the dark, snuggled under the covers, whispering and giggling. Tomorrow they were going to the Academy of Music with Aunt Clara and Mommy to be part of the live audience for a radio program called "Amateur Hour with Bob and Ray." Both of them were wide awake, too excited to sleep.

"Do you think Billy Cranston is good looking?" whispered Betsy.

"No, no, no. His hair sticks up in the back and his ears are too big." Marie giggled.

"I saw him looking at you in Geography class. You should have seen his eyes bug out when you bent over to pick up the stuff that had fallen out of your book bag." Betsy made circles with her thumb and forefinger and put them over her eyes. In the faint light from the street lamp outside, Marie saw the gesture and pulled Betsy's arms down.

"He did not. You're making it up." She huffed and then she giggled. "Did he, really?"

"Would you let him kiss you, if he tried?"

"I don't know. What do you think?" Marie hesitated.

"I don't know either. Have you ever been kissed by a boy?" Betsy asked.

"No, have you?"

"No, but I think I might like it."

Both girls started laughing, loud enough for Angela to call up the stairwell, "You'd better get to sleep if you want to go to the show tomorrow."

✶ ✶ ✶ ✶ ✶

Tillie folded up the cards and put them in the box. "Something big is going to happen soon, isn't it? I could tell from listening to Edward R. Murrow, couldn't you?"

"*Oui, ma coeur*, I think so. I've been reading all the papers very carefully and I'm sure of it. Pete must know, but he can't tell us in his letters because the censor would just black it out."

"I'm so worried about him," Tillie sighed. "I've missed him all the while he's been over there, but at least he wasn't in the fighting like Clara's friend Ray. I guess I knew it was coming, that he'd have to go fight, but I wish he'd broken a leg or something before it came to that. Is it awful of me to think that?"

Edward reached for her hand and patted it gently. "*Non, non.* Of course it's not awful to think that. I just wish he had never gone, but at the same time I'm proud of him for standing up like a man and doing his part. He would have been miserable watching others go while he stayed behind."

"I pray for him every day, every time I think of him, I send up a little prayer. Do you think the mothers of those German soldiers are praying for their sons, too? And who will *le bon Dieu* choose to spare? How does He decide which prayers to answer? Father Lebeau got angry with me when I asked him that question." Tillie got up and put the cards away in a drawer and turned back to her beloved husband. "How will I bear it if he.....if he doesn't come back to us?"

"Let's not think about that. Pete is a smart man. He knows how to take care of himself and I know he'll be careful because he wants to come home to his family." Edward put his arms around his wife and stroked her back gently. "Whatever happens, we will bear it because we have each other."

# CHAPTER 19

## JUNE 6, 1944

Pete was ready. This was it. It was the morning of June 5. They were supposed to go yesterday, but the weather was really lousy. Not much better today, but they were going anyway and he was damn glad of it. He checked his equipment one more time and made sure he had the pictures of Angela and the girls in the protected pouch, along with the message from General Eisenhower.

*Soldiers, Sailors and Airmen of the Allied ExpeditionaryForces: You are about to embark on the great crusade, toward which we have striven these many months. The eyes of the world are upon you..........I have full confidence in your courage, devotion to duty and skill in battle.......let us all beseech the blessing of Almighty God upon this great and noble undertaking.*

He was scared, but like all the other guys, he was determined not to show it. While they were waiting to board the vessels that would take them in a convoy to the designated rendezvous point, called by the code name Piccadilly Circus in the invasion plan, there was a lot of horsing around, yelling at friends leaving on a different ship, strained laughter at bad jokes. Pete's unit was landing on a beach, code-named Omaha, and he would not be going in with the first wave. He was going in with a small contingent of tanks, modified to be amphibious, that would support the initial push into Normandy, held back until the beach was secured. With any luck, that would mean on the same day. More would arrive later.

He saw Stanley way up ahead of him. He sure hoped they gave Stanley extra vomit bags, because the sea looked rough and Stanley was a very poor sailor. Pete guessed that Stanley would go in from one of those new landing craft with the skirt that dropped down close to the beach so the men could rush ashore in hordes.

Fortunately, Pete didn't have a seasickness problem, but he brought the vomit bags anyway, just in case.

And he'd eaten very lightly as well. When he's looked around and saw guys wolfing down huge amounts of food before they embarked, he shook his head at the foolishness of it.

"Hey, Pete, I came down to say goodbye and good luck. I won't get to go until later, next week, probably." George put one hand on Pete's shoulder and gave it a squeeze.

"Too bad, George. You'll miss all the fun. Maybe the war will be over by the time you get there."

"Hey, you big Canuck, save some of it for me." George knew he'd be staying close to the Colonel and there wasn't much chance of his seeing any action at all, but he kept up the pretense. "Where's Stanley? I want to give him a sendoff, too."

"I just saw him up ahead of me three lines over." Pete pointed. "He'll be glad to see you. And George, thanks for coming down. I appreciate it."

The sea was as rough as it looked and few men escaped the indignity of the vomit bag. Pete, though, was lucky. He felt a little queasy for a while, but it passed. Most of the time, he stood on deck, looking out at the vast flotilla around him, awed at the sight of so much raw power. A very tall, skinny, young-looking blond lieutenant stood next to him and, other than a few desultory words, they were both silent, thinking about what lay ahead. When they reached "Piccadilly Circus," both Pete and the lieutenant were stunned by the incredible size of the fleet assembled there. Over five thousand vessels were converging.

The two men, so different in rank and in physical appearance, separated in age by ten years or so, looked at each other and instantly knew they were feeling the same pride in the power and determination of their mother country. "Would you like to use my binoculars?" The officer held them out to Pete. "Thank you, sir." Pete responded. It looked like a nightmare of a traffic jam, but the planning had been carefully detailed and, with maneuvers worthy of the ballet, five separate convoys headed for five beaches on the coast of Normandy. It was shortly after midnight, June 6.

Pete slept on the deck as best he could, resolved to get a little rest before the attack began. He woke when he felt the change in the sound of the ship's propellers and checked his watch. It was nearly 5:30. Dawn could be glimpsed through the cloud cover, just barely coming up on the horizon. In the distance, he could see the beach that was their target and the landing craft moving into position. He ate a biscuit and some fruit paste from his K-rations while he watched. Larry Winters, one of the men in his tank crew, came up alongside him and said, "I can't wait to get off this gutbucket. I've been sick all night."

Ray looked at him. He did look pale. "Have a biscuit. It will help."

"Are you crazy? I'm not eating a damn thing. It will just start the heaves all over again."

"I'm telling you. It's better to have something in your stomach. And keep looking out, across the water at the horizon, so your eyes adjust to the ship's movement."

"Bullshit!" Larry walked away.

While Pete watched, hundreds of men clambered down cargo nets from ships up ahead of him and into the waiting landing craft to be transported as close to the beach as possible. He could see the flash of ammo coming from the cliffs and knew this would be no piece of cake. The big guns on the battleships were targeting the top of the cliffs and the noise and the firepower were awesome. He felt the rush of adrenaline when it came his turn to disembark, and he was damn glad he'd be protected by the walls of a tank when he hit the beach.

The next few hours were a blur of activity as the troops pressed on with the battle plan, resolutely putting out of their minds the terrible scenes of death and gore and devastation on the beach. They were intent on gaining ground against the enemy, even if it was inch by inch.

It had become Clara's habit to snap on her little brown bakelite radio as soon as she got out of bed, listening to the news even before she headed into the bathroom to get ready to go to work.

A couple of days ago there had been a false report that the invasion had started, but it was retracted five minutes later. Somebody had left a message, written in anticipation of the actual landing, on an open teletype machine and it accidentally got transmitted. Skeptical now, when she first heard the announcer declare that the invasion was underway, she sat down on the edge of the bed to listen for something that would convince her it was real. When more details were broadcast, she ran downstairs to the kitchen, where Tillie was already making breakfast.

*"Mon Dieu, mon Dieu*, it's started." Tillie was agitated, having already heard the news. "Edward and I are going to the church right after we eat something to pray for the safety of all the men and especially Pete, and for a quick end to this war."

Angela came down the back staircase already dressed and asked, "Would you please take the girls with you? I have to go to work. It's more important than ever that we make the bombs for them to fight with."

*"Oui, oui.* Do you think they won't have any school today?"

"Whether they have school or not, I want them to say their prayers for their father, but anyway, I don't think there will be any school."

Clara was thoughtful. "I don't know if the store will be open, but I think it will be. If it's not, I'll walk over to the church. I wonder if Ray knows that the invasion has begun? I haven't heard from him for two weeks, but I'm not surprised since he's been in the battle to take Rome."

"I heard that Rome fell yesterday, but that there's still fighting going on from the fleeing German troops. I don't know exactly what that means, but it doesn't sound like it's all over yet." Angela was struggling into her coat, looking at Clara anxiously. "It may be the beginning of the end, but that's all it is."

In Rome, Ray was fast asleep on a cot in a tent pitched in the beautiful Borchese gardens. When he brought his platoon here last night, it was too dark to see much of anything and anyway, they were all too tired to care.

A bright-eyed lieutenant woke him. "Good morning, sir. A messenger just arrived, looking for you. You're supposed to be billeted in a palazzo a mile or so from here. That's where the major is now. The messenger is supposed to take you there."

"OK. Tell him to give me a few minutes to shave and clean up a bit." Ray stretched his aching body and ran his hands through his hair.

"And, sir, you might want to know that there's mail call this morning. The men are pretty excited about that."

Ray's smile wiped the weariness off his face. "Well, hallelujah, I'm pretty excited, too. Pick up my mail while I go see what the major wants, will you?"

"Yes, sir, will do."

The front of the palazzo was badly pockmarked. Probably hit by shell fragments during the bombing, Ray thought. When he stepped through the open door, he was surprised to see that the elaborate marble floor in the foyer looked undamaged by anything more than time. Niches in the walls that probably had held beautiful works of art were empty and there was no furniture. A sergeant stepped out of a doorway and came to attention, saluting with crisp, military precision. "Good morning, Captain, sir. General Truscott is in the room to your left."

Ray was astonished and a little embarrassed. The private who came to get him did say he was meeting with a major, didn't he? Or did he say major general? Too late now to go get a clean shirt and a shoe shine.

"Come in, come in, Captain Carpenter. There's some halfway decent coffee over there." General Truscott responded to Ray's salute with a vague wave of his hand in the direction of his forehead and indicated a seat at the table. "We're here to talk about the battle plan for taking the fight into the mountains. Your platoon will be in a forward position and I want your candid thoughts on how this can work. Mind you, son, I did say candid. I want no deference to rank to get in the way of complete honesty."

Ray started to apologize for his appearance and then thought better of it. It would serve no purpose and would divert the discussion. For the next two hours, strategies were discussed openly, requirements reviewed, obstacles raised and finally, a plan agreed upon by the group of senior officers, as well as two majors and one other captain. Ray felt privileged to be included.

As they were leaving the meeting, Major Webster, to whom Ray reported directly, reminded him, "You've got a room assigned to you in this palazzo. Get your gear and move in. They've got big bathtubs and hot water. Some of the windows are shattered. But that shouldn't be a problem. There are balconies with overhangs and shutters on the casements if it rains. Oh, in case you're hungry, there's an officers' mess. Decent food. Hot, too."

"It doesn't sound as if I'll be here very long." Ray took out a pack of cigarettes and offered one to the major. "Have you heard whether the big invasion of France has happened yet?"

"My God, you didn't know? Where have you been? It was two days ago. A bloody business. Lots of casualties, but our guys have a toehold and they're pressing on."

"I just got in last night. We were mopping up some sniper activity on the outskirts of the city. Nasty stuff. So, no, I hadn't heard. I've got a good friend in the tank corps with the 1st Army. I sure hope he made it. He's got two little girls." Ray felt a sudden wave of lightheadedness. He didn't know whether it was because he hadn't eaten all day or if his fears for Pete were overwhelming him.

319

When he stepped outside a Pfc. jumped out of a jeep and saluted. "My orders are to take you to get your gear and bring you back here, sir."

"Great. Let's go."

Ray returned with his gear and an armload of mail, most of it, including a package, from Clara. He found his room luxurious, especially compared to sleeping on the ground or on the floor of an abandoned building, and threw the pile of mail on the bed. He was hungry, but he needed to feed his soul first. There were letters from his sister, also, and two from his mother. They would wait. He read every letter from Clara twice and then opened the package. It was full of dark fudge with walnuts and six boxes of Smith Brothers Cough drops. He whooped when he saw that, remembering that he had complained of a scratchy throat a while back and the awful tasting stuff the medic told him to spray in his throat. He needed to go get some food or he'd fall asleep right here and then wake up in the middle of the night starving, with only the K-rations in his pack available.

Later, after some excellent spaghetti and fresh bread, he sat down to write Clara.

*Clara, my darling,*

*You've probably heard by now that we have taken the city of Rome. That's where I am now, put up in a palace. No kidding. You should see this bed. It looks like something out of a movie. The bathroom is all marble with the biggest bathtub I ever saw. If only you were here, we'd really enjoy it.*

*I got lots of mail today, mostly from you, but some from Anna and my mother. The package you sent is wonderful. I laughed when I saw the cough drops. Leave it to you to pick up on my complaint about the scratchy throat which is gone now. I'll be well supplied the next time I get one, though. And, really, sweetheart, I know that sugar is rationed. I love the fudge, but I feel guilty about you using up your coupons for me.*

*I got invited to a meeting with the big brass today. I felt honored. It was very interesting to hear how carefully they plan every step. This war is much more complicated than anyone knows, especially because we're fighting on so many fronts at once. When I was a kid reading history, I had all these romantic notions of two armies coming at each other across an open field, shields in place and lances at the ready. This is a far different kind of warfare.*

*I don't have any idea how long I'll be here, but probably not long. There's still a lot to do. Have you heard anything about Pete? I've been thinking about him a lot. We hear a lot of rumors about the invasion but very little hard facts.*

*How I long to see you, talk to you, hold you, bury my face in your sweet smelling hair, taste your skin, feel your soft body next to mine. Stay well for me. I think this war is coming to an end and then we'll be together again.*

*All my love always,*

*Ray*

# CHAPTER 20

## SUMMER, 1944

Pete was pretty much ticked off that none of them had been told about the hedgerows in Normandy. They sure as hell weren't like the hedges in England that the foxhunters jumped over. These were seven or eight feet high and impenetrable, great hiding places for German gun crews. Hacking at them with an ax did very little and anyway, took forever. Then he heard that some sergeant had suggested attaching steel teeth to the front of a tank and tearing the hedges out from the roots, so he had just finished improvising an attachment to his tank when the word came down that they were moving out to the next town.

A few miles down the narrow lane he was standing in the turret when a looey came running up yelling,

"Corporal LaPointe, I just heard you understand French. Is that true?"

"Yes sir, I do. But not too well. I'm French-Canadian and the language is a little different here."

"Come on, then. There's a kid trying to tell us something and he's real excited, but nobody can figure out what he's saying. Something about a bush."

"Maybe he's saying Boche. That's what these people called the Germans in The Great War." Pete jumped down off the tank and followed the lieutenant at a run.

The boy was maybe ten or eleven and pitifully skinny. He was yelling and pointing and talking so fast that Pete put his hands on the kid's shoulders and said, "Lentement, mon brave."

"What are you saying to him?" A major had come up behind Pete.

"I'm just telling him to slow down. He's talking so fast, he's not understandable."

When Pete got the message, he turned to the men behind him and said, "There's a German ambush in the *bocage*, the hedgerow, you know, just up ahead, less than a kilometer. Machine guns and mortars. A lot of them. They've been hiding in a barn up there, just waiting. I'll go warn the front of the column." And he took off at a sprint.

Warned, the column halted and Pete started jogging back to his tank when he heard a barrage of gun fire behind him and he fell forward, hitting his shoulder on the hard-packed dirt. Instinctively he rolled under the nearest truck, as men scattered for cover. The enemy must have heard the column stop and came out of their hiding place to spray the vehicles in the lane with gunfire.

Pete realized his leg was hurting and he looked down to see his left pants leg torn and drenched with blood. "Oh, shit, oh, shit, I've been hit." He looked over to his right and noticed that one of the guys who had rolled under the same truck looked dead. Another one called out to him, "Hey, Corporal, are you Ok?"

"I've taken a hit in the leg. It hurts like hell but I don't know how bad it is. A lot of blood, though."

"Medic! Medic! Over here." Pete heard people yelling. Some guys were in worse shape than he was. He could hear his buddies returning fire. Dear God, he thought, Angela is going to be so worried when she gets the word. Don't let me die right now. I want to live to see my girls again.

A medic rolled under the truck, looked at the dead soldier, who had been shot in the chest, and came over to Pete, quickly put a tourniquet on his leg, fashioned a quick bandage, gave him a couple of sulfa tablets and a shot of morphine. "I'll get a stretcher for you as soon as I can." He patted Pete on the arm and took off.

Tillie heard Angela cry out and she sat up in bed, rubbing the sleep from her eyes. Then she heard loud sobbing, a pitiful noise. She got up and crossed the hall, knocked on the door softly and turned the knob. Angela was sitting up, her shoulders hunched over and shaking.

"*Cherie*, what's the matter?" Tillie hurried across the room and sat on the edge of the bed. She reached over and patted Angela's back, then slowly moved her hand in circles, soothing her daughter-in-law as she would a young child.

"I dreamt that Pete was in some dark place, a cave or a pit or something like that, and he was all bloody. And I could feel him hurting but I couldn't reach him. I couldn't do anything. Oh, I'm so worried," and she started crying and shaking again.

"*Pauvre femme.* It will be alright. *Le bon Dieu* will protect him. Let's say a little prayer right now. Wipe your tears and say a little prayer with me." Tillie slid off the bed and got to her knees. Angela wiped her face with a handkerchief that was lying on the bedside table and joined Tillie on her knees, elbows propped on the bed.

The bowed their heads and each of them prayed silently for several minutes, then Tillie rose. Angela rose with her. "Thank you, Mama Tillie, I feel better now. I'll go over to the church after work tomorrow and light some candles. Maybe there'll be a letter tomorrow."

Pete barely remembered the trip to the field evacuation hospital since he was mostly unconscious. When he woke up he was lying on a cot in a tent and two men were poking at his leg. His pants were gone and his bandage was off. One man with a husky voice, sounding very tired, spoke to him. "There's a lot of damage to the muscle and we're going to have to get those shell fragments out of there if we're going to save the leg at all, soldier. I think there's a good chance we can do that. You'll have to wait your turn, though. Busy day today." Abruptly, both men walked away.

A pretty nurse with short curly dark hair came over to him, smiling. I'll bet Angela's hair would look like that if she cut it, Pete thought. "Hi, Corporal, my name is Maxie. I'm going to re-bandage you for the time being, until they call for you in the operating tent. Meanwhile, how do you feel? Much pain? Would you like another morphine shot?" She bandaged up his leg while he was asking questions. "Did we get those bastards? How did we make out? I know one guy is dead. He was under the truck with me. Anybody else?"

Maxie tucked a blanket around him. "I don't know the details, Corporal, but I'm sure someone from your outfit will come see you after you come back from surgery."

Pete started to doze off when he remembered the doc saying "save the leg." Did that mean they might have to amputate? Shit, shit, shit. Was he going to lose his leg? Please God, no. Then the morphine sucked him under and he was hardly conscious of the stretcher bearers taking him into the operating tent.

When he opened his eyes he realized he was on a cot, but in a different tent with fewer men so he must be back from surgery. His mouth felt fuzzy and his eyelids were heavy. Nausea overwhelmed him and he tried to sit up. A ward boy came running over with a basin not a second too soon. He fell back on the pillow. "My leg? See my leg? Is it...?"

"Yessir, you've still got your leg. Want to look?" And the ward boy lifted the covers so Pete could see he still had his leg. Tears leaked out of Pete's eyes and he fell back asleep.

The new nurse was a redhead, older than Maxie and looking very uptight. She said her name was Peggy and she would get him some water to sip on. She took his temperature and told him the only danger now was infection, so don't get any ideas about prowling around in the night (as if he could) because there wasn't enough staff to watch out for him if he fell down. Pete really didn't know what the hell she was talking about, but maybe just letting him know there'd be no coddling here. The ward boy was always there with the basin and the urinal, so all he had to do was holler for him.

He dozed and vomited most of the night. Dawn was just coming up when the doc stopped by. "I hope you're pleased to note that you've still got that leg, soldier. We got all the shell bits out of there, but a fair amount of muscle was damaged. You'll stay here until all risk of infection is over and then you'll go to a hospital in Britain for physical therapy."

"Will I be able to walk?" Pete's voice was a croak.

"I figure if you work at it hard enough you'll walk again, maybe even without a cane, although I don't guarantee it. That will be up to you. You're a little older than some of these hotshot kids, so maybe you've got more sense. Do not try to hurry this process. I mean it. It will take time and a lot of effort on your part. Physical therapy is hard work, especially in a case like this."

"How long before I can go home?"

"I can't answer that because I don't know how you heal or how hard you're willing to work, but maybe a couple of months and then you can continue more therapy back in the US."

"Thanks, doc, I'm glad you could save my leg."

"You're welcome, soldier. That's what I'm here for." The doctor walked away quickly, stopping two beds down on the other side of the tent.

Sometime later two of the guys in his tank crew came to visit. "Hey, Pete, you caught the gold ring. You're not dead and you get to go home."

"Yeah, and I got to keep my leg, too."

"We heard about that. You know that major who operated on you has a rep for saving arms and legs. Somebody told me the doc told him he felt like a failure every time he had to amputate, so he does the most careful operating job of any medical guy in the whole army. You were lucky."

"Did we lose anybody?" Pete was almost afraid to ask.

"Four dead and six wounded. Could have been a lot worse. I don't know what happened to the kid that warned us."

"Try to find out if the kid is OK, will you? He took a hell of a risk talking to us. If the Germans saw him or some SOB collaborator ratted on him, he's dead and probably his whole family, too."

331

Pete's tone was sober and a reminder that this was a rotten situation for kids in an occupied country, some of them so eager to help that they took unbelievable risks.

"We're heading into Belgium in a couple of days, so I don't know how much we can find out about him, but I'll talk to somebody and see what I can learn."

"Hey, would you do something else for me? See if you can find out anything about two buddies of mine. Stan Borowski went in to the beach with the first wave. I've been asking and I haven't been able to find out. And George Corelli was with Colonel Wesley. He probably didn't get to come over until a few days after the first assault. He may even be somewhere around here. I'd sure like to know that they're both OK."

"I'll see what I can do about that. I remember Borowski, big guy, always cheerful, great bazooka man, right?"

"Yeah, and a good friend to have, too."

When the front doorbell rang, Tillie was slicing onions for a vegetable soup so she took a minute to wash her hands before she answered it, calling out, "I heard you. I'm coming." She couldn't imagine who was at the front door in the middle of the morning. She wasn't expecting anyone.

Father Dumont was standing there next to a young man in a Western Union uniform. "Oh, no, no no, no." Tillie reached for the door frame to steady herself even as Father Dumont reached out for her arm.

"Wait, wait, *ma chere* Madame LaPointe, there is only one red star. See, look here, there is one red star."

Tillie looked and through the glassine in the envelope, she could see that it was addressed to Mrs. Pierro LaPointe, not to Mrs. Edward LaPointe. So it was for Angela, not for her.

"This is addressed to my daughter-in-law, not me."

The Western Union delivery boy spoke up, "Well, Ma'am, we try to deliver directly to the person it's addressed to, but Mr. Obie knew that Pete's wife is working at the bomb factory and he said you could sign for it, especially since Father Dumont was available today."

"Come in, come in.  Where do I sign?"

 The delivery boy held out his clipboard and indicated the place for Tillie's signature. "Thank you, but I have to go.  I have other deliveries."  He got on his bicycle and wheeled off.

"I drove right over when I got the call from John O'Brien.  I thought you would probably be alone at this time of the morning.  Why don't you open the telegram and see what it says?"

"I don't think I should do that, since it's not addressed to me."  Tears were running unchecked down Tillie's cheeks, but she was in control, now that she realized the envelope was stamped with one red star and not two, which meant a death.

"I think she'll understand if you open it, Madame."  The priest's voice was soft and gentle.

"Are you sure it's not against the law for me to open somebody else's mail?"

He wasn't sure about that, but Father Dumont said, "Open it."

In the typical style of Western Union, strips of words, no punctuation marks, pasted onto a form, it read:

THE SECRETARY OF WAR DESIRES ME TO EXPRESS HIS DEEP REGRET THAT YOUR HUSBAND CORPORAL LAPOINTE PIERRO E WAS SERIOUSLY WOUNDED IN FRANCE 30 JUNE 44 UNTIL NEW ADDRESS IS RECEIVED ADDRESS MAIL FOR HIM QUOTE RANK NAME SERIAL NUMBER (HOSPITALIZED) 2628 HOSPITAL SECTION APO 698 CARE POSTMASTER NEW YORK NEW YORK UNQUOTE NEW ADDRESS AND FURTHER INFORMATION FOLLOW DIRECT FROM HOSPITAL=

J A ULIO THE ADJUTANT GENERAL

Tillie Looked at Father Dumont, "It doesn't say where he was wounded or how seriously. And it happened two weeks ago. Why did it take so long for them to let us know?" Her voice was strangled, the deep anguish readily apparent. "Oh *mon Dieu,* there isn't enough information. Why, why? I don't understand. Why send this and make it worse, the not knowing?"

The priest held Tillie's shaking hands. "I'm sure you'll get all the details soon. See, it says, 'further information direct from hospital.' You'll be getting that in a few days, I'm sure."

Before the expected information came from the hospital, Angela received a letter from Pete and his mother and father received one as well. He made light of the wound, assured them all he was doing well and that he would be home in a couple of months. Angela's letter included a paragraph she shared with no one.

*Nothing really vital was damaged, sweetheart. The first thing I'm going to do when I get home is get started on making a new baby for us to love. As long as the equipment works and the doctor promises me it will, I can live with a limp or use a cane if I have to. It was the only thing I worried about because I promised you we would make a new baby and I intend to keep my promise.*

When the postcard arrived from the hospital, it was an anticlimax although it put into question Pete's assurances of the minor nature of his wound. In the section called Diagnosis, it read: 'Severe wound of right calf, deeply imbedded shrapnel.' It did note, however, that Corporal LaPointe was making normal improvement.

✯ ✯ ✯ ✯ ✯

Pete was lying on his bunk writing a letter when he saw Colonel Wesley come in to the tent.  Oh, shit, he thought, I look like a slob.  I haven't even shaved yet today.  When the Colonel reached him and extended his hand, Pete clasped it firmly and apologized for the absence of military discipline in his attire and unshaven face.

"Don't worry about it, Corporal.  We don't stand on ceremony like that when you're in here.  I'm just very glad to see you sitting up and in good cheer.  You took a bad hit, but your doc assures me you'll make a good recovery.  After a bit more time in a hospital in Britain, you'll be going home.  You've been a good soldier, hardworking, dedicated to the cause of your country and a source of pride to the Army, your government and your family."

"Thank you, sir."

"My purpose here today is to tell you that I've put in the paperwork for a Purple Heart and I've also made a recommendation for a Bronze Star.  That sprint you made to the front of the convoy to warn them of the German ambush was done without being ordered by

337

anyone and was a qualified act of heroism. I'm proud to have had you in my command. Good luck, Corporal and God bless." He patted Pete on the shoulder, shook hands again and was gone.

Dammit, Pete thought, I never got a chance to ask him about George Corelli.

The guy in the bed next to Pete's said, "Jesus, you not only get to go home, you're a goddam hero, lucky SOB."

"Yeah, what do you know about that?" Pete was dazed. "How did that happen?"

# CHAPTER 21

## FALL, 1944

Angela was expecting to hear any day that Pete had arrived in New York. She mused about all the changes that were happening around her. She was going to have to face coping with it all, not least of which was whether Pete would let her keep working. The idea of a new baby was exciting, but she already had two girls who were growing and facing different challenges in their lives.

Marie was excited to be going to the high school this year, an almost new one on Elm Street. Since she had completed grades seven and eight in junior high, she would enter as a high school sophomore and she was fretting about the unknown. Of course, she had already expressed her pleasure at having a locker for her coat and books and she was both looking forward to and scared of meeting a lot of new kids from all over town. She'd be starting Latin and French and geometry, all new subjects to learn and teachers she had never heard anything about. She and her friend Betsy had spent all summer talking about this new adventure. I hope it goes well for her, Angela thought, especially since most, if not all of the kids in her class will be older. Not for the first time she worried about Marie being the youngest in her class. The difference between 13 and 16 was enormous.

Amy was going into second grade. Hospital Hill School was closed now so she'd have to go to Hawley Grammar. Angela worried a little about such a long walk to school for Amy without Marie to watch over her, but nothing could be done about it except to admonish her about not talking to strangers or dawdling on the way. Hard to believe her baby was already in the second grade.

Men who had been wounded in the war had started to return. It was usually announced in church when it was a man from the French-Canadian community. And, of course there was always a Mass for the men who had died. In a town that had been depleted of its young men, it could be noticed just from walking on Main Street that they were coming back. Angela heard talk that some of them were drinking heavily and seemed dejected and disoriented. I sure hope Pete will be OK, Angela thought. She understood how it would be difficult to return to the old life after the experience of war. It was clear that there was a powerful sense of being involved in a great cause and being a crusader for justice. And the shared miseries often led to friendships between men that sustained them in the worst of times. But, also, there was a lot of cruelty, deprivation and pain they experienced and some became hardened by it. She knew all of this from Pete's letters.

Would Pete be the same man she loved? Would he still think she was pretty? On the one hand, Angela wanted Pete to be the same darling she had married, but on the other hand she wanted him to appreciate how she had changed. Especially she wanted him to accept her new independence and competence. She knew that didn't make a lot of sense. If she had changed, he probably had, too.

Tillie was setting up the stretchers for the lace curtains she had just washed. The bright sunshine would bleach them out nicely. They'd be dry in no time so she could get them back on the windows before supper. She glanced up to see one of the Poudrier boys walking by.

He'd been home for three months now. She knew he'd been wounded but she didn't know where. Nothing visible, anyway. His mother told Tillie he seemed angry all the time. He couldn't keep a job for long, what with the fights and the drinking. Tillie prayed Pete would not come home with those kinds of problems. She knew he limped and was using a cane because he already told them that in his letters.

She also knew that Angela had been very careful with the money the government sent and the money she earned at the bomb factory. And she knew they wanted a house of their own. It would be hard to see the girls go. There were so many things changing now. Clara and Angela both drove cars. Angela was managing money, wearing slacks and last week she got her hair cut. Not as short as some of the young women she saw, but still, not long enough now to put up in a bun. Clara would probably get married to Ray when he came home and maybe even move to Hartford. Edward said there would be more changes when the war was over and the men returned. He reminded Tillie of how it was after the Great War when the veterans couldn't find jobs. *Mon Dieu*, she thought, I hope we don't go back to the Depression.

✯ ✯ ✯ ✯ ✯

Standing at the rail of the ship taking him home, Pete fell into conversation with a guy with a patch over his left eye. "Sure feels good to be heading back to the good old USA, doesn't it?"

"Maybe for you, but I'm not so sure how it will be for me when I get home."

"Where's home?"

"Louisville, Kentucky. I used to work on a horse farm, tending thoroughbred horses. You know, the ones who race. Most people don't know how valuable they are and how hard a job it is to take care of them. I doubt I'll be able to get my job back with this bum eye, though."

"What's the matter with your eye?"

"Shrapnel. The doc says there's a slim chance it will work its way out, but they couldn't remove it without risking permanent damage to the eye, so he said wait and see. Ha, wait and see. Get it? That's a joke."

"Well, you never know. You have to do what they tell you, but somebody at the hospital in Surrey told me a lot of healing has to do with what's in your head. Look at me, I'm up and walking when there was only a 50/50 chance I would."

"In your head? What do you mean? Sounds to me like mumbo jumbo. It's God who will decide whether we get better."

"Yeah, well, I always heard that God helps those who help themselves." Pete smiled

"What are you going to do when you get home?"

"I've got a wife and two girls. First thing I'm going to do is make another baby. Then I'm going to look into starting my own business. I've got a terrific wife. She's been working in a bomb factory and saving money, so we're going to have a little nest egg to start with. Everything is going to be great."

"You don't think that leg is going to slow you down?"

"Hell, no. It's no big deal. I'm alive and my pecker works. What more could I want?"

"Good luck to you, then." The guy turned and walked away.

Edward finished mulching the hedges in front of the library and started gathering his tools into the wheelbarrow. He looked up from his task at the sound of footsteps coming along the sidewalk. "*Bonjour*, Gaspar, I haven't seen you in a long while. Have you been gone somewhere?"

Gaspar Ouimette held out his hand to Edward. "*Oui, mon vieux*, I took my wife to visit our son at the hospital in Boston. We stayed with her relatives near there so we could see our boy every day."

"And how is he doing? I heard he'd been wounded, but nobody knew anything else about it."

"Not too good. Thanks for asking. He took a round in the back that tore up one lung. He's not healing the way he should. That's why they asked us to come visit, to cheer him up, *tu comprend*? He is depressed, they say. That damned girlfriend he had, Suzette Picout, she wrote him a letter telling him she's got a new boyfriend. That didn't help any." Gaspar was clenching his fists and scowling.

"*Mon Dieu*, that's terrible. Were you able to cheer him up?"

"A little, I think. He was really glad to see his mother. She brought him cookies and *tire lire* and some applesauce she made from our own apples. I don't think I needed to be there, but my wife made me go. My son and I never did get along too well, so I didn't know what to say to him."

Edward had no idea what to say to that, so he put his hand on Gaspar's shoulder and said, "*Bonne chance* to all of you, then. I have to get going with my work on the grounds here, preparing it for winter."

Clara was folding sweaters on the Autumn Sale table, musing about her last letter from Ray. He was back with his unit fighting Germans in the mountains of Italy. Not that he'd been able to write that in his letters, but that she had figured it out from the news reports she read and listened to on the radio, as well as Edward's big map. That map was well-used and marked to trace the paths of Pete and Ray. It had proved to be a valuable resource for all the family.

Ray always seemed so upbeat in all his letters. She hoped that was so, but she doubted it. Seeing the newsreels at the movies showed her that, even when the camera caught soldiers grinning, most of the men looked weary, grimy and living in terrible conditions. She remembered the letters she got from Gus when he fought in the Great War. They told her how men get used to the chaos and the extreme discomfort after a while. She didn't think that was a good thing. How would that change them? What would it mean for them to come home to order and comfort in their lives?

"Mrs. Pelletier, Mr. Barron sent me to tell you a new shipment just came in. He wants you to go down to the Receiving Department to check the inventory." A young boy who had just started working after school stood there, looking awkward and uncomfortable.

"Thank you, Robert, I'll tell Mr. Clark I'm leaving and be right there." Clara hurried over to let her co-worker know she would be off the selling floor. Not much customer traffic now so close to closing. He could manage alone.

Clara had been gradually assuming more responsibility at the store, helping Mr. Barron, sometimes choosing merchandise to mark for sale or deciding what color sweaters to buy for a new season. It was a gradual thing, but it pleased her to be recognized as a good worker. She wondered if she would have to give it up when Ray returned.

Marie was overjoyed. Her locker was next to the best looking boy in her class. He was new so nobody knew much about him, except that his family came from Belgium and his father was a professor at Smith. They were renting a house on Massasoit Street. He touched her hand once to get her attention and she almost jumped out of her skin. It was only that he wanted to ask a question about a Latin assignment, but she blushed like a dope when she answered him. He must think I'm some kind of dummy, Marie thought.

School had only just gotten started and already she was shocked at all the changes. Figuring out what to eat and where to sit in the cafeteria was as important as any of the academic work. She was only a sophomore but she already signed up for a couple of clubs, the school newspaper and the drama group. No meetings scheduled yet, though.

Her daddy was on his way home from the war and Mom said he would be using a cane, but she and Amy were not to worry about it. Marie was so proud of him. He was a hero and had gotten a medal and, although she would have loved to tell everybody about it, she knew it would sound like bragging and some people in her class had dads that would never come home. Maybe the Gazette would write a story about Dad and then kids in her class would notice and ask her about him.

Everybody said the war would be over soon. Marie hoped that was true. Then the men would come home and there would be no more rationing. She supposed there would be other things that would change, but she wasn't sure what. Maybe the men who run the governments would get together and decide never to have another war. Wouldn't that be something? When she said that to Aunt Clara, her aunt said, "Yeah, I'm sure they'll do that and probably mean it. But then, something will happen somewhere and they'll decide they have no choice."

When the phone rang after supper, Angela ran to get it, sure it must be Pete calling to say he'd arrived in New

York. But then, she called out, "Clara, it's Ray's sister Anna calling long distance."

Clara had a moment of panic that made her heart beat pound in her chest. She picked up the phone with hands that were shaking. "Hello, Anna, this is Clara."

"Clara, I'm so sorry I didn't call right away, but my mother had a stroke and she's in the hospital now. I've been running back and forth every day. We got a telegram from the Army three days ago telling us that Ray is missing in action." Anna's voice was thick with tears. "When my mother read it, she had the stroke. I don't know if you knew she is a diabetic and has high blood pressure besides. She's not careful about doing what the doctor tells her, so we weren't surprised when the doctor at the emergency room connected the stroke to her condition. Anyway, my husband noticed that the telegram didn't say "presumed dead" so maybe Ray is a prisoner of war." Clara could hear Anna blowing her nose. She sounded tired and frazzled. "I'm sorry if I'm not making sense."

"Anna, did the telegram have a date on it for when Ray went missing?" Clara asked.

"Oh, I didn't notice. Wait a minute. I'll ask Randy."

After a short pause, Anna came back on the line and said, "September fifth.  Why do you ask?"

"Because last week I had a bad feeling, like a premonition, but then the next day I got a letter from Ray so I didn't think any more about it." Tears were rolling down Clara's cheeks, but she was in control of herself.  "I wonder what we have to do to get more information."

"Randy is going to try to get in touch with our Congressman and see if he can find out anything more. Randy went to high school with him and he thinks that will get him to take his call.  I'll let you know as soon as we hear anything more.  I'm sorry it took me three days to call you, but it's been a little crazy around here.  On top of everything else, our son Edward just turned 18 and he wants to enlist..." Anna started to sob.  "We're trying to persuade him he'd be more valuable if he went to college, even for a year.  And, of course, I'm hoping it will be over by then."

"My dear Anna, you have a heavy burden.  I'm so sorry about your mother and your son, too.  If there is anything I can do for you, please ask me.  I'm going to pray for Ray and for your mother, also. We have to believe Ray will be alright, that he's maybe in a prisoner of war camp or even in hiding behind enemy lines. I've heard of that. I just know he'll come back. Don't give up hope."

Clara put down the phone, turned to Tillie and Angela and Edward standing there and said, "Ray is missing in action, but that's all we know. We have to pray he's OK and that he'll turn up soon."

All three of her dear ones chorused their agreement and silently praised Clara for her calm belief it would turn out right even though they feared the worse.

Clara thought it was one thing to assure everyone else that Ray would come back to them, if only she could believe it herself.

# CHAPTER 22

## FALL, 1944

As soon as he got off the ship, Pete ran around looking for a phone booth and when he found one it had a line six men deep. The guy in front of him turned and asked, "Hey, Corporal, have you got a dime?"

"Yeah, I've been saving it to make this call, though. Sorry."

Finally, it was his turn. He controlled his disappointment when his mother answered and told him Angela was at work. "I have to report in at a hospital here in New York before I can come home. It'll be a few days, maybe, and then I'll get the first train I can get a seat on, so I'll see you soon."

That evening, he called again and this time Angela answered. Pete's anticipation of seeing his wife after over two years had him nearly tripping over his own words. "I've got to be here a couple of days, sweetheart, while somebody does some tests and some f-ing paperwork and I can't wait that long to be with you. There's a guy here that has some pull and he says he can get us a hotel room, so can you get on a train tomorrow morning and I'll meet you and we'll have some time alone before I come home?"

"Yes, yes, of course. I'll figure it out. How will you know which train to meet?"

"I just thought of something, Angela. Put my Pa on the phone, will you?"

Edward picked up the phone and said, "We're so glad to have you back. When will you get here?"

"Hello, Pa. I'm not exactly sure how long this mustering out stuff is going to take but I really need to ask you to do something for me, Pa. Please put Angela on a train to New York first thing tomorrow morning. I'll call later and you can tell me what time the train will arrive and I'll be there to meet her."

"Will they let you do that? Your mother said you had to go to a hospital. Are you sick? How will you get out of the hospital to meet the train?"

"No, Pa, I'm not sick. They just have to do some tests on my leg. It has something to do with the disability payments. And they'll understand if I explain I have to meet my wife's train. And Pa, I really need to be with my wife. I promise we'll be home in a couple of days."

'Oh. *Oui.* I understand. I'll go right down to the station now and see what I can do. We are so glad you are coming home to us, *mon fils. Au'voir.*" Edward started to hand the phone to Angela, but took it back for a moment and whispered, *"Je t'aime."*

Pete was a little startled by the words. It was very rare for his father to convey his emotions in any way and even more rare for him to tell the adult Pete, "I love you."

There was a great flurry of activity on 144 West Street that night with Angela making calls to alert her car pool and her supervisor at the plant that she would be gone a few days and Clara packing Angela's bag and Edward using precious gas to drive down to the railroad station and get a ticket for a train that left at 7:45 the next morning.

Angela was caught up in worry about how she looked and happy anticipation of seeing Pete in a few hours. The train was almost full, but she was able to get a seat. A very young-looking Marine helped her put her bag in the rack overhead and disappeared before she could thank him. The woman sitting next to her was red-eyed, dabbing at her tears with a lace-edged hanky. Angela decided not to intrude on the lady's privacy. When they reached New Haven, the lady got off. A young boy got on with no luggage other than a small canvas bag slung over his shoulder. It turned out he was going to visit his father in Manhattan, just for overnight. They were going to a show on Broadway; he didn't know what. He lived with his grandparents because his mother was dead. His father was a musician. He chatted on cheerfully, not even noticing that Angela was hardly listening. At their arrival in Grand Central Station, he jumped up, said goodbye and plunged into the crowd.

Angela looked around, awed at the size of the station and the hordes of people moving fast in all directions.

Then she saw Pete standing a few yards away, leaning on his cane and she ran to him. He dropped the cane with a clatter and opened his arms wide. They held tight to one another, tears unchecked, kissing and murmuring of love and need and gratitude. They parted when an elderly man tapped Pete on the arm and said, "Corporal, you dropped your cane and I'm sure you don't want to lose it in this hubbub."

"Thank you, sir. Let's go, Angela. The cabs are over this way."

Pete kept touching his wife, running his hand over her hair, rubbing her neck, squeezing her arm, kissing her in the cab and holding her hand while he registered at the Astor. When they got in the room, they were surprised to find a bottle of champagne in a bucket of ice and a little note that said, "Welcome home, soldier." Pete had no idea who arranged that, but he was grateful, anyway. Opening the champagne gave him something to do that kept him from tossing Angela into the bed immediately. He need not have given any thought to slowing down. Angela stood there and removed all her clothes while he was struggling with the cork. He took his cue from that and undressed with the same haste.

357

Thank God, Angela had not changed in this very important part of their marriage. They were totally in tune with each other, back to familiar rituals of lovemaking, no reticence, no shyness, no hesitation. just taking and giving with joy.

"Sweetheart, was I too rough? Are you OK?" Pete handed Angela a glass of champagne.

No, *caro*, not at all. I am as glad to be with you as you are to be with me. We are both fierce lovers."

"All I could think about when I was in the hospital was coming back to you, holding you, loving you. I asked the doc first thing whether my dick was ok. He laughed at me."

"Well, Pete, *mi amore*, you have nothing to worry about. All your equipment is working very well." Angela grinned and then her expression changed, "That's a big scar on your leg, Pete. Nothing to joke about. You're lucky to be walking again," Angela spoke soberly.

"I can only walk because those physical therapists at the hospital in Surrey were tough as nails. They make you do stuff you swear you won't be able to do and you can howl with pain when they start some of the treatments, but they ignore you and make you stick it out. As long as they think it's a possibility that you can walk again, they keep at it."

"Well, I'm real grateful for that. But, Pete, even if you couldn't walk, even if you lost the leg, that wouldn't change how much I love you. I really need you to know that."

Pete sat on the bed and took her hands in his. "I do know that, sweetheart, and I'm grateful for it." He kissed her tenderly, then he tumbled her back onto the pillows and snuggled her up against him. "Are you hungry? Want to find someplace to eat? I want to talk about some things I've been thinking about and we can do it over dinner, OK?"

"Clara told me about an Italian place not far from here that Ray took her to when she came down to spend a weekend with him." Angela started to get dressed, choosing a frilly blue blouse she had borrowed from Clara and a gray wool skirt.

Pete paused in his own dressing to watch Angela put on her garter belt and stockings, aware of how much he had missed the simple pleasure of observing such a feminine act. "I haven't heard from Ray in a long time, but that may be because my mail had to get forwarded if he was writing to the old address and not the hospital. How is he doing?"

"*Deo Meo*, I forgot to tell you, Clara just got a call from Ray's sister, Anna, a few days ago. He's missing in action. That's all they know. Anna's husband is going to try to get their congressman to find out more."

"If the telegram didn't say 'presumed dead,' he's probably been captured. I hear the Germans treat officers decently, unless they try to escape. Then they shoot on sight or worse. I sure hope Ray doesn't think he has to try to escape. That's what they tell you, you know. You're supposed to try to escape." Pete's expression was bleak, "Shit. I hope he wasn't wounded."

"You'll be surprised at how calm Clara is being. She's says she would know if he was dead because she would feel it in her heart."

"I agree with her. Anyway, this is no time to give up hope. Come on, sweetheart, let's go find this restaurant."

The fragrance of olive oil and oregano made both Angela and Pete realize how hungry they really were. Of course, they had given no thought to lunch and Angela had a quick piece of toast and coffee for breakfast, so the idea of an Italian feast was very welcome. They were greeted effusively and seated in a quiet corner with a bottle of chianti. A basket of fresh bread was brought immediately. Angela raised her eyebrows at the butter on the table. Pete shrugged.

After dispensing with the task of choosing from a menu that dazzled them both, Pete reached across the table and squeezed Angela's hand. "I've got some big plans I want to talk about, but first, tell me how much money we've got in the bank right now. I remember being surprised at how much it was when you wrote to me about it a while back."

"Four thousand, eight hundred and eighty-four dollars." Angela said with no little bit of pride in her voice.

"Wow, how did you do that?" Pete was astonished. This was much better than he had hoped.

"I put every cent I earned at the bomb factory in the bank. And then, after I gave your mother money for our room and board, I put a little in an envelope for stuff for the girls and a little for gas and cigarettes and things like that for me. The rest of the government allotment check went into the bank, too. I've been doing a lot of overtime so that helped."

"Angela, you didn't need to deprive yourself or the girls to save this money."

"I know that, but there hasn't been much to buy since so much stuff is rationed."

Pete frowned. "Are you smoking cigarettes now?" His voice came out a little more harsh than he meant it to.

"No, I quit as soon as I knew you were on your way home. It made my mouth taste terrible in the morning and I didn't really like it, but all the girls at the plant did it and they gave us some smoke breaks, which was great."

"I'm sorry, sweetheart. I didn't mean to jump on you. If you want to smoke, go ahead."

"No, I'm done with that. Tell me why you asked about the money."

It came out all in a rush, then. Pete had been thinking about it all the way home across the ocean. He wanted a business of his own, a motor repair business, where he'd work on cars and trucks and tractors and all kinds of farm machinery, maybe even construction vehicles, too. He was excited about it, the words tumbling out so fast, Angela was having trouble keeping up with him.

"But, Pete, that money was to buy us a house, remember?"

"And we will, we will. That's the beauty of it. We'll buy the house and then use the house as collateral to get a business loan. I have to talk to Mr. Cooper at the bank, but I think this will work. There'll be lots of guys coming home when this war is over and the first thing they'll want is a car. Well, maybe not the very first thing, but right away. Guys are going to get married and start having kids and they'll need cars and they'll start businesses that need trucks and my motor repair shop will do it all. People will come to me because I'm a vet. Maybe the government will even get us vets special rates on loans."

Angela caught his enthusiasm. "I could still work, you know. We could save more."

"OK, you can still work, at least until the baby comes."

Angela sobered, "I don't know, Pete. Maybe I can't have another baby. Maybe the same thing would happen again."

"I talked to Dr. Boucher while you were still in the hospital and he says probably not. It was just a freaky thing. Think about it, we may have already started a new baby. I hope so. That would be the most wonderful homecoming present I could get. To find out you got pregnant on my first night back. Wow! That would make me feel like a million bucks."

He leaned across the table. "Let's go back to the hotel and try again."

Later that night, as Angela was slipping into sleep, she remembered something. "Pete, what time do you have to go back to the hospital tomorrow?"

"Oh, I'm done with that. They finished with me the first day back."

Angela sat up in bed. "You said I should come down here while you were detained at the hospital." Her voice was accusing.

"Yup, I lied. I just wanted us to have a couple of days alone, that's all. I think Pa knew." Pete pulled his wife into his arms and hugged her to him. "Don't you think that was a good idea? And telling a little white lie will make it OK that I didn't come rushing home to see my Ma."

Angela sighed and wriggled closer. "Uh huh. It was a good idea."

# CHAPTER 23

## THANKSGIVING, 1944

Clara was finding it difficult to keep smiling at the celebrations of Pete's safe return. She knew it was irrational, but she somehow resented that he was home with his little family, so happy and excited about their future, while she didn't know whether Ray was alive or dead. Pete got around just fine with his cane, except for going up stairs and he seemed to have new purpose in his life. They were looking for a house of their own and had already seen some that looked like they might work out. She was ashamed of herself that she couldn't just be happy for them.

Anna called to let Clara know that Mrs. Carpenter was going into a nursing home. Her stroke had severely affected her left side. She no longer could walk, talk clearly, feed, dress or use the bathroom by herself. At first, Anna thought she could keep her mother at home, but Randy persuaded her it would be an impossible task because Mrs. Carpenter was not only disabled, she was angry and combative. "I'm so sorry to bring you such depressing news, Clara. I do have news that's a little better. Randy did get to talk to our Congressman, who will try to find out more about Ray. As soon as we hear something, I'll let you know."

Angela was so caught up in family stuff that she didn't have time to spend with Clara. The closeness they had developed in the last two years was fading. Some days it felt to Clara that she was bracing herself for bad news all the time. Her muscles ached from the tension. Her teeth hurt from clenching her jaw. But she put one foot in front of the other to keep going, smiling at the customers in the store, greeting people she knew with a friendly wave, every day waiting and hoping.

Charlie had just about decided that he would accept his friend's invitation to Thanksgiving dinner. Every year he had been asked and every year he made some excuse. But Steve always sounded so disappointed when Charlie declined, it seemed rude not to go at least once. When Steve told him that his kids wanted to meet the man who made the wooden toys, Charlie was embarrassed but pleased at the same time. So it was agreed that he would come to their house at one o'clock on Thanksgiving Day.

Charlie went into town on Wednesday night to get a box of Whitman's chocolates. While he was there, he passed a store window that had ladies' silk scarves and he remembered how Clara had always loved the bright ones with swirly designs, so he got one for Steve's wife. Then he stopped in the liquor store and got a bottle of Canadian Club for his friend. He looked through the collection of wooden toys he had made this year and picked out three for the kids. He was ready.

Thanksgiving Day was bright with no signs of snow. Charlie realized he was nervous, going to someone's home. He hadn't worn a tie in a long while, so it felt strange. He wasn't sure if he should wear a jacket or not, but settled for wearing a fairly new cardigan sweater one of the nuns had made for him.

When Steve opened the door, he greeted Charlie with such enthusiasm, it surprised him. The lovely smell of roasting turkey filled the little house. Three children, all boys, the oldest about eight years old, came forward to shake his hand. The little one couldn't be more than three, Charlie thought. Without hesitation, he picked up the tot in his arms and said, "*Bonjour, chouchou*, my name is Charlie. What's yours?"

The boy giggled and said "I'm Charlie, too. Are you really the toy man?"

"Yes, I am and I brought toys for you and your brothers. Would you like to see them?"

Charlie opened his canvas bag and took out the toys first; one was a three car train, one a tractor and one a motorcycle, which went to the oldest boy. The children were very vocal in their appreciation for the gifts and Charlie was pleased. He could see also that Steve's wife, whose name was Olga, really liked the scarf. Steve opened the bottle of Canadian Club immediately and poured for himself and Charlie.

The meal was delicious, the day relaxed, the company friendly. When Charlie left in the early evening, he realized it was the first time in years he had not let the calamitous events at his mother's interment keep him from enjoying the day.

It was a source of great pride to Tillie that she had managed to save enough rationing coupons to be able to present a magnificent feast for Thanksgiving. Maurice and Simon drove from Connecticut to join them for the day. Nobody asked them how they got enough gas coupons, although Edward privately told Tillie that the fuel must have come from the black market. Edward was much opposed to people using the black market, but he held his tongue since this was such a special occasion.

The day was cold, but clear. It took two cars for them to go to church. Pete was dressed and ready to go before anyone. He'd been going to Mass ever since he got back and no one made any comment about it. The lovely old church looked different to Pete now, a place to think and to give thanks rather than a place to incite rebellion, as it had in his youth. As the priest went through the rituals of the Mass, Pete remembered all he had to be thankful for, especially his life and his family.

Outside, on the portico, old friends stopped to chat, trading news of family members who were ailing, getting married, having new babies, away in the service of the country and those returning. Many people who had not seen Pete since he returned came up to greet him and wish him well. He used the opportunity to tell them his plans to start a business. They were his best potential customers.

Marie was the first one in the door when they got back home. "Ooh, it smells wonderful in here. It's a Thanksgiving smell." The sage and thyme in the dressing, the butter on the turkey in the oven, the cinnamon and ginger, nutmeg and cloves in the pumpkin pie, all combined to fill the house with anticipation and memories. In the dining room, the table was already set with precious linen smelling of starch. The silver was shiny, the crystal bright, the peacocks in place.

Tillie, Clara and Angela hung up their coats and put on their aprons. Although little remained to be done, still, delivering it all to the table at precisely the right moment would require the organization and leadership skills that Tillie had in abundance. But first, drinks would be served in the parlor. Just as Tillie was about to start fretting about Maurice and Simon, they twisted the round brass bell set in the middle of the front door. Edward, who was closest to the door at the moment, greeted them.

"*Bonjour.* How was the drive up here?" Edward gathered up the coats to hang them on the rack just inside the door.

"Very few cars on the road. I suppose people don't have enough gas to drive very far. We've been saving our coupons so we could come for Thanksgiving and Bobby gave us one of his. It helps that I'm in a car pool." Maurice embraced his brother-in-law and looked at his face. "You don't think I'd buy black market gas, Edward, do you?"

"*Non, non, mon ami.* I know you to be an honorable man. You'd never do that."

Pete, standing just behind his father, suppressed a smile and came forward to put his arms around his Aunt Simone. "I'm so glad you're with us today. It's been three years since I last saw you. A lot has happened, *n'est-ce pas?*" He kissed her on both cheeks and turned to his Uncle with the same affectionate embrace.

Simone headed back to the kitchen while the men settled into the comfort of the front parlor. As soon as Pete was seated, Amy climbed up into his lap. Maurice was eager to hear Pete talk about his war experience, but he didn't know how to ask or even if it would be rude to do so. Edward saved him by bringing up the topic, recounting the story of the D-Day landing as Pete had already told him. Pete picked up on it and elaborated, but watched his words so as not to frighten Amy. Mostly he confined himself to describing the awesome sight of so many men and ships, the general look of the beach, the sky full of planes and the success, glossing over the killing fields and the pain. When Uncle Maurice asked him, "Did you see for yourself the hundreds of men the papers say fell that day?" Pete lifted Amy down from his lap and gave her a little pat on the rump, telling her to go get her mother.

"'Little pitchers have big ears, *mon oncle*. I don't want her to have nightmares, you know?"

With Amy gone, Pete described the incredible bravery and the horror of viewing the carnage. He talked about the Nazi guns and the effort it took to silence them. He was sure that no one who had not been there could possibly realize the chaos, the fear, the smell of death and destruction and how the memory never leaves the person who was a witness to it. As he talked, he could view it in his mind with alarming clarity and, in that moment, decided never again to speak of it.

Angela came into the parlor, bearing a tray of drinks and the conversation about war stopped immediately. She left and Pete asked his uncle what his plans were for after peace was declared, knowing that many factories making military supplies and equipment would either turn to something else or shut down.

"I feel fortunate that I wound up working in a plant that makes airplane engines because I think there will be many more uses for airplanes after the war, especially for transporting freight. Maybe ordinary people will begin to fly from one place to another. I don't think the plant will close down. Sure, there'll be changes, but they will be good ones."

Edward scoffed, "You'll never get me in one of those things. I don't see any future in flying machines other than giving rides at country fairs."

"Not even for delivering freight?" Pete asked.

"Well, maybe that, and maybe for movie stars or people like that, but not just anybody."

Pete was sure his father was wrong, his uncle right. A lot of things would change. Airplanes made the world smaller. The average guy had never been out of his hometown before the war. Many guys were awed at the great cathedrals in Europe, the majestic mountains, history books come to life. And many families would want to go to visit the graves of their fallen members.

"I saw some pictures of Roosevelt in the newsreels at the Calvin Theatre and he wasn't looking too good. Did you see that, Edward?" Maurice knew Edward was a strong supporter of the President.

"*Oui*, I noticed he is looking tired, maybe a little frail. It must be hard to have all these responsibilities on his shoulders. I'm not sure this guy Harry Truman has the moxie to take on the job if Roosevelt were to get really too sick. *Mon Dieu*, I hope that doesn't happen."

Marie, sitting on a hassock in the little alcove between the parlor and the dining room with her book on her lap had been half-listening to the men talking. She thought about the changes she believed were coming and the changes that had already happened. Most of her friends' mothers were driving now. Nobody got shocked at women wearing slacks. Lots of ordinary people had gone somewhere on a train. She noticed that change crept up on people without their hardly noticing and there was really nothing they could do about it when it was already a part of life.

Clara came in to call the men to the table. "Come on, dinner's ready. Are you starving?"

After everyone was settled, after compliments were given for the splendid looking turkey, gloriously brown and smelling delicious, Edward gave thanks, first for the food, then for the safe return of Pete. He beseeched the Lord for the safe return of Ray and for the safety and serenity of Charles, his lost brother-in-law. He prayed for the souls of his mother-in-law Rose and his brother-in-law Oscar and asked for God's blessings on the family assembled at the table. And he prayed for a quick end to the war and a lasting peace. He ended the prayer with his own gratitude for Tillie, "a wife beyond compare."

Amy giggled and her mother shushed her.

Bowls and platters of food were passed and murmurs of appreciation went around the table. They all tasted silently before Edward asked Pete to tell his aunt and uncle about his plans for the future. This launched an enthusiastic description of Pete's ideas for a new business and Angela's recalling of the house hunting expeditions. The decision was almost made. They were down to two houses off Bridge Street, not far from the Bridge Street School. One had a big garage, big enough for two cars, but a small back yard. The other had a very big back yard and a one car garage.

"Who needs a two car garage unless the house is a duplex." Maurice asked.

"Well," Pete said, "I'm thinking we may need a car and a truck. I figure Angela will need something to drive and I'm sure I'll need a truck for my business."

"It's not like there's no back yard at all. It's big enough." Angela chimed in. "But that house is more expensive."

"It's a decision we'll have to make after I see Mr. Cooper at the bank next Monday. But the other thing is, I think I've found the perfect property for my business. It's out toward the end of King Street, nearly out to Bridge Road. There's a piece of land out there with a dilapidated building on it, used to be a car dealership that went under. It's been vacant for three years now. I think the building could be made usable with a few repairs to the roof and the plumbing. I'm trying to find out more about the owner. Not someone who lives here now or a name I know. The sale is through a lawyer. Anyway, that's where we are with the big plans."

Maurice was clearly impressed. He was too polite to ask questions about money, but privately he wondered how Pete and Angela could manage it. Then he remembered that Angela had been working in a bomb factory, so maybe she had saved the money she earned there. He couldn't imagine Pete would want her to keep working, but you never know what people will do.

Clara had been listening and eating, not saying much except to compliment Tillie on the feast or murmur answers to questions from Amy, but now she said, "It is so good to have a dream of what you want to do and to begin to see that it could all happen. I am so very happy for you two."

All around the table, the rest of the family voiced their agreement with Clara and their good wishes for the success of Pete's business. Pete thanked them and then held up his hand, "We have something else to tell you."

Angela and Marie spoke up almost in unison, "You weren't supposed to tell yet."

"I know, but I'm so happy I can't wait anymore to share this special news. Angela is pregnant. We're expecting a baby in June."

Tillie jumped up from her chair to kiss Angela and hug her son. Edward followed seconds later. All of them exclaimed and chattered and smiled. The anticipation of a new life was an affirmation of the strength of the family. More than survivors of the Depression and the war, they were thriving.

# CHAPTER 24

## SPRING/SUMMER 1945

When Pete first approached Mr. Cooper at the bank right after Thanksgiving, he learned that GI loans with special rates would be available after the first of the year so he and Angela delayed the house purchase until January of 1945. They decided to keep some of their savings for emergencies and took out a small mortgage. The house cost $3,900 and after Pete had done some basic repairs, they moved into it in March. It had a big kitchen, a front parlor and a dining room, a wide screened porch on the side, four bedrooms (one of them very small) and one bathroom. Angela loved her new house and Amy her new school. Marie was less enthusiastic about leaving the house on West Street and needing to take a bus to school in the morning, but she was very happy to have a room of her own.

The house purchase was quickly followed by acquisition of the property on King Street for Pete's new business. May 7, the day the Germans surrendered and the war in Europe ended was also the day Pete hung the new sign up announcing he was ready for business. **Pete's Motor Repair Shop**, the painted wooden sign read, and in smaller letters underneath, **Cars, Trucks, Tractors**. Black letters on a light gray background. The old building was spruced up with a coat of red paint, the roof repaired, the windows cleaned. The weeds had been whacked and most of the lot covered with gravel.

On a bright sunny day in late June, Pete slid out from under the body of a truck when he heard a familiar voice call out, "Hey, Corporal LaPointe, I heard you were a hero. Does that make you too high and mighty to talk to old buddies?" Stanley Borowski was standing there with a huge grin on his face. Pete had to swallow fast to keep the tears from coming.

"*Mon Dieu*, when did you get out? Are you OK? Why haven't you written me or called me? I didn't know what happened to you after you hit the beach in Normandy."

"Yeah, I'm OK, not a scratch on me. I just got home a couple of days ago. I was driving by and I saw the sign. I figured it must be you."

Pete had to finish the job he was working on, but then he joined Stanley down the other end of King Street for a lunch break, leaving the shop to his summer helper, a kid from the Smith Vocational School.

Stanley told stories about his experiences. He had made sergeant at one point, but got busted back to private after a drunken brawl, ending up as a corporal at the end of the war. He had seen the concentration camps when they liberated Buchenwald and he described the scene to Pete with a shudder. "If guys ever thought we were nuts to fight that war, believe me, they would change their minds when they saw what those Nazis bastards did."

"Whatever happened to George Corelli? I tried to find out, but I never did." Pete asked.

"I don't know. I tried, too, but no luck. I was going to call his family, but then I thought it might be intruding, you know?"

"Maybe he'll turn up one day, just like you did."

Stanley surprised Pete by suggesting he'd like to take a course in motor repair under the GI Bill and then, maybe, come to work for Pete. "Great. I'd love to have you. Maybe you could work part-time here while you go to class. There's a lot to learn just from doing it."

On June 1, 1945, Angela gave birth to a healthy, robust baby boy in the Maternity ward of Cooley Dickinson Hospital. They named him Peter Edward. Pete was absolutely ecstatic. Ordered by Dr. Boucher to remain in bed for the last month of her pregnancy, Angela had argued and appealed, but she complied. Neither Angela nor Pete admitted they were worried, but Pete's relief on seeing the baby boy in his bassinet through the glass of the hospital nursery was clearly evident to Pete's mother and father, who had sat in the waiting room with Pete all night, watching him fidget and sharing his anxiety. Angela came through childbirth, if not easily, at least with no more than expected laboring. She was euphoric over the sight of her sturdy, eight pounds and eight ounces of hungry outrage.

Tillie found that she had to adjust her shopping and cooking to a smaller household now that Pete and his family had moved to their own house. She kept telling herself she was glad for them. They needed to be by themselves, to have a little more privacy. Angela certainly wanted a place of her own, to fix up the way that suited her. And she needed some place to put her energy after she quit working. But for Tillie, it was a loss. She missed the girls coming home from school to tell her of their day. She had no reason to bake cookies for eager little hands looking for after-school treats. She wouldn't be able to watch the new baby boy, Petey, grow up.

She and Clara returned to their former closeness, helping each other with little projects, listening to each other's worries, giving and taking advice. It was Clara's suggestion that Tillie might enjoy helping with a Brownie Scout Troop that appealed to Tillie. When she took on that task, she again had reason to bake cookies for little hands and took great pleasure in teaching cooking skills to the young girls.

Marie and Amy came to visit often and Tillie went to their house as well. Marie was growing up so fast, not a little girl anymore. This new generation was different and Tillie didn't know what to make of it. Sometimes

Tillie thought Marie was too bold, arguing with her *Pepere* over something they both read in the paper or in a book. It would never have occurred to Tillie to contradict something her husband said. And Marie talked all the time about what she was going to do when she finished college. Tillie was sure there was only one thing to do and that was get married and raise a family. Maybe it would be all right to be a teacher for a little while before she got married, but not for long.

Edward was very proud of Pete. A man with his own house and his own business was a man of substance. Now that he had a little boy, his family was complete. Edward was very glad when Angela quit working in the factory. He never did think it was proper, even though he knew it was necessary for winning the war. It was different for Clara. She was a widow.

Ah, Clara, his beloved sister-in-law. It was so sad that she didn't get to marry her friend, Ray. Such a nice man, a good man, so polite. Would they ever find out what happened to him? Wars tore up the whole fragile structure of the family. He had heard many stories of tragedy from this war. They may talk about the end of all wars, but sooner or later, Edward thought, it always gets started again.

Edward's interest in maps developed from the map he bought to track Pete and Ray when they were overseas and he continued to be fascinated by them. This interest took a new turn when a casual conversation with one of the Smith College professors he knew from church led him to start looking into old maps. Soon he was a collector. It became a source of pleasure, serious study, and pride.

Angela wanted her house to be perfect, beautiful, organized and a place to show off to friends and family. She made lovely curtains, painted the walls when Pete turned out to be too busy with the new business to do it, even figured out how to put up wallpaper when she decided that's what she needed in the kitchen. She had learned a lot from helping Mama Tillie in the kitchen, but she wanted to branch out to different kinds of cooking. Cutting out recipes from women's magazines, trying them out, she started a file of foods that were a success with her family.

She was saddened that Clara visited her so infrequently and understood that it was painful for her to see them in their new house, getting on with their lives while Clara's own life was caught up in waiting to find out if Ray was ever going to come home.

Petey was an easy baby, hardly ever cranky (except when he was wet or tired) and gurgled happily at everyone. Angela loved to take him in his carriage downstreet, stopping to talk to anyone she knew, letting them admire her little boy.  She had hopes that her father or brothers might see her out walking and stop, admire her child, talk to her, treat her with courtesy.  If only that could happen, she could invite them to her new home and show them that she had made something of her life.

Marie loved her baby brother and her sister Amy as well, but she was so busy with new friends, a summer job picking green beans at a farm in the Meadows and a load of books she wanted to read before her junior year in high school began in the fall, she had no time for them. Sometimes when her Mom wanted her to take care of Petey and Amy, Marie got frustrated that her

Mom didn't understand how important it was for her to spend time with her friends.

She read <u>*Seventeen*</u> magazine avidly, even the ads, for clues on what was considered important. Clothes, hair style, makeup, behavior were all dissected minutely by all the girls she hung out with. Betsy was still her friend, by now there was also Joanie and Fanny and Shirley. They sat on the swing in Fanny's back yard in the evening, surrounded by fireflies and the scent from Fanny's mother's flower garden and traded secrets, assessed the merits of each of the boys they fancied and planned their lives. Marie knew that she would probably be going to Smith and Betsy, too, shared this expectation. The free tuition for Northampton girls made it unlikely their parents would let them pass up Smith for some other college. Fanny wanted to be a nurse like her mother, who worked part-time at Cooley Dick. Joanie had dreams of being a fashion model, but no idea how to do that. Shirley was thinking she would go to Northampton Commercial College to be a secretary. While they all expected to get married someday, not a single one of them planned to do that right after high school.

Clara's friend Ruth's husband was somewhere in the Pacific, but she didn't know where and the war with the Japanese was not yet over. Often, Ruth received his letters in batches. And when they arrived, she was ecstatic for days, repeating bits of the letters to anyone who would listen. In between the receipt of this bonanza, Ruth remained serene, optimistic and full of life. To Clara, Ruth was a very gentle person and a supportive friend, with a strong belief in the power of positive thinking.

Ruth noticed that Clara's hair had begun to look different, thinner. She had no idea what could have caused it but, ever practical, suggested it was time for a short haircut. The suggestion was met with horror. Ray had always loved Clara's long hair. However, it was impossible to ignore that she was losing her hair. The comb and brush showed her that. She asked Tillie and Angela if they had any ideas of what could be done. They both thought it might be something in her diet, but Clara rejected that, saying she hadn't made any changes in what she ate. She tried different shampoos and treatments with mayonnaise and eggs. Nothing worked. Desperate, she went to see Dr. Boucher, who told her it was a condition caused by extreme stress. There was no known treatment.

Clara and Ruth spent a lot of their free time together. They went to concerts together as often as possible, even student recitals at Sage Hall, which were wonderful opportunities for Clara to learn more about classical music. At Ruth's urging, Clara bought a Victrola for her bedroom and started to buy records of the pieces she loved.

One night, when Clara was playing Beethoven's Eroica Symphony, Marie knocked on her door and asked, "Can I come in and listen, too?" It became a source of pleasure for Clara to introduce Marie to the great classical composers. And Marie's presence in the shared cocoon of the music gave Clara some solace as she struggled to maintain hope.

Anna and Clara stayed in touch, mostly by phone. Although frugal Clara thought this an extravagance, she welcomed every bit of news she was able to learn, even if it usually wasn't much, mostly platitudes from the congressman.

Mrs. Carpenter had another stroke and was not doing well at all. Anna fretted over it because her mother refused to cooperate with any of the therapies to improve her condition. She continued to be combative, frustrated with her inability to communicate her needs and angry with her daughter for putting her in the nursing home. Anna often thought about how Ray would have been able to soothe their mother, if only he was there.

In July, with the war over for two months already, Clara had begun to despair. Then, on the 18th of July, the phone rang and it was Anna.

"Clara, I got a letter today from a Major Breen. He says he spoke to one of the men who was with Ray in the battle at that mountain pass in Italy. The guy was left for dead. He's been in a coma for months, but Major Breen says he's conscious now and he told the story of the battle. Ray was injured, but he doesn't know how seriously."

Clara sank to the floor, tears running down her face, her throat too clogged to reply.

Anna spoke, "Are you there, Clara? I'm so sorry to bring you bad news, but I was sure you'd want to know."

Recovering her voice, Clara answered, "I do want to know, Anna. Please forgive me for not responding. You're saying Ray was injured but alive when he was last seen and that he was captured by the Nazis?"

"Yes, that's what the letter says. It's a long letter about how brave Ray has always been and how strong and how we should keep hoping he'll turn up in a hospital somewhere. Major Breen says all of Europe is in confusion now."

"Does he say anything about what they are doing to find Ray?"

"Well, he says 'we are doing everything possible,' but I don't know what's possible." Anna sighed heavily.

Clara was angry and frustrated with empty reassurances and lack of action. "I can't understand why they can't find him if he is still alive. He must have been wearing those dog tags all the servicemen wear, so even if he can't speak...." Clara could not continue; her throat was closed with the weight of her tears. After a few seconds, she said "Anna, I am forgetting that this news is hard on you, too."

"I guess the dog tags could have been lost." Anna offered.

"*Mon Dieu,* I can't bear it anymore. I feel so helpless. What can we do?"

Anna was crying now, little hiccups in her voice, "I don't know. I don't know. I guess we just keep praying."

Clara recovered herself. "Thank you for calling to tell me, Anna. I appreciate hearing from you more than you can know. If you get any more information please call again."

They said their goodbyes and Clara got up from the floor. Edward and Tillie were out. She was alone in the house with her thoughts. Upstairs in her room, she put a recording of Sibelius's Second Symphony on the Victrola and sat in the rocker to think.

Had Ray's wounds been treated? Was he in pain? Was he dead, buried in an unmarked grave? She started to pray and, after a few words of prayer, she stopped. All the prayers over the last two years hadn't been answered; what good could it do to keep praying to a God who didn't pay any attention to her prayers. Hadn't she always known that Ray was never going to come home, that once again it would be just like it was with Gus?

Clara hit her fist on the arm of the chair. It wasn't the same. She could feel him in her heart, hear him in her head. She could not afford bitterness. It took away hope. Often, in the quiet of the night, when she couldn't sleep, she felt sure he was still alive. Somewhere. Calling her name.

Lying on a narrow cot in a tiny room that looked like it had been carved out of the earth, with one wall of shelves full of baskets that smelled like they probably once held potatoes and beets and turnips, Ray tossed restlessly. He had escaped from the POW camp and run into the forest, eluding his pursuers by running in the middle of a stream, where the dogs could not follow his scent. He'd been hit in the shoulder by a rifle shot as he cleared the fence and he knew he'd need to get some help to take care of it, but it was more important to get as much distance from the camp as he could while he still had some strength.

The shot in the right buttock he had gotten during the battle in the Italian mountains had healed nicely with the efficient care he'd received in a German hospital. The POW camp he got sent to later was another story. There was never enough food or warmth; a few thin blankets had to be shared. Spirits were low because none of the prisoners had any idea what was going on with the war. They were hungry all the time. Some of the guards were disgruntled with their lot and had taken it out on the prisoners with beatings over any imagined infraction of the rules. Ray, especially, had been the target of repeated beatings.

He guessed that the camp was in Poland, maybe near the Russian border, but he didn't know. He did notice it was almost completely surrounded by forest. He thought about it for a long time and then decided to take a chance at escape. The first part of his plan worked well. He ran in a stream for a long time and finally, the enemy had given up. When he thought it was safe, he crawled under a giant fir tree to rest a bit.

Ray didn't know how long he had slept. Maybe he had lost consciousness, but suddenly he was aware of being carried through the forest in the arms of a guy who was huge, at least seven feet tall, maybe more, and brought to this dwelling. An old woman cleaned his wound, clucking her tongue and shaking her head, all the while talking in a language he didn't recognize. Clearly, though, she was scolding the big guy, who never said a word. Ray figured she was Big Guy's mother and that he was mute.

Obviously, Ray thought, she knows that the bullet has to come out. If she's been living out here in the forest, she probably has some rudimentary knowledge of medical treatment and is aware of the dangers of infection. He was right. While the Big Guy held him down, Old Woman removed the bullet. Ray didn't know how because he passed out from the pain of it quickly. When he came to, he was lying on this cot in a room with two walls of packed earth and stone and two of rough hewn wood. He had no idea how long he had been there. He noticed a bowl near the cot and a jug of water. He was aware of light coming through the knot holes in the wood and there was a lantern on the table. He tried to sit up, but was unable to summon the strength for the task.

Ray could feel the sweat trickling down on his neck and realized he was feverish. He closed his eyes. Oh, Clara, sweetheart, I really need you, he thought. He heard a sound, maybe a gasp or a sigh and he opened his eyes. She was there, right there, at the end of his bed. "Clara, you're here," he called out. Her image faded and he closed his eyes.

## ABOUT THE AUTHOR

Louise Appell was born and raised in Northampton, Massachusetts. Her father, Romeo Fortier, was French-Canadian. She graduated from Smith College and went on to earn a doctorate in education at the University of Kentucky, She had a distinguished career in special education as a teacher and university professor before moving to the private sector to lead a team in the development of curriculum materials for people with disabilities. Dr. Appell is the author of several works of non-fiction and is currently at work on the third book of the trilogy about the fictional Billieux family.

Printed in the United States
67267LVS00001B/1-72

Front cover photo: Women working in bomb-making factory in Florence, Mass. during WWII.